LOST & FOUND

by

Sharon Ledwith

Pandamonium Publishing House
Publishing Made Simple.
www.pandamoniumpublishing.com

ISBN: 978-1-998467-23-5
Published by: Pandamonium Publishing House
Publishing Made Simple.
www.pandamoniumpublishing.com
pandapublishing8@gmail.com

Printed in Canada

For permissions, inquiries, or additional rights, please contact Pandamonium Publishing
House at the information listed above.

*For my wonderful friend, Susan.
You taught me that every animal who wandered into the shelter
always had something to say.*

Follow us on social media for giveaways, contests, and more:

Facebook: Pandamoium Publishing House
Instagram: @Pandamonium_Publishing_House8
YouTube: Pandmonium Publishing House
TikTok: Pandamonium Publishing

Pandamonium Publishing House
Publishing Made Simple.

1. Leader of the Pack

"Silly, stupid humans!" Whiskey hissed.

Creeping through the ductwork was becoming harder on her old bones. Layers of dust tickled her pink nose and made her facial whiskers twitch incessantly. Her stomach retched at the stale odors. However, Whiskey, a fifteen-year-old calico cat, ignored these annoyances and persevered. She had to, knowing that she was the only link, the only form of communication, between the cat floor and the dog floor at the Fairy Falls Animal Shelter. This was what made her special, gave her life purpose. This quiet night was no exception.

What the humans called a *crisis* had happened at the shelter today and Whiskey had to relay this information to the canine pack leader. Nearing the entrance above the dog floor, the thick fur on the back of her neck rose. Some of the dogs she tolerated, some she abhorred. Her ears flattened. Whiskey knew she would have to scale across the top of Mary Jane's gate in order to get to Nobel's cage and deliver her report. She also knew to be extra careful not to shake the little bells attached to her red collar that would jingle out her presence. Reaching the opening, Whiskey extracted her long claws and pushed the dusty register aside.

Looking down, she sighed, thankful that Mary Jane, a black and white pit bull terrier, and a long time resident of the shelter, was asleep. Carefully, Whiskey jumped down, balanced on the top of the fenced gate that faced the hallway, and started to slink across it. Then she sneezed and her bells jingled.

A growl and a snort sounded from below. "Who dares to wake me?"

Whiskey peered down. Mary Jane's eyes were rolled back, her tongue hanging limply out one side of her mouth. A quilted blanket on the cement floor was half-shredded and inches away lay a rubber toy, which would normally be stuffed into Mary Jane's powerful jaws to exercise the constant frustration of being incarcerated for so long. Whiskey watched Mary Jane lunge for the toy, shaking her thick head and neck in anger.

Whiskey leaned over into the cage and purred, "Someday, I hope you choke on that thing."

Mary Jane dropped the toy and lunged at the smug cat. Whiskey had just enough time to recoil and land feet first on the hallway's cement floor. She groaned, feeling her arthritic back legs cave slightly. She was not a kitten anymore, that was for sure. Mary Jane rattled the kennel door, snapping, growling, and barking. Slobber ran down the white patch on her neck and dribbled onto the floor, making it too slippery for her to balance on her hind legs. She slipped and fell with a loud thump and knocked the water bowl, spilling water all over. Whiskey flattened her ears and shook her head. This dog could easily have been the pick of the litter when it came time to receive the sleep needle, but since this shelter had a 'no kill' policy in place, all of its residents, including Mary Jane, remained safe and alive.

Suddenly the kennel next to Mary Jane's came alive and the one after that. Whiskey heard a whimper from the cage down the hall where the new dogs were kept. These were the dogs whose owners would either still rescue them or would condemn them to live here in the shelter until they were adopted by a new human.

"You sure know how to make an entrance, Whiskey."

Whiskey's ears pricked up. The right ear had been badly frostbitten once upon a time, but her left ear was still intact. Half her face was masked in black; the other half a mixture of white and orange. The rest of her small body was a patchwork of black and orange fur, with the exception of a white belly. She preened her whiskers, licking the pad of her front right paw until she realized all she tasted was watered down bleach. Cringing, Whiskey slowly sauntered over to Nobel's kennel—the biggest—at the very end of the hallway. She plopped her bottom on the cool concrete floor and stretched.

"You're certainly a deep sleeper, Nobel. Are you sure you used to be a watchdog?" Whiskey asked, preening the area above her yellow eyes.

There was a low growl, and then a high pitched bark. It was Nobel's way of laughing. "I'm part Husky, part Doberman, and part mystery mutt, so sometimes I get all messed up about my job. Do I run as fast as I can or do I stand and fight? It's darned confounding, I say."

Although it was dark, Whiskey could see the amusement in Nobel's light blue eyes. His fur was a mixture of black, tan, and grey, and standing on all fours he would be at least three cats tall. Nobel's kennel was well-kept, with a thick, comfy blanket set up in front and a pan full of water at the back. He'd been at the shelter for as long as she had, so Whiskey felt a sense of oneness with Nobel, even though he was canine.

"I smell feline! Feline! Feline! Feline!" a dog from the middle cage barked.

Nobel rolled his eyes. "You're dreaming again, Louis. Go back to sleep!"

Whiskey heard a snort from the big Rottweiler mix, followed by a whine. "Dreaming? Hmm, yup, silly me. Must be dreaming. No felines on the dog floor. Silly me."

She heard Louis yawn, fart, and then settle back down on his papered floor. Louis tended to pee in his kennel, so he wasn't afforded the luxury of a cushy blanket like Nobel's.

"Dumb as wood, that one," Nobel muttered.

"Yet he trusts you completely," Whiskey mewed, scratching her chin.

"That's because I'm the pack leader. It's not a choice, you know."

Whiskey nodded. She understood all too well. Dominant and submissive. There were leaders and there were followers. It was the same for cats as it was for dogs. The problem was that there were far too many cats in this shelter, so most tended to break off into separate colonies. Poppy, the fat, white Persian was one leader. Boscoe, a slick black domestic short-hair was another. Then there was Shadow, a grey tabby mix, and the meanest leader Whiskey had ever encountered in all her years.

"You have some news?" Nobel asked, cutting into Whiskey's thoughts.

She jumped. "Yes," she answered, and then decided to lick her leg. "This morning, while I was curled up on the chair in the office, I heard the Bossy One talking into one of those small, shiny things humans call a phone."

Nobel lay on his blanket and crossed his big paws. "Did you understand any of her words?"

Whiskey stopped grooming. "Some, but you won't like it."

Nobel's ears rose. "I don't like the Bossy One to begin with. What comes out of her mouth is mostly garble and she stinks like a dead skunk."

"I think you've just insulted skunks everywhere, my friend," Whisky mewed.

Nobel growled impatiently. Whiskey sighed and said, "From what human words I know, I heard 'no money' repeated many times."

"Money?" Nobel asked, inclining his furry head. "What is money?"

"Something humans need to survive on."

"Survive on? Explain."

Whiskey frowned. Sometimes dogs were thick-headed. "Money, my friend, allows the humans to eat well, sleep in a safe place, and cover their bodies with the strange hairless outerwear they call clothes. Clearly, 'no money' means the humans cannot function very well."

"So how does 'no money' affect us?" Nobel asked.

"I also heard the word 'shelter' after 'no money', meaning that the humans who care for us can no longer provide us with the food we eat, the blankets we sleep on, and all the comforts we've come to expect of this place." Whiskey's ears lowered. "No money, my friend, means this shelter will not be around much longer."

"What?!" Nobel howled. "But this is our place, our sanctuary! She can't make it go away!"

"The Bossy One will if she doesn't come up with enough money soon. I sensed her fear, her desperation. She sounded broken."

Nobel snarled. "The Bossy One has become weak! Her weakness endangers the pack! Do you think the other Ones who take care of us will do something about this?"

Whiskey sat silent for a few moments. *Who might challenge the Bossy One?* She thought about it. *The Kind One? The Loud One? The Quiet One? The Quick One? Which human might be dominant enough to do this?* The whimpering had dulled down and snoring replaced the barking. Her body twitched as if electricity surged through it.

Louis stirred in his sleep. "Get her. Bite her. Chew. Chew. Chew." He snapped his jaws and flailed his long legs.

"Shut up, you fool!" Mary Jane growled. She picked up her rubber toy and shook it viciously.

Whiskey's ears pricked up as she realized something. "Fool, no. Genius, yes."

Nobel leaned closer to his kennel door. "I don't quite follow."

"That's because you're the pack leader. You never follow. Don't you see?"

Nobel gave her a vacant look. His whiskered brown brows bobbed up and down in thought.

Whiskey fluffed her jowls. "It's simple. The shelter needs a new pack leader to survive. In order to do that all the animals must join forces to help find a stronger human who can stand up to the Bossy One."

"And how do we do that, seeing as most of us are in cages?"

"By using what nature gave us," Whiskey meowed, locking eyes with Nobel. "We send our thoughts to any human who will listen."

Nobel's brows rose. "But...what if it doesn't work?"

Whiskey stretched again, allowing her paws to knead the air before her. "Then, my friend, we will need what humans call a *miracle.*"

2. Community Hours

"This town sucks!"

"Now you listen here, young lady, your father entrusted me with you and I'm not going to let him down! Are you listening to me, Meagan? Meagan! Stop that damn texting and put your phone away this minute!"

Meagan Walsh cringed at her Aunt Izzy's grating words, but she didn't put her phone down. She was too busy texting her best friend Cassie back home in Happy Valley-Goose Bay about how stupid she'd been for getting caught breaking into Aunt Izzy's superintendent's car's glove compartment last night to steal a pack of smokes. *There. Done. Send.* The shiny, red cell phone had been a gift from her father—including the costly monthly fees—so that she could call him any time, day or night. Meagan barely called him, though. She'd rather chew raw whale blubber.

It had been two weeks since her father had shipped her to Fairy Falls—a small, boring, northern tourist town—just because he wanted to keep her out of trouble and provide a better education. So without much of a warning, Meagan was flown hundreds of miles to an aunt she'd only met a handful of times. Now here she sat, in her aunt's apartment building lobby on a warm, sunny afternoon in June, waiting for Aunt Izzy's wrath. The brown faux-leather chair Meagan was planted on stuck to her jeans in all the wrong places, so she wiggled from side to side in an attempt to get comfortable. When that didn't work, she stared at her bejeweled sandals resting on the brown tile floor to avoid her aunt's caustic stare.

"Well? Don't you have anything to say to me, Meagan? It took a great deal of groveling to my super, Mrs. Arbuckle, for her not to call the police."

Startled, Meagan looked up. She brushed her raven bangs away from her blue eyes and tucked the red phone in her back jean pocket. Her slender nose flared. "Eww. Is that dog crap I smell?"

Aunt Izzy stiffened. She checked the green scrubs she wore, lifted one foot, and then the other. There it was. A clump of brown poop wedged in the bottom of her sneaker. Compliments of the Fairy Falls Animal Shelter, where Izzy Walsh worked scooping litter boxes, wiping dirty animal butts, and cleaning up after the messy dogs and cats for minimum wage.

"I was hoping for more of a 'thank you'," Aunt Izzy replied, placing a chubby, pale hand against the beige wall. She slipped her shoe off. "Oh, and a 'please don't tell dad'."

Meagan zipped up her thin, purple hoody to conceal the pink T-shirt she wore underneath and shrugged. "Tell him. Maybe he'll ship me to another relative in a less boring town."

At first Aunt Izzy glared at her, and then her features softened. She hunkered down to face Meagan and rested a hand on one of her knees, but Meagan was too busy staring at the shoe with the poop on it. Was Aunt Izzy going to slap the side of her head with it? Or worse, rub it into her nose like a disobedient puppy? Meagan clenched her teeth.

"Meagan, dear, I know it's been hard for you, especially with the loss of your mom in that terrible car accident."

Meagan's stomach tightened. Her mind replayed that night five years ago that had changed everything. It was the yearly award night at her grade school. Even as Meagan walked across the school's stage to accept the *Most Improved Student Award*, she kept glancing at the empty seat next to her dad, wondering why her mom was so late. As soon as the ceremony finished, two constables with the Royal Canadian Mounted Police were waiting outside the auditorium's doors to escort Meagan and her dad to the office to let them know why mom never made it to Meagan's special night. She swallowed hard, tasting sour bile. *Tractor trailer. Cut a sharp corner. Mom never saw it. Sheared off the top of her car. Killed instantly.*

Meagan lowered her head. Her bottom lip quivered. She shoved her hands into her hoody's pockets and her right hand toyed with the nail clipper she'd used to break open the glove box.

Meagan raised her head and frowned at her Aunt. "Since you think I've been through enough, then why don't you cut me some slack?"

Aunt Izzy sighed. "Meagan, I know you're in a strange place with stranger people, and believe me, I've made tons of mistakes myself. Bad relationships. Bad habits. Bad choices." She paused to lightly touch the long scar running down the left side of her face. "Look, your dad is giving us both a chance to start over, make things right. Only this time, I'm the teacher and you're the student."

Meagan inclined her head. "What do you mean?"

Aunt Izzy smiled, making her facial scar crinkle like a jack-o-lantern's sardonic smile. Meagan pursed her lips. She had heard rumours about how her aunt had received that scar. A bar room brawl over a man. Thrown beer bottles. Blood spattered everywhere. Drugs had been a factor, too. After it was over, the other woman had needed over a hundred stitches—her aunt had gotten away with only fifty.

"I mean, I don't want you to make the same mistakes I have. That's why your dad sent you to live with me for a while. So you don't walk in my shoes."

Meagan glanced at the poop-encrusted sneaker. "I totally agree. I never want to walk in those shoes."

Aunt Izzy smiled. "Good. Then it's settled." She slapped Meagan's knee affectionately, stood up, and then turned and walked toward the doors leading to the apartment building's parking lot. Meagan noticed that the afternoon sun from the glass doors lit up her aunt's auburn, frizzy hair in an almost angelic manner. She looked for the horns anyway.

Then Meagan's stomach twitched. "Wait…what's settled?"

Aunt Izzy opened the door, turned, and said, "Why, your community work, Meagan. I've talked it over with Mrs. Arbuckle and she won't press any charges if you agree to complete two hundred hours of community service. "

Meagan jumped out of the chair. "Two hundred hours! But...but that's practically my whole summer! I only tried to steal a pack of smokes!"

Aunt Izzy frowned. "You make it sound like it's no big deal. Stealing is stealing and besides you've got to be nineteen to legally buy smokes. If memory serves, you're still fifteen."

Meagan scowled. "Only till the end of August! And BTW— weren't *you* smoking at my age?"

"The past is the past, Meagan, and this is now. And now, you have to pay for your crime through community hours. There's no negotiation here. You'll be putting in your time while making a worthwhile contribution to the community and I know the perfect place."

Meagan's face burned. She balled her fists. "And where's that?"

In the time it took Meagan to take a breath, Aunt Izzy pitched her shoe straight at her. Meagan's reflexes were sharp and she caught the shoe with both hands. Without looking down, she knew her palms were baptized in dog poop. Meagan gagged.

"Better get used to that smell, my dear. You're going to be scooping a lot of poop up during your time at the Fairy Falls Animal Shelter."

3. Meeting Meagan

illy, stupid humans! Whiskey deliberately kicked extra litter onto the floor. Whoever forgot to scoop her litter box in the bathroom where they put her every day at closing hours would have to deal with the mess. It had been a long week of informing the cats and dogs about the Bossy One's threat of closing their beloved shelter. Some of the cats were nervous and went to seek out hiding spots so the humans might never find them to take them away. Some were indignant and vowed to get adopted as soon as possible. But the majority of the cats seemed to ignore Whiskey's warning, opting to play and eat, rather than sending their thoughts to every human who wandered through the shelter.

Even Nobel had a hard time convincing the dogs. Since there weren't as many of them, it was easier to send messages through the fenced runs outside, but harder for them to grasp the gravity of their situation. It took more 'money' to take care of a dog than a cat, as Whiskey understood, so she was insistent that Nobel must try to get this message across to his pack. All the animals in the shelter were in danger of losing their home and those who were old or sick or unadoptable were in even more peril of losing their lives to the sleep needle if the shelter closed.

Suddenly, the front door beeped twice. "Whiskey, come on out! Mama Gail's here!"

The bathroom door flew open and Whiskey scurried out, meowing complaints to the Loud One, who bent to stroke her. Whiskey let out a single purr so she would stop and get on with the day. It didn't work, though. The Loud One continued to pat her until she had a palm full of orange and black fur. Standing up, the human, who must be past child-bearing and half Whiskey's age in cat years, wiped the fur across her bulging blue scrub top, and then turned and walked through the door of the main cat room to get to the stairs at the back. The dogs started barking and howling the moment her feet hit the stairs.

Beep, beep, the front door sounded again. Sighing, Whiskey lifted a back leg in the middle of the hallway and proceeded to groom herself. She heard a familiar voice. *The Kind One is here. Good. I'll get my litter box done first.* She stopped grooming and instantly regretted the extra mess she'd made. Then Whiskey heard another voice. This one belonged to a human who was younger and female, yet there was a rough edge to her voice, like she had just swallowed a handful of litter. Curious, Whiskey sauntered over to the reception area, jumped on the grey chair that waited there for her, and proceeded to do what she did best— observe.

"Stop whining about it, Meagan, or suck it up, as you would say. You're doing these hours and there's no getting out of it."

"Isn't there a child labour law on this?" the younger human asked.

"You're not being paid."

"Okay, isn't this considered some kind of abuse, then?"

The Kind One smiled. "Only if I feed you to Mary Jane."

"Mary…who?"

Whiskey snorted in laughter, but to a human, it would sound more like a strangled meow.

The Kind One jumped and turned around. She giggled, and then moved to scratch Whiskey under the chin. "Good morning, Whiskey-girl. I hope you didn't leave too much of a mess for me this morning."

The girl's face twitched. "That cat is named after booze? Nice."

"She was found near the liquor store," the Kind One said, smiling. "It seemed appropriate."

Whiskey sneezed, causing her collar bells to jingle, and purred to appease the Kind One. She was Whiskey's favourite human and she didn't like it when the felines of the shelter made more of a mess than usual for her to clean up. However, last night, a full moon had graced the skies. Tempers were higher at this time of the month, so it wasn't unusual to find upturned litter boxes, vomit in the cages, or clumps of fur all over the floor. The pull and power the moon had over animals was out of their control, so when it waned, things got calmer, and their home was kept cleaner.

"Mary Jane is our pit bull," the Kind One was saying. "She's the last one left in the shelter since the government banned the breed. I wish we could find her a suitable home. I think she's going a bit bonkers being in the shelter twenty-four seven."

The girl's mouth fell open. "I don't do dogs."

The Kind One shrugged. "Fine. There are over seventy cats that need attention and care. I'm sure you won't be bored."

The girl frowned. "I don't do cats, either. I'm...I'm allergic."

"Oh, haven't you heard, my dear? There are pills for that," the Kind One said, laughing. "Go into my car's glove compartment and grab a couple of allergy pills, and then get your lily-white butt back here so you can help me start cleaning."

The girl moaned. She pulled at the oversized pink scrub top she wore as if protesting the Kind One's orders, and then opened the door to go outside. Beep, beep.

"Well, Whiskey, shall we get this party started?"

Whiskey meowed, and then stretched before getting down off the chair. She ran straight to the door and let out a long-winded meow. She wanted out so she could roll on the driveway to loosen any fur the Loud One had not purged from her. Two beeps accompanied her departure. Whiskey heard a car door slam and looked across the lot. The young girl had a white stick stuck in her mouth and was heading for the side of the building, near to the dog runs. Whiskey watched as she snuck behind the lone shed and sat down.

Interesting, she thought. *I wonder if the Kind One trusts her?*

Whiskey decided to observe this young human. Carefully, she skulked over to the tall grass that was never cut and pushed her way through it. Closer, closer, closer she got, until she was about a stone's throw away. The dogs were barking like the lunatics they were. Louis was in the run closest to the forest that backed onto the building, while a new dog, a Lab mix, she guessed, was in the middle. The run next to the driveway had always been reserved for Mary Jane. Whiskey glanced back at the girl who was sucking on her white glowing stick. Whiskey sniffed, and then sneezed. Her bells tinkled. *Poison,* she thought, pawing her face to dissipate the stench.

"Who's that?" the girl asked, quickly removing the white stick from her mouth.

Whiskey sneezed again, sounding off her bells as she jumped out of the long grass. She gave the young human a long look of disdain, like one a cat might make while having the squirts in a litter box.

"Oh, it's just you," the girl mumbled, and then resumed sucking on her white glowing stick.

Silly, stupid human, Whiskey thought. She turned to saunter away.

"I'm not silly, and I'm certainly not stupid," the girl responded nastily.

Whiskey froze and then sat down. She turned her head around to watch the girl blow smoke out of her mouth. Her long legs were stretched out in front of her and she seemed relatively relaxed. Whiskey shook her head. Had she imagined it? Did this girl really pick up her thoughts? This was a real conundrum. No human had ever come as close as this one to understanding her; to actually communicating with her. The exception, of course, had been the Kind One's instinct to know when a cat was ill and take care of the matter, but instinct was instinct and this was something more.

"What's the matter, Whiskey?" the girl asked, sucking on the white stick once more before rubbing it into the ground. She blew out ringlets of smoke. "Cat got your tongue?"

4. Steady Patterns

"You can understand me, can't you, girl?" the calico cat said, staring straight at her.

Meagan stretched, much like a cat, and then crossed her arms. "So what if I can? And FYI—cigarettes relieve stress for me. I need them like you need food."

Whiskey's ears flattened. "I do not need poisoned food, thank you very much. And what is stress, girl?"

"Meagan."

"What?"

"My name is Meagan. How would you like to be called 'cat' all the time?"

"It is what I am." Whiskey preened her head with a paw. "You humans are the only ones who need to give out names. In my lifetime, I have had three different names, though I like Whiskey the best. Now, what is this 'stress'?"

"Stress is something adults do to kids all the time. It's that push-push-push feeling that gets up all inside you. Stress makes your stomach bunch, neck tense, and head ache."

Whiskey stopped grooming. "So why don't you just walk away from this stress? Cats do it all the time."

Meagan sighed. "I wish it were that easy."

Whiskey sneezed, making her bells ring. "It's easier than poisoning yourself with that white stick. If you could smell what I can smell, then you'd never pick up another white stick."

Meagan laughed. "Maybe, but when I first walked into the shelter, you should have smelled what I smelled. It was ripe! Whew, you animals are disgusting!"

Whiskey grinned a cat grin, and then laid down on the gravel. "Does the Kind One know?"

"Kind One?"

"The human you came in with. Does she know that you can talk to cats?"

"Aunt Izzy? No. Only my mom knew. She used to work for a veterinarian, but…" Meagan paused, shook her head, and then cleared her throat, "Nobody does now. I used to talk to animals all the time when I was younger. It seemed natural to me, picking up pictures or feelings or emotions from a stray cat, a wandering dog, or a friend's pet, and then sending a message back to them. I remember it being fun."

Whiskey's yellow eyes widened. "You can understand dogs, too?"

Meagan nodded. "Sure. I just pick up their signals, the same as I would for cats, and connect with them. I stopped doing it when I was around ten 'cause—" Meagan paused for the second time, and sighed deeply "—kids were making fun of me and adults didn't believe me. I honestly thought I'd lost the ability until I picked up on you."

The dogs started barking wildly again. "Okay, okay, hold your bits and pieces, Mama Gail is coming!"

"What's going on?" Meagan asked, peering around the shed.

"It's feeding time for the dogs. The Loud One is rotating them so they all get a chance to relieve themselves before eating."

"The Loud One? For not caring about names, you animals sure have some strange ones for us."

Whiskey's tail twitched. "We go by the steady patterns we pick up from a human."

"Steady patterns?"

Her tail flicked again. "Yes. Every human is different. The Loud One booms in everything she does. She uses her voice far too much and her ears far too little. The Quiet One is the opposite. She listens and rarely speaks, but knows more about what's going on at the shelter than anyone else. Then there's the Quick One. She speeds through the shelter, cleaning, watering, and feeding us as if she's doing the job of ten humans. It's all so disturbing to watch, darting here and there like a lost puppy on the road."

"I see," said Meagan. "So how did you come up with the oh-so-wrong name for my Aunt Izzy?"

Whiskey jumped up on her lap and stared into her blue eyes. Meagan shrunk. "If you can communicate with me, then you should know why."

Whiskey was a light-weight cat, no more than a furry bag of bones, yet there was something intimidating about her, like an old-school teacher smacking a ruler against her palm. The truth was, this elderly cat knew her aunt better than she did and it made her a little on the jealous side. Other than the stories her dad had shared—the bar fight, the drug addiction, the rebellious big sister—she knew nothing else.

Meagan shook her head. "I haven't a freaking clue, Whiskey."

The cat almost looked disappointed. "Then may I suggest that you start paying attention? You'll learn more about humans that way."

"Meagan! Where the hell are you?" Aunt Izzy bellowed across the parking lot. "It doesn't take fifteen flipping minutes to down some pills!"

Meagan grinned. "You might want to exchange her name for the Impatient One."

Collecting Whiskey in her arms, Meagan jumped up and ran out from behind the shed. "I'm here, Aunt Izzy. I was just catching Whiskey before she got lost."

"Liar," the cat whispered, and then whipped her tail across Meagan's face.

"Whiskey is allowed outside, which is more than I can say for you," Aunt Izzy said, wagging a finger. "Now put her down and get inside. Hey, is that cigarette smoke I smell on you?"

"Er...no, of course not," Meagan replied. "Must have rolled over a few butts trying to grab Whiskey."

"Double liar," Whiskey meowed, swiping a paw over Meagan's mouth.

"Ugh! That's not funny, Whiskey!" Meagan yelled tossing the smart-ass cat to the ground.

Aunt Izzy giggled. "Honestly, my dear, the way you just spoke to her you'd think Whiskey actually understands you."

Meagan shrugged, then ran up the cement stairs and into the shelter. Beep, beep. Whiskey followed her every step of the way. "Go away, I've got work to do," she whispered.

"Did you say something to me, Meagan?" Aunt Izzy asked, coming up from behind. Her face was flushed from trying to keep up with the pair.

"Um, no, I was just talking to myself, seeing what needs to be done first," Meagan replied.

"Save the animals!" Whiskey meowed loudly.

"Save the animals?" Meagan asked, looking down at her.

Aunt Izzy eyed Meagan strangely. "Well yes, dear, that's why we're here, so let's start by collecting all the water bowls and topping up the food dishes."

Beep, beep. The door flew open. Aunt Izzy looked up and smiled. "Oh, hi, Karen. We're not open until ten."

"Well, I need to talk to someone about the stray cat spraying around my store front. It's bad for business, you know!"

"And you know as well as everyone else in Fairy Falls that there's no by-law in place to take care of stray cats. We only collect lost dogs. My suggestion is that you catch the offending tom in a live trap and bring him here."

Meagan glanced over toward the door. A woman, dressed in a green and white outfit that looked like it came from a glamour magazine, stood in the doorway with both hands on her hips and lips pursed. Her short brown hair was perfectly styled and the colour of her lipstick matched her fingernails. *Raging red,* Meagan thought, giggling.

"Is there something funny about a cat spraying all over my real estate office, young lady?" the woman inquired.

"Er, no, ma'am. Nothing funny about a cat spraying your office," Meagan said sheepishly. She wiped her clammy hands across the front of her jeans.

Aunt Izzy cleared her throat. "Karen, this is my niece, Meagan. She's staying with me for a while. Meagan, my dear, this is Ms. Karen Bean."

Meagan grinned, and then waved at the elegantly-dressed woman with the beady brown eyes. Whiskey rubbed up against Meagan's leg. "I know of this tom. He's crusty, but not unreasonable. Tell her to stop parking in front of his favourite napping place during the day and he'll stop spraying her store at night."

"I'm not telling her that," Meagan said between clenched teeth.

"I beg your pardon, young lady? Tell me what?"

Aunt Izzy swung around. "Meagan, go collect the water bowls, please."

"Tell her, tell her," Whiskey mewed.

"Um, Ms. Bean, this may sound a little crazy, but—"

"But what?" Karen Bean cut in.

"Well, do you think you could park your car in another spot? My guess is that you're probably blocking the poor cat in during the day while he's sleeping and he's just showing you how pissed he is by spraying your office at night."

There. I said it. Meagan's stomach bunched.

"Meagan, don't be so presumptuous! Ms. Bean donates quite a lot of money to the Animal Shelter. Now apologize this instant!"

Karen Bean held up a slender hand. "No. Wait, Izzy. Seems to me the spraying started when I changed parking spots a couple of weeks ago. Yes, it does make sense. I'll park in my old spot today and see what happens. If your niece is right and the tom ceases to spray, then by the end of this week, I'll drop off a substantial donation for the shelter. Deal?"

Izzy nodded, but still looked puzzled. "Deal."

Then Ms. Bean smiled a perfect smile, turned, and walked out the door. Beep, beep.

5. The Chosen One

Whiskey spent the morning following Meagan, who was trying to avoid the Kind One any way she could. Scooping and scrubbing litter boxes, washing water bowls, and sweeping and mopping were jobs that were starting to run thin, so Meagan decided to hide out in the nursery. Whiskey tried to contain herself. *If Meagan thinks I'm a chatty cat, wait until she gets an earful of fifteen hungry kittens and their testy moms.*

Viewing Meagan through the glass door was like having a front row seat at a tom's neutering. Priceless. The kittens all mewed in unison while the moms were busy jumping up on the highest shelf for a break. Meagan covered her ears in the furry sea of creams, oranges, tabbies, and blacks. Raising her undamaged ear, Whiskey tried to get snippets of what the kittens were saying.

"Wanna play, wanna play, wanna play?"

"Catch me, catch me, catch me!"

"Food, food, food! Bring us more food!"

"What the devil is going on in the nursery?" the Kind One asked, coming up from behind Whiskey.

She meowed to try to keep her attention away from Meagan, but it was too late. Meagan was caught in a live trap. The Kind One rapped on the door. "Meagan, get your butt out here now! I want to speak with you!"

The door creaked open. Whiskey could still hear the little monsters bantering. "Don't leave, don't leave! Stay and play, stay and play! Bring us treats, bring us treats!"

"Good Lord. I've never seen, nor heard those kittens act like that before. What did you do in there, Meagan?"

She shrugged. "Nothing. I just went in to check on their water."

The Kind One moved her mouth to one side. "I see your allergies, or whatever problem you had working with cats and dogs, has been miraculously cured."

Meagan grinned. "Yup. It's a miracle."

Whiskey's ears pricked up. *A miracle? Yes, that's what's needed to save the animals!* Meagan would be proclaimed the Chosen One to take over from the Bossy One—the new pack leader of the shelter. However, Whiskey would have to convince Meagan that she had what humans called 'the right stuff' to make a good pack leader before there was no money left.

"So are you going to explain to me how you knew what to say to Karen Bean?"

Whiskey jumped up to paw at Meagan's leg. "Tell her you are here to save the shelter. Tell her you are here to challenge the Bossy One."

"No!" Meagan shouted down at Whiskey.

"No?" the Kind One asked.

"Uh, not you, Aunt Izzy. It's Whiskey. She wants up again."

"Ignore her, she's a cat, I'm a person. Now speak to me!"

"Woof, woof," sounded from the open door leading down to the pound section of the shelter. Whiskey's fur bristled. She turned with claws out, ready for a fight. Then her whole body relaxed, seeing it was Nobel. His light blue stare was on her, trying to pick up her thoughts. Then, as if understanding completely, he looked up at Meagan and howled in pleasure.

"Is it true?" Nobel asked. "Can she understand us?"

Whiskey glanced up. "Tell him. Use body language if you like. Scratch your head."

As directed, Meagan began scratching the top of her head like it was infested with fleas.

"Sorry for startling your niece, Izzy. I know Nobel can be a bit of a brute at times," the Loud One explained.

"That's okay, Gail. Meagan has to get comfortable with dogs if she's going to help you too. Meagan, say hello to Gail Winn."

Continuing to scratch, Meagan smiled and said, "Hi, Gail."

The Kind One reached over and pulled Meagan's hand away from her head. "Stop that, blackfly season is over."

Gail laughed. "Yeah, but mosquito season has just begun!"

"True that," the Kind One said, grinning. "Meet you outside for coffee in ten?"

The Loud One stuck one thumb up in the air, and then tried to pull Nobel toward the door leading outside, but he wouldn't budge. He continued to stare up at Meagan in fascination. He wagged his tail, then whined, wagged his tail again, and then whined again. His leash was taut, his manner calm.

"Take me for a walk?" Nobel whined to Meagan.

"Honestly, what's gotten into you, boy?" the Loud One asked. "Don't you wanna go out for a pee and stretch your legs?"

"Er, I'll take him," Meagan blurted.

"Oh, I don't know, my dear, he's a puller," the Kind One said.

"It's okay. I'm stronger than I look," Meagan offered.

"It's fine with me, if it's fine with you, Izzy," the Loud One said.

Nobel barked. He pawed the chipped flooring.

"Good'nuff for me, Meagan," the Kind One said, nodding. "Take Nobel up the path to the top of the hill, let him do his business, then bring him back."

As soon as the Loud One placed the leash in Meagan's hands, Nobel dashed for the door. Beep, beep. Whiskey took a deep breath and lunged for the open door too. Her old joints were no match for Nobel's young ones and her lungs had to work overtime to keep up.

"Slow down, Nobel! I'm not as young as I used to be!" Whiskey called after the bouncy Husky-cross.

Nobel cocked his leg on a thorny bush, and then scratched the ground with his back paws.

"Feel better?" Meagan asked, raking her shoulder-length raven hair out of her face.

He gave her a toothy grin. "Much."

Whiskey wheezed. "Would you stop pulling that poor girl every which way? She is going to be the new pack leader of the shelter and I don't want her hurt!"

Meagan jerked. "Now, wait a minute. I'm here to do my two hundred hours of forced labour and that's it. No one said anything about being a pack leader, whatever that is."

Nobel licked Meagan's hand. "Pack leaders are born, not made, and I see qualities of a born leader in you already."

Meagan frowned. "I'm not following you."

Nobel howled. "Of course not, you're a pack leader, like me!"

Whiskey groaned. It came out more like a sad-sounding meow.

"Look, kid—" Nobel began.

"Meagan. Call me Meagan."

"See? Already you're asserting your dominance. You walk like a top dog, your head's alert, your chest is out—"

"Stop staring at my chest!" Meagan blurted, covering her ample bosom with her arms.

Whiskey let out an onerous yowl. "We need you, Meagan! The shelter needs you! Be the leader we need and challenge the Bossy One!"

Meagan sighed. She crouched down and said, "Whiskey, at the end of this summer, I'll be sixteen and my plans don't include Fairy Falls. Besides, I have no clue how to run the shelter or be this pack leader you're looking for. Why is it such a big deal to find a new leader, anyway?"

Nobel growled. "The shelter is in need of money and from what Whiskey found out, there's not enough of this money to take care of all of us. Even the Ones who feed, water, and clean us are in danger of losing their jobs."

Meagan's eyes bugged. "No money? Does my aunt know any of this?"

"I doubt it," Whiskey hissed. "So, you see, if we don't find a new pack leader soon we will all lose our home."

Meagan chewed her bottom lip until it bled. Cringing, she wiped her mouth and said, "If the shelter needs money, then I think I can be of some help."

Whiskey's whole body shivered. A charge of energy went through her, as if she were a kitten again. "How can you help?"

"By doing what I did for Karen Bean. Remember? I solved her problem by telling her what you told me. So if it's true, then the shelter will be richer by the end of the week."

"But...what will the Kind One say? You've never told her or anyone else but your mother that you can talk to animals. Why start now?"

Meagan sighed. "I wasn't planning on telling Aunt Izzy, or anyone else."

"Well then, how do we get people to give us money?" Nobel yipped.

Meagan's shoulders sagged. She stared at the ground, strumming her fingers against her thighs. Something caught her eye and Whiskey turned to see what Meagan was looking at.

"OMG! I've got an awesome idea!"

Whiskey squinted. She knew her eyes weren't as good as they used to be, but she was sure Meagan was kneeling close to where Nobel had just relieved himself. She began to dig up the earth where Nobel had struck the ground with his back paw. To her, it looked like a sparkly, white rock. Whiskey blinked several times.

"A rock?" Whiskey hissed. "Humans are so silly!"

Nobel started to pant. "It's a pretty rock though, Whiskey."

"And dogs are so thick-headed!" she meowed.

Meagan laughed. "You see a pretty rock, Nobel. I see a funky kind of cell phone that only I can use to communicate with the dogs and cats. Get it?"

"No," Nobel and Whiskey woofed and meowed in unison.

Meagan rolled her eyes. "It's only gonna be used as a prop."

"But how will this save the shelter?" Whiskey asked.

"By using magic," Meagan said, scraping dirt from the stone.

"Magic? What's magic?" Nobel asked, lying on the cool grass. He stretched as if he had all the time in the world.

Meagan stopped scraping. "Look, if I tell people that I can talk to animals I'll be laughed at, called a freak, and my aunt may even lose her job. But, if I say I found this hunk of rock near the shelter and suddenly I could understand you and Whiskey, then it would be considered magic. It's no worse than someone using a crystal ball to predict the future."

Nobel rolled in the grass. "So, you're going to fool humans? Trick them into thinking that you can talk to us using that rock?"

"Yeah. Think about it, Nobel. I'm willing to bet people will donate big money to the shelter if they know I can help them solve a problem with a dog or cat, like I did for Karen Bean. And then, when the shelter has enough money, I'll just lose the rock."

Whiskey meowed. "It's brilliant! Genius, even!"

Meagan scratched her small, furry head. "Thanks, Whiskey."

"For what?" she asked, purring.

"For believing in me. It feels good inside."

"No stress?" Whiskey asked, still purring.

Meagan closed her eyes, and then opened them. "Nope. None. No pressure, no problems, just a good feeling."

"Well, as much as I'd love to stay and roll in the smells, we'd better go back. The Loud One probably has my breakfast ready," Nobel said, standing. He licked Meagan's face full on.

"Eww, stop that," Meagan said, grimacing. "I know where that tongue's been!"

As the trio left to go down the path and back to the shelter, a pair of intense, green eyes followed them closely. Once he knew it was safe, a huge grey and white tomcat, triple the size of Whiskey, jumped out of the bushes adjacent to the path. He clawed at the spot where the girl had dug up the rock. His kinked tail whipped from side-to-side. Suddenly, a large, black bird swooped down to land on the closest branch.

"Morning, Brutus," Raven cawed. "Who were they?"

Brutus looked up at the huge bird, his tattered ears lowered, his eyes now slits. "Meddlers, Raven," he growled, "and you know how much I hate meddlers."

6. The Magic Rock

"Okay, so you're telling me that this piece of quartz allows you to communicate with cats and dogs?" Aunt Izzy asked, waving the jagged crystal in Meagan's face. "That it was *Whiskey* who told you why a tom cat was spraying around Karen Bean's office?"

Her aunt wore a poker face, so Meagan had no idea how much of her tale, if any, she believed. Maybe this wasn't going to be as easy as she thought. Meagan took a deep breath, and said, "That's right. I knew you wouldn't believe me. I knew it sounded too freaky and out there, so I just avoided you all morning."

Aunt Izzy crossed her arms. "Where did you say you found this rock?"

"Quartz. You called it quartz."

She rolled her eyes. "Whatever. Where?"

"I already told you, by the back of the shed, while I was trying to get Whiskey."

"And as soon as you picked up this particular quartz, you could understand fully what Whiskey was saying to you?"

Meagan sighed. "Yes, that's right."

Aunt Izzy scratched her chin with one hand and rolled the glittering rock in the palm of her other hand. Then, looking down at Whiskey, who was stretched out next to Meagan's feet, she smirked and said, "Okay, Whiskey, we'll test this. Tell me something you like and something you don't like that I do for you."

Silence. Whiskey sat there flicking her tail.

"I don't hear anything, Meagan."

Meagan reached for the crystal. "That's because it only works for *me*."

Her aunt arched a thin, ruddy brow. "Enlighten me, then."

Meagan nodded, and then like an old-school magician waving a wand, she grasped the stone, squeezed it hard, and asked Whiskey the same question Aunt Izzy had. "Tell my aunt something you like and something you hate that she does for you."

Whiskey perked up. "Is that what she asked me? It sounded like garble."

Meagan giggled. "Answer the question."

"What'd she say?" Aunt Izzy asked, inclining her head.

"Sshhh! I'm concentrating," Meagan replied.

Whiskey's pink tongue came out to lick her equally pink nose. "Well, I like when the Kind One shares her turkey sandwich with me, but I hate when she chases me around to stick the white pill down my throat."

"Got it," Meagan said in an ominous tone.

"Got what?" Aunt Izzy asked.

"Your answer," Meagan replied, smiling. "She likes it when you share your turkey sandwich, but hates it when you try to stuff a white pill down her throat."

Her aunt balked. Then her face began to twitch.

"Aunt Izzy? Are you okay?"

"But...Whiskey needs her white pill. Without it she'll get sick and die."

"What did the Kind One say?" Whiskey asked, pawing Meagan's leg. "I sense deep sadness coming from her."

"She said if you don't take your pill—" Meagan licked her lips "—you'll get sick and die."

Whiskey sat down, appearing to mull over what Meagan had just told her. A paw came up to preen her whiskers. "Tell the Kind One I will take my pill without any fuss from now on."

Meagan nodded. "Whiskey says in future she'll take her pill, no problem."

Aunt Izzy's poker face returned. "Should I start making her an extra turkey sandwich, too?"

"Fine, I'll prove it. Where are her pills?"

Without a word, Aunt Izzy walked over to the medicine cabinet by the kitchen to retrieve a brown vial and a long plastic tube resembling a straw. She walked back, opened the vial, took out a single pill, and stuck it into the top of the plastic tube.

"No, wait," Whiskey meowed. "I hate that thing. I'd rather take it from her hand."

"Whiskey wants it from your hand," Meagan said.

Aunt Izzy laughed. "That'll be the day. Whiskey always needs a pill popper."

Meagan shrugged. "Trust me. Try it."

Taking the pill out of the popper, Aunt Izzy bent down with the pill in her open palm. Whiskey didn't even give her a chance to reach the floor. She sprang up, placed her two front paws on Aunt Izzy's hand, and gobbled up the pill as if it were a cat treat. She licked her lips as proof of swallowing it, and then began to groom her white tummy.

Not taking her eyes off her hand, Aunt Izzy stood up. "I...I don't believe it."

"Seeing is believing, Aunt Izzy. Is that proof enough?"

Beep, beep. The front door flew open and with it came a balmy breeze, as if a storm was brewing outside.

"Are we paying you to stand around, Izzy?"

She was still staring at her hand. Meagan nudged her. "Aunt Izzy, there's someone here."

"Someone?" the woman bellowed. "I'm the *Manager*! Who are you?"

Aunt Izzy snapped out of it. "Oh, Katrina, this is my niece, Meagan. She's here to do her community service hours. Meagan, as you heard, this is the shelter's manager, Katrina Smith."

Meagan shrunk like a mouse being sized up by a hungry alley cat. *So this is the woman who's called 'the Bossy One' by the animals.* She quickly gave her a once-over. No scrubs for this woman, just dark dress pants, high heels, and a printed blouse. Meagan smirked. Not too smart for Animal Shelter attire, unless the lady figured no outfit was complete without cat hair. Her short, blond hair was cut close to her head, her brows were too thin, and her piercing green eyes gave Meagan the impression that she wasn't from this planet.

Katrina nodded curtly. "I hope you don't stare at the customers that come into the shelter like you're staring at me. You may make them feel uncomfortable and leave, and we need as many animals adopted as possible."

"Er, sorry," Meagan said. "My bad."

The side door burst open as Louis pulled Gail Winn up the stairs. "Louis! Settle down, boy, hold your pipes until we get out...oh, hi, Kat, didn't see you there," Gail said, huffing to catch her breath.

"It's Katrina, not Kat."

Gail's face fell as if Katrina had blown down her sails.

Louis whined, but it didn't sound like a whine to Meagan. "Gotta pee, gotta pee!" Louis repeated.

But the dog's pleas went unheard as Aunt Izzy piped up to ask, "Did you get to speak to the Fairy Falls Council about extra funding for the shelter?"

Katrina waved a thin hand in the air. "I did. They'll get back to me at their convenience. Damn them! Since Joy MacGregor's untimely death last month, it seems that every piece of town business has been put on the back burner!"

"That's not fair, Katrina," Aunt Izzy said. "Joy has been an upstanding member of this community for years. The town needs time to grieve, that's all."

"Well, I say get over it!" Katrina spat. Aunt Izzy flinched. "What about *our* needs? The Council's nothing but a bunch of whiny lolly-gaggers if you ask me!"

Meagan noticed her aunt wasn't comfortable around Katrina. She rocked back and forth on her feet, wringing her fingers together. Aunt Izzy's shoulders were higher than normal and her posture appeared slouched. Meagan's eyes widened. *She's being dominated by that witch!* She balled her fists. *I wish that woman would piss off!*

Louis's dark ears perked up and his big, wide head inclined. He locked eyes with Meagan. "Piss, piss. Me do, me do!"

Whiskey meowed. "Uh-oh. No, Louis, not on her!"

But it was too late. Louis promptly lifted his leg and peed all over Katrina Smith's pressed pants. Stunned, Ms. Manager looked down and found she was standing in a pool of warm dog pee. "Ugh!" she screamed and tried to hop out of the puddle which only made her slip and fall back into it.

Louis jumped all over her. "Me pee more? Me pee more?"

"No, Louis!" Meagan yelled. "No more pee! Now, get off of her!"

Louis slobbered and he looked disappointed. "Me do good? Me do good?"

Meagan rubbed her face. "Yes. Good dog, now get off."

"I don't know what got into him," Gail said, tugging on Louis's leash. "He's never done that before, but he sure listens to Meagan."

Izzy looked at Meagan. "Yes. It seems my niece has a newly acquired way with animals."

"Will somebody get this mess cleaned up before people start coming through that door?" Katrina bellowed.

"Yes, of course, Katrina," Izzy said in a soothing voice. "Meagan, go get the mop please."

Meagan's shoulders sagged. "Fine," she said, heading for the kitchen. With her back facing the office, one last thought entered her mind. *If Ms. Manager thinks I'm taking her clothes to the dry cleaners, she can bite my...*

Louis perked up again. "Bite ass, bite ass?"

Before Meagan could finish the thought, a high-pitched scream followed her down the hallway. She stopped dead in her tracks and instantly regretted what she had just thought. Meagan's mouth opened, but no words followed because she knew it was too late. Louis had bitten Katrina Smith's butt. Meagan sighed. This was all her fault. The stress returned and she craved a smoke. Now Meagan not only had to pay attention to what she said, but to what she thought as well.

7. Bad Meat

he next day proved even more of a challenge. Whiskey waited impatiently to be let out of the washroom. She had hardly slept all night, going through the ductwork system to let the others know that she and Nobel had finally found the Chosen One—their new pack leader. Unfortunately for Louis, he had punctured the Bossy One's behind and she had to be rushed to the local hospital. Whiskey knew, without a doubt, what was going to happen to Louis—ten days of quarantine, no visitors, and off the adoption list until his sentence was over.

Beep, beep. The front door sounded.

Good, Whiskey thought. *It's about time Meagan got here.*

The bathroom door opened and Whiskey flew out.

"Wow, Whiskey, you're sure in a hurry to get somewhere."

Whiskey froze. That didn't sound like Meagan. She looked up. *Oh, it's just you.*

"Hey, old girl," said the young man, bending to scratch Whiskey behind the ears.

Hello, Reid, Whiskey said. Of course, all he heard was a tiny meow.

Beep, beep. The door opened again. Whiskey spied the Kind One and Meagan walking in. Today they were both wearing matching lime green scrub tops and pants. Whiskey started preening herself immediately. She wanted to be presentable to the shelter's new leader.

The boy laughed. "Hey look, it's Shrek and Shrek Two!"

Meagan scowled at the red-headed young man. "You should talk wearing those blue scrubs, *Smart-ass Smurf.*"

The Kind One stifled a giggle. "Let's see how full of chuckles you are after cleaning out the dog kennels, Reid."

Reid grinned. "Who's the pretty young thing with you, Izzy?"

Meagan dropped her scowl. Whiskey swore the girl's face turned as red as Reid's hair.

"Meagan, this is Reid, Roberta Robinson's son. Meagan's my niece and she's here to do her community hours," the Kind One explained.

"For high school?" Reid probed.

"Er...not exactly," Meagan replied, stuffing her hands in her scrub top's pockets.

"Oh, you're probably here getting extra co-op hours like me. I want to be a veterinarian when I'm done high school, so I figure this is the best place to start. It's all good."

Meagan fell silent. *Is this guy for real?* Whiskey heard her thoughts.

"Do you want me to bite him for you to see if he is real?" Whiskey asked.

"No!" Meagan yelled, pulling out her hands and waving them.

Reid backed away. "It's not all good?"

Meagan shook her head. "No, I mean, yes, it's all good. Um, I have to work now, bye."

"Start in the main cat room. Collect the water bowls," the Kind One shouted after her.

"I told you to be careful with your thoughts. At least you knew I wouldn't actually attack him," Whiskey said, running after her.

"This is going to be harder than I thought," Meagan said, grabbing the trolley and rolling it out into the next room. She flinched. "Ewww! Cat pee, cat poop, cat vomit, and cat farts! Maybe I was wrong. It's not all good."

Whiskey ignored Meagan's rant. "It's nothing to do with being hard. You just have to learn some discipline." She jumped onto the top of the trolley from a nearby scratching post.

"Discipline? That sounds an awful lot like school."

"Excuse me, Whiskey?" a small white cat with grey markings on his head and tail asked in a low voice.

Whiskey looked down. "Oh hello, George. Where's Tess?"

"I was going to ask if you had seen her. We usually go around together to scoop out any meat leftover in the cages. I'm worried about her."

"Maybe the Chosen One can help," Whiskey offered.

Meagan clenched her teeth. "Would you quit calling me that? It's getting annoying."

George's yellow eyes widened. "Can you find Tess for me, Chosen One?"

Meagan rolled her eyes. "I'll try, but only if you call me Meagan."

George rubbed up against her leg. "Thank you, thank you, Chos...I mean, Meagan."

"What does she look like?"

"There's a picture of her on the big play cage over there," Whiskey replied.

Meagan scanned the images. "She's black. So are at least twenty others on the floor."

"She's got a yellow collar on," George offered.

"I guess that will have to do."

Pushing the trolley aside, Meagan got down on her hands and knees.

"What are you doing?" Whiskey whispered.

"I'm pretending to be a cat. It's something I used to do when I was younger," she whispered. "Now quiet, I'm concentrating."

Meagan brought her nose to the floor. It flared instantly, but she remained silent. Then her nose twitched as if she had whiskers. Still on knees and hands, Meagan moved like a cat would; sleek, graceful, confident. She wiggled her behind as if she possessed a tail. This amused Whiskey, but she dared not speak to Meagan. Calmness flowed through her body; Whiskey could feel it and so could the other cats on the floor.

Meagan prowled into the back room, sniffing, twitching, and wiggling her body. It was truly a thing of beauty. Whiskey was so caught up in the moment that she hadn't heard the main room door open. A pair of blue-clad legs passed her before she snapped out of it. Startled, Whiskey decided to take matters into her own paws before Reid found Meagan on her hands and knees.

"Stop the boy from going into the back room!" Whiskey yelled. "Poppy, have your gang surround him!"

Poppy meowed loudly, and then pointed to Carol, a diluted calico with an attitude, and Olivia, a black cat with one torn ear. "Start a fight amongst yourselves, girls. Circle around the boy and keep him in it!" Poppy commanded, too fat to move herself.

A high-pitched yowl cut through the room as Carol and Olivia pawed at each other. The black cat went through the middle of the boy's legs, making him stumble and fall to the floor. Carol jumped on his chest and growled. Poppy caught up with the action and hissed in his ear. The boy jerked and tried to shimmy away, but Olivia was there to bat him across the head.

"Help!" Reid yelled, trying to wiggle away.

The air was charged with excitement. Other cats, not of Poppy's gang, started to swarm the boy. They were feeding off of his fear and anxiety. The growling went up a notch and suddenly Olivia took a swipe at an innocent bystander—an older grey feline. She spat in defense as blood trickled from her right front leg. Whiskey's yellow eyes widened. *Uh-oh, this is getting ugly. Meagan better wrap up her search for Tess, and fast.*

The door flew open. It was the Kind One. Instinctively, she grabbed the closest broom and ran toward the floundering boy. "Carol! Olivia! Poppy! Move!" the Kind One commanded as she pushed the rowdy gang of cats away from the boy. Then she helped him up.

"Reid, are you scratched or bitten?" the Kind One asked.

Visibly shaken, he shook his head. "And you wonder why I prefer dogs."

"Aunt Izzy!" Meagan screamed. "Get in here, now!"

Whiskey perked up. So did George. "Meagan found Tess! Meagan found Tess!" The little white cat with grey markings ran off toward the back room.

"George, wait!" Whiskey cried after him.

She knew there was something wrong. Meagan hadn't sounded positive. Had she found Tess? Whiskey high-tailed it to find out. When she arrived in the back, she saw Meagan crouched in one corner. Reid and the Kind One were hunched over her. George had managed to get close enough to see that it was Tess in Meagan's arms. But she was still. Whiskey sighed. That wasn't a good sign.

"Now, George dear, move along," the Kind One said, waving him away.

"Meagan! What's wrong with Tess?" George asked, moving around to her other side.

"I found her behind the cabinet. She's barely breathing. She needs medical attention, Aunt Izzy, and she needs it now!"

"Oh, my dear sweetness," the Kind One said, taking Tess's weak, limp body out of Meagan's arms. "I fear we'll never make it to Doctor Van Stock in time."

"But...but we've got to do something!" Meagan pleaded.

"I just got my license and my ride's outside. Meagan and I can take her to the vet's," Reid said, backing out of the room.

George crawled onto Meagan's lap. "Lift me up. I want to see her."

Meagan scooped up George and stood. She brought him closer to Tess.

"What are you doing?" the Kind One asked.

"He wants to see her," Meagan said.

"You're wasting time, Meagan," Reid said. "He doesn't know what's going on."

"Yes he does," Meagan said softly.

She brought George within inches from Tess. Suddenly, Tess stirred, her eyes fluttered open, and she pawed George's face. Then Tess managed to let out a weak meow, before she went limp in the Kind One's arms.

"My poor sweetness," the Kind One sobbed, cuddling Tess.

Whiskey sat in silence, taking in the emotions, the feelings, the smells, and the sounds. She knew what she had heard. George had heard it. Meagan had too. Tess's last words. "Bad meat, George. Bad meat."

8. Staff Meeting

Tess's body was placed in the freezer and an urgent call was sent out for Katrina Smith to okay an autopsy. Meagan tried to listen in on the conversation between her aunt and Ms. Manager. One point, Aunt Izzy's voice got higher, more defensive. Her face reddened. She rubbed her forehead, then slammed the desk with her fist. Things didn't seem to be going well.

"What's happening?" Whiskey asked. "All the cats want to know, especially George."

Meagan sighed and shrugged. She had no idea.

"Pack leaders know what to do," Whiskey said, whipping her tail from side to side.

"Then ask Nobel," Meagan replied in a snippy tone. "I don't have any power here. I'm just the pooper scooper. And stop reading my mind, it's incredibly creepy."

"Then stop thinking and start doing!" Whiskey hissed.

Meagan's dark brows narrowed and she twisted around to look down at Whiskey, but she wasn't there. Glancing around, it seemed Whiskey had disappeared. *Finally, some peace,* she thought.

"I can't believe it! I just can't believe it!" Aunt Izzy yelled, obviously in a fluster.

"Believe what?" Meagan asked.

"Katrina said there are no funds for an autopsy for Tess. In fact, she says there's barely enough money for any medications we may need. I don't understand. We just had our yearly dinner-auction fundraiser last month. I know at least twenty-thousand dollars were raised that night alone." Aunt Izzy began wringing her hands, rocking back and forth.

Beep, beep. The door opened slowly.

A tall woman with hard features walked in. She wore bleach-splattered jeans and an equally bleach-splattered blue scrub top. Her shoulder-length red hair was streaked with grey, yet there was something almost gentle about this woman. In her hands were four steaming cups of coffee in a cardboard holder.

"Reid phoned me. I'm sorry about Tess, Izzy," the woman said in a quiet tone.

Aunt Izzy stopped wringing her hands. "Thanks, Bertie. Though it seems our glorious leader won't pursue an autopsy. Apparently there's no extra money to do so."

Bertie wrinkled her long nose, which made her look like she was about to sneeze. "But… what about last month's fundraiser?"

Aunt Izzy shrugged. "Your guess is as good as mine."

Bertie's jaw moved back and forth. "Do you think we'll get paid this week?"

Meagan perked up. *Did I hear Bertie right? Not get paid?*

"Now, Bertie, that only happened once."

"Once is too much for me. I'm a single parent with a seventeen-year-old son who wants to go off to university in another year." Bertie's chin quivered. "I'll never get to retire to Florida at this rate!"

It was the quietest yell Meagan had ever heard.

"Feel the Quiet One's fear? Now do you see why we need a new pack leader?"

Meagan glanced down to find Whiskey rubbing against her leg. "Still mad at me?"

"Why would I be mad at you, Meagan?" Aunt Izzy asked, unclasping her fingers. "You were the one who found Tess."

Meagan recovered. This was getting tricky. She reached for the quartz in her scrub pocket and flashed it at her aunt. "I wasn't talking to you."

Bertie's deep brown eyes locked with Meagan's blue eyes, but she remained silent.

"Meagan, this is Roberta Robinson, Reid's mom. A.k.a. Bertie to us grunts."

Bertie's features softened. She nodded. "Reid's right. You are pretty."

Meagan's stomach flipped and her face heated up. *I'm going to shove Reid's head in a pile of dog poop,* she thought.

"Would you like me to arrange that for you?" Whiskey asked.

"Nooo!" Meagan yelled.

Bertie balked. "Sorry. I didn't mean to embarrass you."

Aunt Izzy rolled her eyes. She reached over for a hot cup. "Never mind, Bertie, I'll explain Meagan's odd outbursts to you during break."

Bertie nodded. "I'll call Gail up for coffee. Sadie's off today, but said she'd meet us for morning break. She sounded urgent."

Aunt Izzy laughed. "Sadie always sounds urgent!"

Beep, beep. The door burst open, almost knocking the coffee tray out of Bertie's hands.

"Sadie, dear, slow down, there's no fire here," Aunt Izzy said, sidestepping a short, skinny woman who looked as if she could have been a bodybuilder at one time.

Sadie pulled a cup out of the tray Bertie was holding and tore the plastic lid off. "Honey, 'slow down' is not in my vocabulary."

Meagan noticed that her long, bleach-blond ponytail twitched like an irritated cat's tail. Instead of scrubs, she wore tight jeans and an equally tight black T-shirt. Her tanned face appeared pinched as she darted around the office in search of something, all the while taking small sips from her coffee.

"Let me guess. The Quick One?" Meagan whispered down to Whiskey.

"The one and only," the calico replied, preening her whiskers.

"Sadie, dear, what are you looking for?" Aunt Izzy asked.

"Proof," she snapped back.

"Proof?" Bertie asked. "What kind of proof?"

Sadie's hazel eyes flew across an open book on the front desk. Her finger struck a page. "This kind of proof."

Aunt Izzy and Bertie walked over to the desk. Suddenly, Meagan heard hard-hitting footsteps bounding up the stairs. The side door flew open. "Okay, gals, the doggies are fed and watered, it's my turn now!" Gail bellowed.

"Gail, did you write this receipt?" Aunt Izzy asked.

Blowing stray strands of salt and pepper hair out of her face, Gail strolled over to the desk and looked at the receipt. She scratched her chin. "Well, that's my signature. Must have, I guess. What's the big deal?"

Sadie scowled at Gail. "The deal is that money is missing for this deposit," she said sharply, "and it's not the first time this has happened. The last time I covered your ass by taking money out of the donation jar!"

Gail's ruddy face fell. She scratched her chin again. Sharp pricks pierced Meagan's legs. She winced and looked down. Whiskey was trying to climb up her leg.

"Why are the Quick One angry and the Loud One upset?" the cat asked.

Meagan hunkered down to pick Whiskey up. "Because" —she whispered in Whiskey's ear— "Gail is being accused of stealing money from the shelter."

"Nonsense!" Whiskey roared. "The Loud One would never do that!"

The women jumped in unison at Whiskey's caterwauling.

"Put that cat down, young lady, you're hurting her," Sadie snapped.

"That young lady is my niece, Sadie, and—" Aunt Izzy turned to stare at Meagan "—if Whiskey has something to say, then now would be a good time to share it with the staff. Isn't that right, Meagan?"

Feeling her throat tighten wasn't helping the fact that Meagan had just been shoved on stage and forced to perform in a play she wanted no part in. Slowly, she squeezed the cool quartz for some kind of reassurance. The con was on and she had an audience now. She brought the rock up to her closest ear and pretended to listen to it while the other women stared at her, all sharing the same expressions of narrowed brows, pursed lips, and sunken cheeks.

"Since when did Whiskey grow a set of vocal chords?" Gail asked.

"Since my niece claims to have found a rock that possesses the magical power to talk to animals," Aunt Izzy answered bluntly.

Sadie burst out into laughter, Gail guffawed, and Bertie almost spit out her coffee.

"Believe me, most of the time I don't want to know what they have to say!" Gail roared.

"Your niece has got quite an imagination, Izzy," Sadie said, shaking her head.

Bertie wiped her mouth. "Now, girls, I've heard that some gifted people are actually capable of understanding and talking to animals."

"Yeah, Bertie. Doctor Doolittle and that Timmy kid on Lassie reruns!" Gail guffawed, slapping her leg. "Is that true, girl? Momma's down the well!" she said, mimicking a young boy.

The four women broke out in laughter.

Meagan shushed them all. *If I'm going to pull this off, I'd better act like I know what I'm doing,* she thought.

"What are you doing?" Whiskey asked.

"Being a pack leader," Meagan whispered through clenched teeth.

"It's about time," Whiskey purred.

Before Meagan could reply to Whiskey's crack, hurried footsteps came up behind her. She glanced over her shoulder to see Reid looking flushed and shaking terribly. His caramel brown eyes wildly darted at first to Gail, and then to Bertie.

"Reid? What's wrong?" Bertie asked, putting her coffee down on the desk.

"Damn, the boy looks mighty spooked," Gail added.

"Quick! Mom, Gail! Something's wrong with Mary Jane. She puked all over her kennel, and then just keeled over! I-I think she's dying!"

9. Sweet Secret

"I'll miss her."

Nobel snorted. "You hated each other, Whiskey."

The old calico stared into Mary Jane's empty cage. It had been cleaned with bleach at least three times. The harsh smell still lingered, making Whiskey's nose twitch like a mouse's. The pit bull's blanket had been thrown away and her rubber toy scrubbed until the smell of her was gone. *Was this all there was to it?* Whiskey wondered. *To be simply washed away as if you never existed?* Over the years, she'd seen dogs and cats come and go at the shelter. Most had gone home with a human companion, while a small portion, like her, would probably live and die here. That was the connection she'd felt with Mary Jane. That was the reason she would miss her.

"Did you find out anything?" Whiskey asked, starting to groom herself.

Nobel stretched before he said, "Only that Louis heard Mary Jane mutter something about her food tasting sweet, before she took her last breath."

Whiskey stopped grooming. Her thoughts turned to Tess and to her last words. *Bad meat,* she had uttered. "Did Mary Jane's food taste bad?"

Noble shook his big head. "She didn't live long enough to say. All I know is that the Loud One fixed all our meals the night before like she has always done. My food tasted fine." Whiskey fell silent. If food was the problem, then all the animals in the shelter were in danger. It didn't matter if you were a cat or dog, a long-time resident like Mary Jane, or a fairly newer entry like Tess—no one was safe. Not even her, or Nobel.

"There's also talk that the Loud One is in trouble," Nobel said, breaking Whiskey's thoughts. "Is that true?"

Whiskey sighed. "Yes. Something about stealing money, but you and I both know that is impossible. The Loud One's feelings are true to us. I've sensed it and so have you. Humans are so silly and stupid!"

"They have their ways and we have ours, Whiskey," Nobel offered.

"If they had our instincts they'd be a lot smarter!" she hissed.

Beep, beep. The upstairs door sounded.

Whiskey's back arched and her fur fluffed, making her appear bigger.

"It can't be morning already, it's still dark outside," Nobel whined.

"Shhh. Listen, Nobel, there are footsteps coming down the stairs."

Nobel sniffed, and then wagged his tail. "It's Meagan and Reid!"

Louis stirred in his sleep and the old hound in the next room howled.

The door creaked open and Meagan and the young man she called Reid slipped into the pound area. Whiskey took herself off alert and her fur went smooth again as the lights switched on. She blinked and her eyes adjusted to the light. Some of the dogs whimpered.

Nobel howled. "What are you doing here, Meagan?"

"And what's *he* doing here with you?" Whiskey hissed.

"I'll explain in a minute," Meagan whispered to the both of them. "Just trust me."

"Hey, what's Whiskey doing on the dog floor?" Reid asked, catching up to Meagan. "Does she have a death wish?"

Meagan stroked Whiskey's back. "Whiskey uses the ducts to move through the shelter, and believe it or not, she gets along with most dogs. It's us humans she doesn't understand."

Reid rubbed his eyes. "So try to help me understand something, Meagan. You text me in the middle of the night to get out of bed, steal my mom's key to the shelter, and drive us over here because you have something urgent to show me that can't wait until morning. Now would be a good time for show and tell."

Meagan took a deep breath in, and then let it out. Whiskey sensed that Meagan was wound up like a ball of string, so she rubbed up against Meagan's leg to remind her that she wasn't alone. It worked. Whiskey felt Meagan ease up and relax.

"Okay, I have to trust someone on this, so I'll just say it. I can talk to animals."

Reid's face twitched. "You could have texted me that."

"I'm serious!" Meagan shouted.

"Me too." Reid yawned. "Can we go now?"

"No. I brought you here to prove it and that's what I'm gonna do. Just give me a second to think of something to ask Nobel, since you work on the dog floor most of the time."

"Tell him the girl he likes is using him," Nobel woofed.

"I can't tell him that, Nobel, that's mean."

"Her name is Kayla," Nobel insisted, his eyebrows bobbing up and down.

"Why is Nobel barking so much?" Reid asked.

"Er, he said this girl named Kayla is using you," Meagan blurted.

Reid's jaw dropped. "Kayla Reynolds?"

Meagan shrugged. "I don't know, is there more than one Kayla?"

"No! How do *you* know about Kayla?" Reid demanded, balling his fists.

Meagan gulped. "I don't know anything." She looked down at Nobel. "But he does."

"What a minute—" Reid raked his thick, red hair "—my mom said you were about to show her and the rest of her co-workers some kind of magic trick with a rock before I told everyone about Mary Jane puking. Is this what this is about? Is this a joke? If it is, I'm not laughing."

"Believe me, it's no joke, Reid." Meagan dropped her chin to her chest and sighed heavily. "And I don't need a stupid rock to talk to animals, just my…imagination."

"Your imagination?" Reid smacked the door to Mary Jane's empty kennel. "Then you've got a real screwed up imagination, playing with people's minds!"

Whiskey could feel his anger sweep through her body like a bad storm and flow out to the rest of the kennels, awakening most of the dogs. Some howled, some barked, some whined.

Meagan raised her chin and glared at Reid. "And that's the main reason why I've kept this ability a secret, even from my dad. Everyone reacts just like you. They make fun of me, tell me I'm lying. The only person who ever believed me was my mom and now she's…she's gone."

Nobel growled his displeasure. "Tell Reid that I sensed Kayla's emotions when she was down here helping him the other day and they were not the same feelings he had. She overpowered him, weakened him into submission."

"Why is Nobel growling at me?" Reid backed away from Nobel's cage. "He…he never growls at me."

Meagan crossed her arms. "Ask him yourself, douche-bag."

Whiskey pawed Meagan's jeans. "Pack leaders do not act—"

"Fine!" Meagan cut in, waving her hands. "Nobel said that Kayla's a big flirt and you're buying into her crap! There. You heard it straight from the pack leader!"

"You could have softened the blow, Meagan," Whiskey mewed.

"I agree. His face just turned redder than his hair," Nobel whined.

"But, I-I thought she liked me," Reid muttered.

Beep, beep.

Both Meagan and Reid jumped. "I thought you locked the front door?" she whispered, which was redundant, since all the barking and howling drowned her out.

"I did." Reid scratched his nose. "Someone else must be here who has a key. It's a good thing I parked behind the shed so no one knows we're here."

"Quick, go shut off the light and hide," Meagan said, pointing.

"Where?" Reid asked, running for the switch.

"In here, with me," Nobel said.

"You're not big enough to hide the both of us," Meagan said as she scooped up Whiskey.

"Tell him to hide with Louis, then," Whiskey said, catching her breath.

Meagan nodded. "Louis, hide Reid, okay?"

Louis jumped up against the cage door. "Me do, Meagan, me do!"

Reid stopped. His nose flared. "You're kidding, right? I think Louis crapped out all his dinner in there."

Whiskey heard footsteps coming down the stairs. "There's no time, Meagan. Tell him to suck it up."

Reid must have gotten the message because he opened Louis's cage and leapt in. Whiskey heard rustling and an odd grumble from Reid as Meagan swung open Nobel's cage, and jumped in. *At least we have a blanket to hide under,* Whiskey thought. *Poor Reid has to settle for soiled newspaper.* By now some of the dogs had calmed down. Nobel howled a few times to tell the rest of his pack to settle down before the pound door swung open.

Curious, Whiskey jumped out of Meagan's arms and onto her shoulders, and then pounced up onto the top of the cinder blocks that separated each kennel. She crept down low, her ears flattened.

"What are you doing?" Meagan whispered.

"Observing," she meowed quietly.

"Go away, go away," Louis barked, then ran in a circle as if chasing his tail.

Whiskey heard a raspy cough. It sounded strangely feminine, but she wasn't quite sure. The footsteps stopped in front of Louis's cage. Whiskey hoped Reid was hidden well enough and that Louis's big body shielded him from the eyes of that human. Peering over the blocks, Whiskey noted this human wore a dark, hooded jacket. Smelling for an identity would prove to be a daunting task given the wide variety of odors and scents surrounding her.

Waiting patiently, the old calico watched the cloaked intruder pull a small wrapped package out of a pocket. A gloved hand ripped open the paper. Her pink nose flared and Whiskey knew without a doubt that a piece of raw meat lay exposed. A needle connected to a tube was extracted from another pocket. An ominous feeling swept through Whiskey's small body. Suddenly, her tail twitched and she sneezed. Her bells jingled.

Startled, the human balked, peered down the hall, and then quickly stabbed the meat with the needle, injecting whatever was inside that tube into it. Withdrawing the needle, the human stepped back and threw the meat over the fenced gate of Louis's cage.

"Meat, meat! Tasty, tasty!" Louis barked, scrambling to sniff out the morsel on the floor of his kennel.

The human coughed again, and then turned, opened the door, and ran up the stairs.

Beep, beep, went the front door.

10. Smoke Screen

"Meagan, tell Reid to take the meat away from Louis!" Whiskey meowed. "I saw the human stick something into it!"

Meagan's shoulders tightened. "Reid! Grab that piece of meat! Now!"

"Give it up, Louis!" Reid commanded, shuffling around Louis's cage.

"My meat, my meat!" Louis barked.

"Let it go, Louis!" Meagan yelled, scrambling to stand.

"Louis, listen to Meagan!" Nobel howled.

Meagan unlocked Nobel's kennel gate. She had to get to Louis before he swallowed that meat. Questions pummeled through her mind. *Is the meat bad? Bad like the meat Tess had eaten? Bad like the meat Mary Jane could have eaten?* Stumbling over her sandaled feet in the darkness didn't help her get to Louis's cage. Finally, grasping for cage's gate, she swung it open and reached in. However, Meagan grabbed a handful of Reid's hair instead.

"Oww! Let go, I almost had it!" Reid yelled.

"My bad." Meagan released Reid and grabbed Louis's collar instead.

"Drop it now, Louis!" Meagan shook the excited dog.

Louis obeyed and released the meat from his slobbering jaws. She heard newspapers rustling while Reid sifted through the ones on the floor. "Got it," he said, jumping out of the cage and almost knocking Meagan over.

"Hey, watch it!"

"My bad," Reid replied, mimicking Meagan's tone. He switched on the lights.

Meagan burst into laughter. "Dog crap and newspaper are a great look for you!"

"No meat, Meagan? No meat?" Louis whined.

Meagan bent down and scratched Louis behind the ears. "No meat, Louis. I don't want you to get sick and die like Mary Jane."

Louis's brown eyes widened. He stared intensely at Meagan. She shuddered, as if the big dog had touched her deep down in some way. Then, he licked her face. Meagan winced. "Eww, Louis, you've still got drool all over your mouth."

"Like you said, great look, Doolittle," Reid said, pulling bits of newsprint from his jeans and black T-shirt.

Meagan straightened, brushing down her black leggings. She shut the gate to Louis's cage and then poked Reid in the ribs. "At least I don't stink."

"I beg to differ," Whiskey meowed, sliding down from the top of the kennel. "Have you checked your feet?"

Meagan looked down. Doggy poop covered most of her plastic sandals. She glanced at Reid. "Maybe you should give Louis clean papers before we go."

Reid nodded. "Maybe you should help."

Nobel growled. "Tell Reid to bring that meat here, Meagan. I want to smell it."

"Did Nobel just say something?" Reid asked.

"He wants to smell the meat," Meagan replied. "My guess is maybe he'll get a whiff of whoever gave it to Louis."

Whiskey rubbed up against Reid's legs. "Tell Reid he can scoop my litter box anytime."

Meagan giggled. "I'm sure he'll appreciate that, Whiskey."

Reid's face twitched. "It's true. It's really true, isn't it? You *can* understand animals."

"I swear, you're as thick-headed as Louis," Meagan snapped. "Do you think I'd drag you out of bed in the middle of the night for a joke? Of course it's true!"

"Does anyone else know?" Reid asked. "I mean, that you're for real, that you can talk to animals without a magical rock."

"No. Just you."

"Not even your aunt?"

Meagan rolled her eyes. "Not even her. The rock was just so they wouldn't think I'm some kind of freak or liar."

Reid smiled. It was more like the silly grin of a child who had been unleashed in a toy store. He nervously pulled at some paper stuck to his pants. "So…why tell me, then?"

Meagan pursed her lips. It would have been easier to text him her answer. *Ur my only choice. LOL.* Yep, that would have been much easier. No adult would have listened to her bantering about communicating with animals, much less kids her age. However, Reid did possess a special connection with the animals here at the shelter. He was kind, caring, and when no one was looking, compassionate by fluffing blankets and giving out extra treats. At least that's what some of the dogs on the floor had told her. Those qualities alone made Reid her safest bet in sharing her secret. Other than her mother, no one else came close.

She stared at her feet. "Like I said, I need to trust somebody."

"Meagan, meat now!" Nobel barked. "Before it loses the scent."

Startled by Nobel's gruffness, Meagan grasped Reid's arm and pulled him down the hall. "Nobel needs to sniff that meat. He thinks maybe he can get a hit on who gave it to Louis."

"You mean like searching for fingerprints like those crime shows do?" Reid asked, holding the meat at arm's-length.

"Yeah, you could say Nobel's like a forensic lab on all fours."

"Nobel's not a Lab, Meagan," Whiskey meowed. "He's part Husky and—"

"Get a sense of humour, Whiskey," Meagan cut in, shaking her head.

Sliding to the entrance of Nobel's cage, Meagan unlocked the gate and let him out. Whining, with his tail erect and wagging, Nobel began to sniff the meat. Suddenly, he backed off, his hackles bristled and his ears flattened. He growled.

"What's the matter, boy?" Reid asked, trying to bring the meat closer to him.

Nobel continued to move away until the door leading to the other kennels blocked his path. He bared his teeth and growled again, louder this time.

"May I suggest Reid retreat," Whiskey said, coming up from behind.

"Reid, Whiskey says to back off," Meagan said in a cautious tone.

Nodding, Reid hid the raw meat behind his back and slowly backed away from Nobel.

"What's up, Nobel?" Meagan asked, reaching over to pat him.

Nobel's ears moved forward. "The meat stinks. It reeks of smoke. Smoke from those white sticks."

"You mean cigarette smoke?" Meagan asked.

Nobel licked his nose. "Yes. By the stench of that meat, the human smokes lots of white sticks. Lots, like the mean human who used to own me."

Meagan thumbed her chin and at the same time Louis barked, "Ohh, me feel dizzy. Ohh."

Nobel's ears perked up. He sprinted to Louis's kennel. Meagan and Whiskey followed. Meagan moved aside the quarantine paper hanging limply over the door and peered in. Louis was a little wobbly—more than normal. He swayed from paw to paw.

"Sit down, fool, before you fall!" Nobel commanded.

"Hee, hee, Nobel stupid looking," Louis barked. Stupid, stupid, stupid."

"Something's not right with him, Meagan," Whiskey said. "It's like he's—"

"Drunk," Meagan cut in.

Both Nobel and Whiskey looked up at Meagan.

"What is drunk?" Whiskey asked, inclining her head.

Meagan sighed. "It's a state us humans get into 'cause we're bored. At least that's the reason I got drunk."

Whiskey hissed. "Humans are so silly and stupid!"

She crossed her arms over her black long-sleeve top. "Don't judge me. It happened only once when I was out at a party with Cassie."

"One too many times, I'd say," Whiskey growled. "A pack leader needs to stay focused."

"Uh, Meagan," Reid muttered. "I think we have a problem."

Meagan looked down the hall where Reid stood. Mimicking an expressionless mannequin, he held up the piece of meat he'd wrestled from Louis. The basement lights were bright enough for her to see a translucent greenish liquid dripping from the meat. Reid ran a finger along the bottom of the meat, then stuck it into his mouth. He closed his eyes then opened them. "Sweet," he whispered.

"Eww, that's the grossest thing—"

"Antifreeze," Reid said, cutting her off. "This meat has been juiced with antifreeze."

Meagan's chest tightened. Panic pooled down into the pit of her stomach as she remembered the time a neighbour's dog had drank antifreeze left in a pail in a garage, three winters ago. Two days later, depressed, weak, and dehydrated, the dog had died a horrible death. She looked at Louis—still teetering—and glanced at Reid. She forced her lips apart, and said, "But, Louis didn't swallow any of the meat."

Reid's shoulders sagged. He turned the meat around. Meagan's eyes bugged. Chew marks had claimed a good portion of the poisoned slab. With a clenched jaw, Meagan pulled out her cell phone and did something she thought she would never do— she called her Aunt Izzy for help.

11. Confronting Shadow

An ominous buzz Whiskey had never experienced in all her years living here charged through the shelter. Since the attempted poisoning on Louis three days before and the deaths of Mary Jane and Tess, the shelter no longer felt like a sanctuary for the lost and abandoned. Whiskey shuddered. It had been a tough job, calming the cats, some of which swore they wouldn't touch canned meat ever again. Even George refused to take one bite and would go and hide when the bowls were being doled out on the floor. Whiskey also noticed that he hadn't been the same since Tess died. Deep down, she knew George needed to move on, to try to find a family who would adopt him and take him away from the uncertainty of this place.

A clatter of dishes sliding across the floor jerked Whiskey out of her thoughts. The Quick One was on duty today and she moved about the peeling blue floor as if a legion of fleas had crawled up her butt. Whiskey was getting dizzy watching her. She spied George, crouched next to Shadow's big metal cage in the corner of the room. Signs were hung around the moody grey tabby's quarters, letting the public know to keep their distance. Whiskey's ears flattened. That miserable cat preyed upon the weak-minded felines on the floor and somehow she managed to control a good-sized colony from inside of her cage. Well, it was Whiskey's job to make sure George wouldn't be one of those swayed cats. She hobbled in George's direction, groaning from the stiffness in her back legs. The Quick One cut her off halfway.

Whiskey sat down to preen herself, not wanting to draw attention to where she was heading. While grooming, Whiskey observed the Quick One placing a bowl full of meat in front of George, and then opening the door to the vacant side of Shadow's cage to place another full bowl inside. She shut the door and slid the divider out so that Shadow could move freely into the clean side of her cage. The Quick One slid it back and true to her nature, wiped down the cage, scooped the litter, and filled the dry food bowl in the unoccupied side before Whiskey even finished combing one side of her face. The Quick One closed the door tight, and then darted off toward the laundry room.

This was the way it had been ever since Shadow had arrived on the steps of the shelter; left in a box with a large log placed on top. Deemed vicious by the Animal Shelter Board, Shadow was destined to live in that divided cage until she calmed down enough to get spayed. Whiskey snorted. That would be the day.

Grunting, Whiskey got up and ambled over to where George lay, vacantly staring into the meat-filled metal bowl. Suddenly, a grey paw emerged from the cage to swipe at Whiskey. She moved in time, wincing at having to make the unexpected movement.

"Leave George be. I was consoling him first, old feline!" Shadow hissed.

"Since you're not in heat, I can't see how that's possible!" Whiskey growled, feeling the fur on the back of her neck rise.

A low growl emanated from the back of Shadow's throat. Whiskey could feel a presence behind her and she turned, her back arched and her tail fluffed three times its size. A black, neutered, year-old male and a snot-nosed, creamed-coloured older male with allergies stared Whiskey down. She relaxed. These two were no threat. All she had to do was call for Boscoe and they'd scatter and hide in different directions. However, seeing as the big, black tom was nowhere to be seen, she'd have to take care of this matter herself. Twisting around, Whiskey reached for George's bowl of meat and with one protruding claw, she flung it at the pair of fraidy-cats.

"Hey, fellows, want to be the shelter's new food tasters?"

"Watch out for that meat!" the black cat meowed. "It...it might be bad!"

The cream-coloured cat fell over his legs and sniffed. "Helph! Bad meath, bad meath!"

The two cats stumbled over each other before they stuffed themselves underneath the closest table near the bucket of cat kibble. Shadow growled again.

"Coward," Shadow hissed.

"Coward?" Whiskey meowed. "If that's the case, then I'd love to see you go down to the dog floor sometime. I know of a couple of dogs who'd love to sink their jaws into your flabby butt."

Shadow growled, her pupils widening, and she crouched low, ready to spring. "One of these days there will be no bars between us, old calico."

Whiskey grinned the best she could, with what few teeth she had left. "I guess you've never heard the human expression 'when hell freezes over'."

Shadow leapt at the bars, flailing claws trying to swat Whiskey, but she sat out of reach by a whisker. "You missed," she mewed.

"Whiskey, you shouldn't make Shadow mad," George whispered, still crouching at the side of the cage. "Sometimes what she says makes sense."

Whiskey snorted. "She is trying to control you, George. It is what that scheming tabby does best!"

George hung his head. "Maybe, but...she makes me feel good. Just like Tess did."

"Idiot!" Whiskey meowed. "It's her scent that's making you feel good. You're lucky she's not in heat!"

George lifted his head. "Don't talk to me like that!" His eyes widened, his back arched. "Shadow is nice, nice like Tess!"

He bolted past Whiskey, heading for the back room where Meagan had found Tess. Whiskey sat in silence. What was happening to this place, her home? The younger cats had never been rude or ignored her before. She was always respected, admired even, by the populace of the shelter. Her word was tuna here. She got along with most of the dogs and for years she had tried to bridge the gap between the two species. So what had changed?

"You're losing your power here, old calico," Shadow purred. "It starts with the young not listening and moves through the shelter like the whispers of fleas until no cat, or dog, will want to listen to a feeble-minded feline like you. It's survival of the fittest and you're no longer fit to lead."

Whiskey's ears flattened. She lunged to take a swipe at Shadow, but as her paw entered the grey tabby's domain, a claw snagged the scratch pad hanging inside. Her eyes widened. Whiskey tried to pull away, but it was useless. The bells on her collar jingled wildly. Shadow hissed. Delight danced within her dark pupils. She held nothing back, her claws digging deep into Whiskey's soft, furry face. Her muscles tensed and she yowled while Shadow viciously yanked out her nails. Then Shadow retreated into a corner of her cage and crouched low, her tail whipping from side to side in preparation for the next strike.

"Let's see how well you observe with no eyesight, old cat," the tabby growled.

"Shadow! Leave Whiskey alone!"

Startled, Whiskey looked up, feeling fresh blood trickling down one side of her face. Meagan stood over her like a crazed cat ready to claim her territory. She grabbed for the closest broom and whacked the side of the metal cage. She did it again and again, until Shadow was cowering in the farthest corner. Meagan moved quickly around Whiskey, opened the sliding panel to the clean part of Shadow's cage, and whacked the side in warning to the nasty tabby.

"Move next door, or the broom handle finds a new home," Meagan warned.

Shadow hissed. "This isn't over, human!"

Meagan slid the divider back into place, and then banged on the side of the cage where Shadow now resided. "When Louis gets better, I'll have to introduce the two of you."

Whiskey's face throbbed. Meagan opened the door and released her claw from the scratch pad. Then Meagan carefully picked Whiskey up and cradled her in her arms. "I guess the cat didn't get your tongue this time," Meagan whispered.

Whiskey purred. "No. But I would have enjoyed seeing that pussy get a broom up her—"

"Meagan! What happened to Whiskey?"

Jolted out of her purr, the old calico turned to stare eye-to-eye with the Quick One.

"Uh, she got into a scrap with Shadow," Meagan replied. "I was going to take her into the bathroom to clean her scratch."

The Quick One sharply nodded. "Use peroxide and the yellow ointment in the drawer."

Meagan smiled. "Okay, Sadie."

Whiskey felt Meagan move to side-step the Quick One, but she outpaced her to stand in front of them. "You know, Meagan, I never got the full story. Why did you and Reid come here the other night?"

Meagan gulped. Whiskey sensed uneasiness in Meagan, as if a pawful of litter was stuck in her throat. "Well, umm, it's like this, Reid and me, you see, we—"

The Quick One's eyes widened. "Ohh! I get it, say no more, say no more, your secret's safe with me."

Meagan wrinkled her nose. "What secret?"

The Quick One winked at her. "Your crush on Reid. Look, honey, I understand the cravings of young love, but couldn't you find a better place to make out than the shelter?"

Whiskey felt Meagan getting hot, then hotter, as if a sun beam was spreading through her. Suddenly, the main room door opened with bang, followed by a harsh cough. "Coffee's gettin' cold, and my nerves need a smoke. Coming, Sadie?"

Whiskey peered over Meagan's shoulder. The Loud One was standing there with a cup in her hand and a white stick bobbing from the corner of her mouth. The Quick One waved at her. "You don't have to ask me twice, Gail." Then she turned her focus back to Meagan. "Go take care of Whiskey, we'll chat later." She winked at Meagan again.

Whiskey detected relief surging through Meagan. It was a strange sensation, this break, this release, like being freed from a cage. Whiskey bounced in Meagan's arms as she followed the Quick One out of the main cat room, and then turned left to enter the bathroom. She switched on the light, plopped Whiskey on the counter, closed the door, and locked it. Rifling through the top drawer, Meagan pulled out a bottle filled with clear liquid, a cotton ball, and a rolled up tube.

"What was the Quick One talking about, Meagan? Your whole body got hot."

"Nothing. Never mind. It's not important," Meagan replied through clenched teeth.

Whiskey decided to let it go and started to purr. "Thank you for saving me."

Meagan smiled while dousing the cotton ball with the clear liquid. "Reid's been banned from the shelter." Her smile faded.

Whiskey's ears moved forward. "For how long?"

Meagan shrugged. "I don't know. A week. Two weeks. Maybe longer."

"Humans are so silly and stupid!" Whiskey hissed.

Meagan's face hardened. She blotted the cotton ball over Whiskey's open wound.

The old cat yowled. "You did that on purpose!"

"So sorry. I'm silly and stupid."

"I didn't mean you!"

Meagan's smile returned. She stroked Whiskey's chin, careful not to come too close to her injury. "How's Louis?" Whiskey asked, purring.

"He's almost back to his crazy, old self. Aunt Izzy isn't as pissed with me as I thought she'd be 'cause Doctor Van Stock told her if it weren't for Reid and me being there, Louis would have been dead in two days. I told her we came here 'cause I forgot my cell phone and wanted to call Dad. She believed me."

"So why did Reid get banned?"

Meagan reached for the ointment and squeezed a little out on her finger. "He stole his mom's key, so apparently he can't be trusted around here anymore, or so Ms. Manager says. There's even talk that he might be responsible for the missing money. It's all a bunch of crap!"

Meagan dabbed the ointment into Whiskey's cut. It didn't hurt as much as the clear liquid had. "Aunt Izzy said the cops will do nightly checks on the shelter, but because there are only animals here and no people in the building it's not much of a priority."

That harsh sound returned in Meagan's voice again. Whiskey rubbed up against her finger. "Only some humans are silly and stupid." She purred.

An urgent pounding on the bathroom door startled Meagan and made Whiskey's fur bristle. "Meagan! Did you leave Shadow's cage open?" the Quick One asked.

Whiskey twitched her nose. The Quick One sounded fearful.

Meagan unlocked the door and opened it. Whiskey sneezed. Her bells tinkled as she pawed her nose. The smell of smoke from those white sticks was overwhelming. Meagan swept her dark bangs out of her eyes and moved a hand up to rest upon her blue scrub top. She strummed her fingers in a moment's thought. "I-I don't think so. I know I made sure I shut the side Shadow was in really tight."

The Quick One rubbed her fair hair as if digging for something. "I've told you again and again to shut both doors. Sometimes the divider doesn't go in all the way. Well, thanks to your incompetence, Shadow somehow managed to move the divider over enough to squeeze through. She's free on the floor and there's going to be a bloodbath if we don't catch her and put her back in. Go grab the leather gloves on the top shelf and follow me."

Whiskey was dizzy from the rapid garble that shot out of the Quick One's mouth. She watched Meagan reach for a pair of leather gloves. "What's this about Shadow?" Whiskey asked, jumping down from the counter. She cringed from the unexpected force of the landing.

"Shadow's loose on the floor," Meagan replied, slipping on the long gloves. "Any suggestions?"

Whiskey froze. She looked up, her tail twitching anxiously. "Yes. But you'll need a bigger broom handle."

12. Getting the Message

Meagan stared out the torn window screen. She was relieved to not have to deal with Shadow, who by now was deep in the forest that backed onto the shelter's property. Tall white pines and drooping spruces dotted the sloped landscape like guards protecting a national treasure. Rocks, saplings, and thick bushes filled in the gaps until Meagan could no longer see over the ridge. In the distance, she heard a woodpecker faithfully drumming on a defenseless tree, pummeling it until there was silence. She slid the window shut, locked it, and stripped off the leather gloves. She tossed them on the nearest table and yawned. She hadn't been sleeping well since the attempt on Louis's life.

"I wonder if Sadie will have any luck finding Shadow out there," she muttered.

"George is gone too," Whiskey said, rubbing up against Meagan.

Startled, she looked down. "Are you sure?"

"Positive. Both Poppy and Boscoe saw George follow Shadow out the window."

Meagan sighed. *Great. This is my fault,* she thought.

"It certainly is not your fault!" Whiskey meowed. "George was being stubborn."

"Stop doing that. My thoughts are my thoughts!" Meagan yelled.

"Who are you yelling at?"

Meagan's shoulders tensed. She turned, almost knocking Whiskey over, to see a girl, roughly about her age, in a metallic blue wheelchair. Her skin was a shade darker than Meagan's fair skin, as if she had applied a spray tan all over her slim body. Short, brown hair with long bangs almost covered the girl's deep green eyes. Her lace-up pink top, black yoga-style pants, and sparkly blue canvas shoes seemed top-of-the-line. Stylish compared to what Meagan usually wore—drab scrubs or jeans, hoodies, and plain T-shirts. Even the girl's makeup was expertly done, including a polish on her nails that was so shiny, Meagan swore she'd need a pair of shades if she kept staring at them.

Meagan heard hard, direct footsteps coming toward her, accompanied by the faint smell of floral perfume. "Okay, Natalie, I'll leave you to socialize with the cats while I go walk dogs."

The girl in the wheelchair glanced over her shoulder. "Sure, Kayla, see you in a bit."

Meagan inhaled sharply. *So that's Kayla—the girl who could make Reid walk through a field of dog crap in his bare feet.* Her brow creased. What did he see in her, anyway? The girl's hair was a deep purple colour and her eyes a light mauve—great look if you belonged to a witches' coven. She was also dressed like she belonged in a fashion magazine. A tight-fitting turquoise top, tapered dark jeans, and chunky black-heeled shoes didn't seem like an appropriate choice for walking dogs. Meagan smirked. Perhaps she'd sneak down and have a word with the dogs on leading Kayla down a more scenic route—like through a muddy ditch.

Meagan stifled a giggle.

"Is Reid downstairs?" Kayla asked Meagan as if she was a lowly servant.

Meagan gritted her teeth. *Control your thoughts, control your thoughts,* became her mantra. She didn't want to think the wrong thing and have the cats start using Kayla's legs as scratching posts. *But then again? Stop, stop, stop,* rippled through Meagan's mind.

"Are you sure you don't want me to give the girl a good swipe for you?" Whiskey asked.

"Nooo!" Meagan yelled and then she realized who she answered.

Kayla jerked. "Fine, I'll find him myself, freak."

Meagan opened her mouth to defend herself, but Kayla was long gone.

"Sorry about that, Kayla's a little high-maintenance," the girl in the wheelchair said.

Meagan closed her mouth and grinned. She liked this girl instantly. "Sorry for yelling, it's been a tough day," she explained. "My name's Meagan. I'm Izzy's niece."

"My name's Natalie, but you can call me Nat. The prima-donna you yelled at is my stepsister, Kayla."

Meagan laughed. Nat rolled her wheelchair forward to the middle of the floor and stopped. She noticed Nat's wheelchair had a knight's helmet embroidered on the back. Suddenly a huge, black cat jumped into her lap. "Hey, Boscoe, there you are. Are you ready for your treatment?" Nat asked as she stroked him.

"You betcha, kid," Boscoe meowed as Meagan heard his reply.

Boscoe head-butted Nat's chin and licked her nose. She giggled and so did Meagan. Then she realized that Whiskey had left her side to go sit by Nat. Other cats seemed to gather around Nat's wheelchair until there was a small crowd. Meagan frowned. *What's going on? Do the cats know something I don't? And what is this treatment Boscoe is ready for? Pedicure? Manicure? Kittycure?* She stared intensely at Nat and her muscles tightened. *By the looks of Nat, she seems more into makeovers than animal care.*

"Looks like you've got quite a fan club," Meagan said, pursing her lips.

Nat shrugged. "I guess."

Then Nat took a couple of deep breaths and closed her eyes. She rested her hands, palms up on her lap, and continued to breathe deeply. Boscoe made himself at home by curling his big body into a tight ball between Nat's legs. He started purring. In fact, most of the cats were either purring or had their eyes closed. Meagan's stomach bunched. This was getting too weird, even for her.

Feeling a little uneasy and deciding it was best to give Nat some space, Meagan reached for the closest litter box under the table and began sifting through it with a scooper. Meagan peered over her shoulder, which caused her to miss the garbage can and drop a scoop full of fresh poop all over her shoes. *Great. This day's getting better and better,* she thought, tensing her jaw.

"Not as better as how Nat makes me feel," an orange kitten mewed.

"Me too," a beige tabby meowed, stretching her long body across the floor.

"Better than better, my bones don't ache anymore," Whiskey said, purring loudly.

Meagan dropped the scooper. It clattered to the floor. She covered her ears. Couldn't she have one thought without the whole room reading her mind? "Stop doing that!"

Nat jerked. She opened her eyes. "Are...are you talking to me?"

Meagan cheeks burned. "Uh, no, I was talking...to myself."

"Do you talk to yourself often?" Nat asked, swinging her chair around to face Meagan.

"Around here I do."

Nat smiled. "I know what you mean. The animals are an awesome outlet for me."

"Outlet?" Meagan thumbed her chin. "What do you mean?"

"Animals just know stuff," Natalie said, stroking Boscoe.

Meagan giggled. "Believe me, I think they know too much stuff."

"No really, I'm serious. I can tell them anything, anything at all, and I know it stays here."

Meagan couldn't contain herself. "Newsflash, Nat, what happens in the shelter, doesn't exactly stay in the shelter!" She snorted in laughter.

Nat's face reddened. Her entire body stiffened. Boscoe put his head up.

"Hey, kid, why'd ya have to ruin a perfectly good treatment?"

"Yeah, I was just starting to relax," Poppy meowed, rolling around the floor.

"More, more, more," a tiger-striped cat with a chewed ear purred.

Whiskey looked up at Meagan. "You have no clue what Nat does, do you, Meagan?"

Meagan's face fell. Usually it was her who knew what was going on, who had an *in* with the animals, a special backstage V.I.P. pass. Her mouth went dry, now feeling invisible, non-existent, as if she were back home in Happy Valley-Goose Bay, doing nothing, being nothing, feeling nothing. It was as if she were standing on that school stage receiving the *Most Improved Student Award* all over again, and it meaning absolutely nothing to her without her mom in the audience. Meagan's chest ached and her chin trembled.

"Are you sure this girl is the Chosen One, Whiskey?" Poppy asked with her fat belly exposed. "She doesn't seem to know anything about the *feel good* energy Nat gives us."

That was it. Freak or no freak, Meagan didn't give a crap what Nat thought. She was tired, cranky, and fed up with being treated like a nobody. She balled her fists and cleared her throat. "Maybe I can't give all of you feel good energy like her, but I'm still your pack leader, so a little respect wouldn't kill you!"

"Meagan, calm down," Whiskey meowed. "You're upsetting the kittens."

"What about my feelings, Whiskey? Don't they count?"

Natalie coughed. "Are...are you okay, Meagan?"

"Of course she's not, Nat. She's a freaking weirdo!"

Meagan's whole body numbed. She glanced to her right, and there standing in the doorway with the cruelest grin on her fake-tanned face was Kayla. She laughed. "No, go on, don't let me interrupt your little chat session with the kitties. Gail told me all about how you think you can talk to the animals around here. So tell me, do they text you, too?"

"Kayla, stop it!" Nat yelled, making Boscoe jump out of her lap.

Suddenly, Meagan's cell phone vibrated in the side pocket of her blue scrub pants. Ignoring Kayla, she reached for it and swiped the screen. *R u busy?* texted Reid. She sighed deeply and quickly texted him her answer. *Save me.* It didn't take long before he answered her back. *Meet me by the shed.* Meagan nodded and pocketed her phone. Suddenly, her nose flared and she looked down. The poop on her shoes was really starting to reek.

Kayla laughed again. "Was that a text message from one of the dogs downstairs?"

Meagan balled her fists. Enough was enough, and Meagan turned to face Nat's evil stepsister. "As a matter of fact, it was Nobel. He told me to give you this present, special delivery." Then, in one swift kick, Meagan flung the kitty crap directly at Kayla's face. Bull's-eye. She hit her mark.

"Ewww!" Kayla screamed as she clawed at her face, making the cats scatter.

Nat covered her mouth, trying not to laugh.

Now was her chance. While Kayla was busy scraping poop off her face, Meagan slipped behind her and ducked out the back door that led downstairs to the dog kennels. Before the door closed, she caught Whiskey squeezing through in pursuit. She just made it.

Meagan twirled around on the landing and crossed her arms. "Oh, so now you're back to following me around. Done with Doctor Nat's feel good energy?"

Whiskey sat down at the top of the stairs. "You sound jealous. A good pack leader never looks at the small things, only the big picture."

Her arms dropped to her sides. "What's that supposed to mean?"

Whiskey preened her whiskers, and then jumped down each step carefully, passing Meagan, and leaving her behind on the landing. She turned at the bottom of the stairs, and flicked her tail. "It means it's time to start seeing with your heart, Meagan."

13. The Standoff

"Slow down, Meagan!" Whiskey hissed, trying to catch her breath.

Meagan stopped and held open the back door that led outside next to the dog runs.

"Slow enough?" she asked.

Whiskey scooted out the door. Her eyesight wasn't the best and neither was her hearing, but Whiskey's nose never failed her. She sniffed the area. *Good. Shadow isn't around.* Scent had been Shadow's strength in the shelter and now that she had escaped, Whiskey wondered how she would use it to benefit her newfound freedom. She shuddered. It was unfortunate Shadow hadn't been spayed. Whiskey didn't want to imagine a litter of feral kittens doing their mother's bidding and feeding off her wicked intentions.

Meagan darted toward the shed and Whiskey followed.

"Reid!" Whiskey meowed, ambling around the corner.

Meagan smiled. "I think Whiskey's happy to see you."

Reid reached down to stroke Whiskey's back. She arched for him. "I'm glad someone around here is happy to see me."

Meagan jabbed him in the ribs. "Hello? I'm here, aren't I?"

Reid winced. "So, who did I save you from? Sadie or Gail?"

"Neither. Try Kayla, the wicked witch of Fairy Falls."

Reid's mouth dropped. Whiskey pawed Meagan's leg. "I believe Reid still likes her."

Meagan snickered. "Betcha he won't like the new makeover I gave her. The kitty litter facial suits her."

Reid smacked the side of the shed. "You're jealous!"

Meagan rolled her eyes. "I'm not the jealous kind, douche-bag, so get over yourself!"

Reid laughed. Whiskey meowed.

"Oh, so what am I jealous of, then? It can't be her personality. She has none."

Reid grinned. "Face it, you're jealous because she's more mature than you."

Meagan's eyes bugged. "That's ridiculous! She's mean, conceited, and have you forgotten what Nobel told you about her? She uses people!"

"Kayla could have been in a bad mood that day," Reid replied, waving a hand. "That's probably what Nobel picked up on."

Whiskey was getting dizzy moving her head back and forth to watch the bantering. Humans were silly and stupid when it came to relationships. Cats might be territorial, but at least most could co-exist with each other in a respectable manner. It was too bad Meagan couldn't mark her territory like a proper pack leader. She sighed. *The Chosen One has a lot to learn.*

"Why did you call me out here, anyway?" Meagan asked, breaking Whiskey's thoughts.

"Not to Kayla-bash, that's for sure," Reid spat.

Whiskey let out a yowl. "Admit that you like him and move on!"

"Huh?" Meagan coughed. "That's crazy!"

"What's crazy?" Reid asked. "What did Whiskey say?"

Meagan's cheeks reddened. "Nothing."

"Admit it," Whiskey meowed, rubbing up against Reid's legs. "You like him, you like him."

"Did Whiskey say something about me?"

Meagan pursed her lips. "She misses you."

"Oh, well I miss you too, girl," Reid said, stroking her again. Then he stood up and stuck his hands in his jean pockets. "Wanna hear some dirt on Katrina Smith?"

Meagan inclined her head. "Go on, make my day."

"Apparently, the woman has got a serious money problem."

"How do you know that?" Meagan asked, frowning.

Whiskey perked up. "Money? Is it about the shelter?"

Meagan waved her off. "No, it's about Ms. Manager. Now quiet, I want to hear this."

Whiskey growled. *Doesn't Meagan realize that the Bossy One is to blame for our shelter's money mess? Sometimes she's as thick-headed as Louis!*

Reid removed his hands from his pockets, crossed his arms over his dark T-shirt, and leaned against the shed. "This morning, I stopped by the bank to grab some money from the ATM. I heard some yelling going on inside. It was Ms. Smith with the bank manager and she didn't look too happy."

"She never does."

"Not Smith. It was the bank manager who was pissed. Her face was all red and she was shaking a file at Smith, telling her there would be no more extensions. The manager gave her till the end of the month to pay up."

"Pay up what?"

"I'm not sure," Reid replied, shrugging. "Smith knocked the file to the floor and left in a huff. I ducked out of the way before she saw me."

"What's he saying, what's he saying?" Whiskey mewed, pawing at Meagan's pants.

Suddenly a brutal snarl, followed by a loud crash, made Whiskey jump.

"Somebody, help, please!" a frightened human female screamed.

Reid jumped. "What the—"

Whiskey darted around the corner of the shed until she caught sight of the familiar animal control van. The human who usually brought in stray dogs was nowhere to be seen. The side door of the vehicle was left open and the dog crate was empty, its gate swinging back and forth. She heard fierce growls coming from the other side of the building. She flattened her ears and pushed them back against her head. Something wasn't right.

"Please! Help us!"

"That's Kayla's voice!" Reid yelled. "Come on."

"Do we have to?" Meagan muttered.

Whiskey turned and half jumped up Meagan's legs. "Carry me! We have to get to Nat before that dog attacks her!"

Meagan's eyes bugged. "Nat's with Kayla?"

Whiskey meowed. "Hurry, before it's too late!"

Reid was ahead of them, but not for long as Meagan passed him with ease, like a trained relay runner. Sailing up the steps and following the wraparound deck that led to the back where the outside lunch table was, Meagan skidded to a stop. She lost her footing, almost tripping over a discarded leash on the deck, and squeezed Whiskey tightly.

"Ease up, Meagan, or you'll pop me like a balloon!" Whiskey hissed.

Meagan apologized and placed Whiskey on the railing. At the end of the deck, where it sloped to meet the gravel, Nat's wheelchair lay empty on its side, its wheels spinning fast. Both of them heard growling coming from behind the building, by the outdoor cat play cage. Reid finally caught up, huffing. A scream, and then a high-pitched squeal, followed his arrival.

Meagan turned to Whiskey. "Stay here."

"Like hell," Reid said.

Meagan clipped him across the back of the head. "Not you! Whiskey."

"Like hell," she meowed, and then scooted across the railing, jumping over the abandoned wheelchair.

"Get back here!" Meagan screamed after her before she dashed around the corner.

Whiskey sensed she was being followed and peered behind her. Reid was on her heels and catching up fast. Suddenly, she hit a deep rut in the ground and rolled a few feet. Reid sailed over Whiskey and landed on his back. Whiskey groaned while raising her head. The fur on her body bristled and her tail flitted as though it were on fire. She spied Nat, sprawled across the floor in the big play cage, while Kayla braced the door shut. The latch on the door still hadn't been fixed yet, so it was loose and lopsided.

The older girl was doing everything humanly possible to keep a huge, black male dog from trying to get at them.

Whiskey heard a vicious growl as the dog lunged at the door. It was hard to tell from this distance, but she guessed the dog was part pitbull, part hound…and part insane. Drool dripped from his mouth, his ears were back, and his hackles up. He charged the door a third time. Kayla's whole body shook and she fell to her knees. Nat screamed and dragged herself toward the opposite end of the cage, pushing aside litter pans and knocking over dishes along the way.

"Hold on, Kayla, I'm coming!" Reid yelled.

Whiskey's chest tightened. Either Reid was the bravest human she'd ever known or the stupidest. She twitched her whiskers. She'd go with the stupidest. Whiskey heard the mad dog sniff and snort long enough to realize there was fresh prey on the outside of the cage. He snarled and bounded around it until he spied Reid, holding up a tattered straw broom.

Suddenly, a shoe flew over Reid's head and hit the huge mutt square on the nose. Caught off guard, he barked, stumbled, and shook his massive body. He sniffed the shoe, growled, and looked up. His dark, red eyes seared into Meagan like claws tearing into flesh. In one hand, she held her other shoe.

"Move away from Reid, Fido, or the next one's gonna hit what's under your tail!"

14. Boggart

"Why are you acting this way?" Meagan yelled at the big, black dog.

The dog inclined his massive head and cocked an ear as if he'd never heard a human voice so clearly before. Snarling, he pawed at the ground. Reid leapt in front of Meagan and held out the straw broom like a legendary lance. His shoulders tensed and his legs widened.

"Back up slowly, Meagan," Reid whispered. "Go get Matt Moody. He's our animal control officer. He'll know how to handle this brute."

The dog lunged and snapped at the broom with its powerful jaws, pulling out a mouthful of straw. Kayla and Nat screamed in unison. Meagan rolled her eyes. "Reid, I've got this. Get out of my way."

Reid shook his head. "I've never seen a dog act like this before! He's out of control! Now go do what I told you to do."

Meagan's nose flared. "No! You go, I'm staying!" She kneed him in the butt.

"Ouch!" Reid yelled. "Whose side are you on?"

"Right now, the dog's side," Meagan replied, skirting around Reid.

"Why are you acting this way?" Meagan asked the dog again. This time she looked him in the eye and showed him no fear.

Spittle dripped from the black dog's jowls and soaked into the ground. "It's my job!" he barked with all the authority his voice could deploy.

Meagan frowned. She juggled her shoe from one hand to the other. "What job?"

"To protect!" the dog snarled, then snapped for the broom again, this time yanking it out of Reid's hands.

"OMG!" Kayla squealed, hiding her face behind her hands. "I-I can't watch!"

"Crap!" Reid yelled, rubbing his hands together.

The dog splintered the broom with his powerful jaws. Reid jumped behind Meagan. "Nice job, Lancelot," she whispered.

"Will someone get us out of here?" Kayla pleaded. "My sister is in obvious pain and I can't get any reception on my cell to call for help!"

"Oh, don't worry about me, Kayla!" Nat spat. "If you'd listened to me in the first place, this wouldn't have happened!"

Meagan heard Nat's response. She looked at the dog. "What did the older girl do?"

Spitting broom pieces out of his mouth, the dog snapped his teeth. "She rattled my cage! It's my cage to protect! Mine!"

"She rattled your cage?" Meagan's brow creased. "Crap, she does that to me too."

The dog howled. "Then let me at her! I'll protect you too!" He twisted around and headed back toward the entrance to the play cage. Kayla screamed again.

"Meagan, may I suggest the need to be in a calmer, more peaceful state when you talk to him?" Whiskey advised. "He's picking up your anger for Kayla."

"Wait." Meagan took a deep breath, let it out, took another deep breath and let it out. "What's your name?"

The dog stopped his assault. "Boggart," he growled.

With the sneaker still in her hands, Meagan moved a little closer to him. "Boggart. Hmm, sounds like a strong name for a mighty dog like you. My name is Meagan."

The dog's droopy ears inched forward.

"What are you doing?" Reid whispered.

"Trying to be a pack leader," she murmured, "and sucking up doesn't hurt either."

"I don't freaking believe it!" Kayla said, slapping her forehead. "Are you actually trying to talk to that dog?"

Meagan squeezed her shoe. "Got a better plan, poo-face?"

"Meagan!" Whiskey meowed. "Be calm! Be assertive! Put out good feelings!"

"I'm trying, Whiskey, believe me, I'm trying," Meagan replied.

"Well, try harder!" Whiskey hissed.

Meagan nodded. "Are you hungry, Boggart?"

Boggart cocked his head. "Must earn my food. Must protect."

"Don't you think you have? I mean, you did capture the girl who rattled your cage. Isn't that worth a reward?"

Boggart inclined his head to the other side as if balancing out what Meagan offered.

"Meagan, energy flows where awareness goes," Nat said calmly. "Whatever you're doing is working. I'll help by sending some healing energy to the dog while you keep talking to him."

"Really, Nat?" Kayla said, haughtily. "Don't encourage the freak with that mumbo-jumbo healing crap your mom teaches. Honestly, sometimes I'm so glad we don't share the same DNA!"

"Hey! You kids get away from that dog!"

Meagan turned to see a man in a blue uniform and black boots standing behind them. He was tall with slick blond hair and a moustache, and held a long metal pole with a looped rope at the end. "I said move! Now!" he commanded.

"Finally!" Kayla clapped. "Someone with some common sense."

Out of the corner of her eye, Meagan saw Reid back away. She grunted. She wasn't going anywhere. "Don't worry, Boggart, I'll protect you," she said.

"Meagan! Do what Matt told you to do and move!" Gail bellowed. "That dog's dangerous!"

Meagan winced. *Great. How I am supposed to assert myself if I'm constantly being dominated by people who don't understand what I'm doing?* She closed her eyes and opened her mind. *Whiskey, go get me the dog leash on the deck.*

Whiskey jumped out of the hole and rubbed up against Meagan's leg. "It's about time you used that mind of yours."

Meagan opened her eyes to catch Whiskey flick her tail, and then skittered around Reid to pass Gail and Mat Moody. *Good. Now all I have to do is show Boggart I'm on his side.*

"If you don't move your feet, then I'll move them for you!" Moody shouted.

Meagan pursed her lips. "Fine. Let's start with this part of my feet!" She spun around and whipped her sneaker at the animal control officer. Unfortunately, Meagan's aim was lower than expected. She whacked him with dead-on accuracy. The poor man never saw it coming. Screaming, he dropped the catch pole and crumpled to the ground, cradling his privates as if they were gold.

Reid's face grimaced. "Oh, that's just not right."

"See? That girl's a freaking nut-bar!" Kayla shouted.

"Meagan!" Gail boomed. "What's gotten into you?"

Meagan cupped her mouth. She'd meant to aim higher. The chest, the neck, the chin. Anywhere but in that region. *Great. I've assaulted a town officer with a weapon. What's next? More community hours? Jail time? Or worse—be forced to live here in Fairy Falls forever?* Meagan's shoulders tightened. She didn't even want to think about it.

"Meagan protect Boggart?" the dog whined, with no snarling or growling.

Meagan dropped her hand and looked at Boggart. Her eyes widened. *It's go time.* She smiled and said, "That's right, Boggart, it's my turn to protect you. You need a time-out from always being on guard. It must be exhausting. No wonder you're hungry. It's time to take a break."

There was a sudden shift in Boggart's manner and he seemed to relax, as if a huge burden had been lifted from him. The sensation of nails digging into her legs made Meagan cringe and look down. Whiskey had returned. A weathered red leash hung from her mouth. She dropped it at Meagan's bare feet and flicked her tail.

"Good enough?" Whiskey asked.

Meagan picked up the leash and made a large loop with it. "Perfect."

Suddenly, a hand grasped her shoulder and squeezed. Meagan flinched.

"Gail, no!" Reid yelled.

"Enough is enough, Meagan! You were told to get away from that dog, so it looks as if I get the honour, seein' as you got no more shoes to throw."

Gail now held the dog-catcher's pole. "Take it easy, Gail, Boggart's not dangerous," Meagan said, squeezing the leash.

"Tell that to the girls in the cage," Gail replied, pulling her back.

Meagan held her ground. "I had this under control until you and Moody showed up!"

Gail grunted. "Yeah, the dog's a real charmer, slobber and all."

"Tell the Loud One the dog will only listen to you," Whiskey meowed, pawing at her legs. "That way no one will get hurt."

Meagan nodded. "Gail, you've gotta trust me, I can help you get the dog safely into a kennel."

"I don't see how, seein' as I got the pole," Gail said.

"Remember that rock I found that helps me talk to animals?"

"You mean that *magical* rock?" Gail snorted. "How could I forget, you made me pee myself silly!"

"Thanks for the visual," Meagan mumbled. "What I mean is that's what I'm using now to talk to Boggart. How do you think I knew his name?"

"From the tag on his collar," Gail said.

Meagan peeked at Boggart's brown studded collar. A bone-shaped silver tag engraved with the name BOGGART dangled from it. This wasn't going to be easy. She glanced down at Whiskey. "Any more advice?"

"Ask the dog where he came from. Then the Loud One will know you're not lying," Whiskey meowed.

Meagan sighed. It was worth a try. "Boggart, where did the man find you?"

Boggart cocked his head back and forth. "In the place that stinks," he barked.

"The place that stinks?" Meagan asked.

Boggart's ears moved forward. "Lots of ugly smells there. Lots of birds."

Ugly smells? Birds? What's he talking about?

"The dump!" Whiskey meowed. "Many shelter animals have come from there!"

Meagan's eyes widened. "Oh, the dump! Boggart was found at the dump."

Gail's hand slid away from Meagan's shoulder. "H-How did you know where Matt picked him up?"

"Not from the tag on his collar," Meagan said, rubbing her shoulder. "I already told you, the rock I found helps me understand him."

Gail's jaw dropped. She scratched her chin. "But...I don't believe...son of a pickle. I could go for a cold beer about now."

Suddenly, Meagan's whole body was uprooted and thrown to one side. She rolled across the uneven ground a few times, clutching the leash tightly to her chest. Her head spun, eyes went blurry.

"Next time I tell you to move, kid, do it!" Matt Moody yelled as he yanked the pole out of Gail's hand and pushed her out of the way. Meagan swore she heard Kayla clap and whistle.

The dog let out a vicious howl. "Boggart protect Meagan!"

The dog eyed Matt Moody and moved slowly toward him with his head down and ears back. The image of Matt's arm being torn out of his socket flashed through Meagan's mind. Blood, mayhem, and the possibility of amputation added to this vision. She had to stop Boggart. Even if it meant exposing herself to all sorts psychiatric evaluations.

Meagan knew she had one chance and one chance only. She readied the leash again.

"Need some help?" Reid asked, lifting Meagan by the waist. His peach-fuzzed face innocently brushed up against Meagan's cheek, making her shiver.

"Hmm, got any shoes to throw?" she asked, leaning against his chest.

"I said help, not hinder," Reid said, grinning. "However, I used to give a mean body check in my days at hockey camp."

Whiskey meowed. "Meagan, the dog's about to charge!"

Startled, Meagan jumped into the line of fur and fangs, and lassoed Boggart around his neck at the same time that Reid slammed Matt Moody into the side of the building. Moody dropped the pole and kissed the earth with a loud groan. Meagan hauled the big, black dog down with all the strength she could muster and covered his body with hers. She slowly ran her free hand along Boggart's lean belly, trying to calm him.

"Meagan protect Boggart," she whispered in his ear. "No more guarding. Rest time."

Boggart let out a deep sigh. He twisted his head around to lick Meagan's cheek.

"You go, girl," Nat whispered to Meagan through the cage.

Meagan looked up to find Natalie leaning against a huge scratching post tree. Her palms were up, resting on her lap, like they'd been in the back room earlier when she gave the cats one of her treatments. A sudden calmness swept over Meagan as if she was wrapped in a cozy, warm blanket. Her whole body tingled. Maybe this was the same sensation the cats had felt that made them feel good. Whatever it was that Nat was doing, Meagan liked it.

"What the hell's going on here?"

Meagan cringed at the sound of Aunt Izzy's voice. She turned her head. Her aunt's face appeared flushed. Uncombed, frizzy auburn hair, baggy sweat pants, and lack of make-up told Meagan that she had rushed to get here. Sadie raced up to stand beside her.

"I didn't want to phone Katrina about this," Sadie said. "After all, she's your niece."

"Thanks, Sadie," Aunt Izzy said. "I owe you one."

Sadie coughed. "By the way this day's gone, honey, you owe me your first born."

Meagan narrowed her brows. What was going on? She'd just saved Matt Moody from being the dog food flavor of the month. "Did I do something wrong, Aunt Izzy?"

Aunt Izzy placed both hands on her husky hips. Her facial scar puckered. "Try to stand in my shoes, Meagan, seeing as you're not wearing any."

Meagan heard Kayla laugh. She ignored her and said, "I don't understand what you mean."

"Then let me make things understandable for you," Aunt Izzy said, clearing her throat. "In the last three days, I've had to explain to the Animal Shelter Board of Directors why you and Reid broke into the shelter in the middle of the night. I've been on and off the phone with Doctor Van Stock about Louis's condition, and I've had to beg, no, make that grovel, to Katrina Smith to keep my job. Then, just when I thought things were smoothed out, I get an urgent call from Sadie telling me to get my ass over here because my niece is in deep doggy doo-doo again. Is that understandable enough?"

"Oh, don't be so hard on her, Iz, the girl's got guts!" Gail boomed. "That magical rock she found really does work! You should have seen Meagan talk down that dog like one of them police negotiators in the movies!"

"You mean with this *magical* rock?" Aunt Izzy asked, as she pulled something from her grey sweater pocket. A piece of crystal quartz glittered in her palm.

Meagan's eyes bugged. She stopped stroking Boggart and patted down her scrub top pockets on both sides. *Empty.* Her face grew hot, her stomach clenched. Then Meagan remembered. She'd left the rock on the bathroom counter this morning.

Whiskey rubbed up against her. "Meagan, I sense anger and doubt coming from the Kind One. What is happening?"

Meagan licked her dry lips, and said, "I-I think the cat is out of the bag, Whiskey."

15. Real Nature

"What does 'grounded' mean, Whiskey?" Nobel asked. "Does that mean Meagan's been buried like a bone?"

Whiskey stopped grooming her paws. Dogs were so thick-headed. She looked at Nobel in his kennel, his light blue eyes on her, waiting for her answer. *Grounded?* What did that mean in human terms? Of course Meagan wasn't buried like a bone, that would be too cruel, and the Kind One was far from cruel. So what then did grounded mean in animal talk? Her whiskers twitched and her tail flicked intensely.

Nobel let out a high-pitched howl. "You don't know, do you?"

"Of course I do!" she hissed. "It means...it's..."

"It's stupid, stupid, stupid!" Louis barked from his kennel. "Meagan not here, not here!"

Nobel yipped. "At least someone knows!"

Whiskey sighed. It seemed Louis was on the mend. No other animals had fallen ill since Louis was rushed to Doctor Van Stock's, but most were still on guard. The canned meat was still barely touched by the cats and the dogs did extra sniffing duty when they were fed, picking up any scent that wasn't normal to them and reporting it to Nobel. Even Boggart had been given a new job since his kennel was the closest to the kitchen. He was tall enough to stand on his hind legs and watch through the window while the Loud One or the Quiet One prepared every dog's meal. So far, nothing had been done out of the ordinary.

"So what's Meagan going to do without her magic rock?" Nobel asked, breaking Whiskey's thoughts.

Whiskey licked one paw, then the other. What indeed? Meagan was in a 'pickle', as the humans would say. A fine mess. Meagan's greatest fear had been confirmed. She had told Whiskey that she had been called a liar by the Kind One, a trouble-maker by the Quick One, an attention-starved crazy-ass kid by the Loud One, a juvenile delinquent—whatever that was— by Matt Moody, and a freak by Kayla. The only humans who did believe Meagan were Reid and Nat.

Whiskey sighed. "I'm afraid Meagan has to learn to be true to herself."

Nobel's ears pricked up. "What do you mean?"

She preened her whiskers. "Cats know what is in their nature. Dogs know what is in their nature. Animals do what animals know, what is natural to them. Humans seem to know nothing at all of being natural, of knowing their real nature. At least that's what I've observed."

Nobel pawed his muzzle. "You mean, although Meagan knows how to talk to us, she chooses to hide from doing what is natural to her?"

Whiskey stopped preening. "By George, I think you've got it!"

Nobel's brows rose. "Isn't George a cat?"

Beep, beep.

Someone had just entered the shelter. Whiskey's fur fluffed out. Nobel sniffed the air.

He growled. "I don't know that scent. It's covered up by a strong odor. Rotting flowers, maybe, and definitely smoke." His wet, black nose flared. "Yup. Smoke from those white sticks."

Whiskey, with her tail flicking incessantly, started climbing the cinder blocks to reach the top of Nobel's kennel. "I'd better get back to my room before I'm caught down here."

Nobel whined. "Be careful, Whiskey. Meagan's not here to protect us."

Boggart growled from his kennel. "Boggart protect! Scare human away!"

Whiskey shook her head. "Do you suppose he's related to Louis somehow?"

Nobel barked. "It wouldn't surprise me in the least."

Whiskey flashed Nobel a catty grin and then scooted across the kennel tops until she reached the open duct. She carefully slipped into the small opening and moved through the duct system as fast as her arthritic legs could carry her. The dust was starting to get to her sensitive nose and she let out a sneeze. Her collar bells jingled. Whiskey pawed her nose and then carried on, turning with the bends and sliding with the dips until she reached the duct entrance to the shelter's washroom. She heard the doorknob rattling and her eyes widened. A human was trying to invade her sanctuary.

Whiskey had just enough time to jump up and slide the register back over the hole. She curled her body into a ball and feigned a catnap, tucking her head into the crook of her stomach. Her heart was beating fast from the journey, too fast for her liking, so she took a few deep breaths just as she heard the door creak open.

Whiskey kept her eyes closed, hoping whoever was there would be satisfied that she was where she was supposed to be and shut the door. Her nose twitched again, full of dust from the ducts, and she sneezed hard. Her bells jingled again. Whiskey opened her eyes, shook her head, and looked up in time to catch the inside of a cloth bag swallowing her whole body. Panicking, she yowled and scratched the inside of the bag. She dug her claws into the thin fabric and wrenched downward to rip a hole in the bag. Her hopes were dashed the moment she realized both her front claws were stuck. She sneezed again, sounding off her bells a third time.

Anger pierced through her old body as if being attacked by a gang of vicious, feral felines. Whiskey hissed and spat, yowling at her attacker, and then something sharp jabbed into the side of her body. She hissed again and tried to pull herself free. Managing to get one paw liberated, Whiskey batted the top of the bag where a human hand clutched it. A sudden weakness ambushed her and Whiskey spiraled into a pit of darkness. The last coherent sound she heard was the familiar beep, beep, of the shelter's front door before she fell into a deep, sedated sleep.

"Ohhh, where am I?" Whiskey meowed.

Her bones ached and her head throbbed. She opened her eyes to stare up at all four paws. Her body curved with the bottom of the bag she was stuffed in, making movement a demanding endeavor. Light surrounded her from all sides. *It must be morning,* she thought. Dampness encompassed her and ate at her bones. Whiskey shuddered, and finding the strength, extracted the claws in her front paws to dig into the thin, white cloth around her.

A sound like a young human screaming echoed through the air. Whiskey's whole body stiffened. She knew that sound, that hideous call. *A brown beast is close by.* Daring not to move, not even to take a breath, Whiskey waited with the patience she had honed over the years. She'd seen a brown beast only twice in her life. The first, on the farm she had been born on. It had entered the chicken coop and viciously killed three of the birds. One hen had been pulled through the wire fencing, leaving nothing but feathers and a pool of blood.

The second encounter had been far worse. Whiskey shuddered, remembering the horrific event as if it were yesterday, envisioning the beady-eyed, bushy-tailed, mangy monster that had destroyed her litter, her family, in the blink of an eye. Whiskey had been lucky to escape with her life. Her old human had saved her, beat the brown beast away with a broom, and then took her to the animal doctor. A deeply etched scar covered by orange and black fur on her back was Whiskey's only physical reminder of that horrible day.

Another scream rang out, this one from farther away. Whiskey let out her breath. The brown beast had moved on, probably to find a tree to sleep the day away. However at night, it would awaken to hunt and this time Whiskey vowed not to be on the menu. She remained still for a long time, suspended in the cloth bag, not moving, until she was sure, without a doubt, that the evil creature was gone.

Satisfied, Whiskey pulled herself upward, grunting and groaning, until her back legs pushed against the bottom of the bag. A tiny puncture let in enough light so Whiskey could hook a claw into it and pull down. Her eyes widened. *Success!* She removed her claw and pushed her nose and mouth through to bite away at the fabric. The sharp smell of pine and stagnant musk made her pink nose twitch. Ignoring these smells, she persevered, and when she was satisfied that the hole was big enough, she replaced her mouth with an eye and peered out of her cotton cocoon. She coughed. *Where am I?* Surrounding her was a sea of green. The bright light in the sky had filtered through just enough to tell Whiskey that morning would soon pass into afternoon. A gust of wind kicked up and made her body sway with the branches. She growled and forced the rest of her head through the hole. Her head popped out like a newborn kitten.

Whiskey's body rocked back and forth before she looked up. Her yellow eyes widened. The bag she was imprisoned in was fastened to a large tree branch. Curious, Whiskey looked down and immediately wished she hadn't. A pool of still water surrounded her on all sides. The water oozed like green slime. Cans and bottles bobbed precariously throughout the stagnant water. A few tires lined the shore and try as she may, the old calico couldn't sense a breath of life coming from the dark water. Whiskey gulped. Her only way out was up.

A movement caught her eye. She squinted. Bushes, not more than twenty feet away rustled. Suddenly she sneezed. A rush of warm liquid rolled out of her nostrils.

"W-W-Who's there?"

Whiskey's ears perked. She knew that voice. "George? George, is that you?"

The bushes rustled again. A small, white cat with grey markings on his ears and tail peered over a stump. He gasped.

"What are you doing, Whiskey?" George asked. "Are you playing a game?"

Whiskey's ears flattened. Honestly, she swore cat brains were wasted on the young.

"Does it look like I'm playing a game?"

George jumped up onto the stump. "Well, yes. It looks like fun, too!"

"If you think it's so much fun, then you come up here and try it!"

George mewed and then bolted for the big tree. He climbed fast, leaping from branch to branch until he skidded to a stop just above Whiskey. Breathless, he pawed at the cloth sack. This made it swing precariously over the black and green water. Whiskey groaned.

"Stop that!"

"But...I want a turn."

Whiskey sighed. "George, this isn't a game and it's certainly not fun."

"It's not?"

"No. I was stuffed in this sack, put to sleep, and hung out here by a human."

George sat on the limb. "But...why would a human do that?"

"My guess is that it's something to do with Meagan's ability to talk to us."

George's yellow eyes became saucers. "Will the human stuff her in a sack too?"

Whiskey closed her eyes. Her patience was starting to wear thin. Then, she thought of the danger that the other animals of the shelter could be in and Whiskey opened her eyes. She had to get back to warn the others—all the dogs and the cats—that their home was no longer their sanctuary, and she needed George to accomplish that feat.

"I don't know, George, but I do know that we have to get back to the shelter."

George struck the bag. "I'll never go back! Tess is dead because of the bad meat there!"

The bag suddenly ripped further, leaving only a few strands secured to the branch. Whiskey managed to get one paw through the hole. "George, help me!"

"Promise you won't take me back to the shelter?"

The bag ripped again. Whiskey pushed her other paw out. "George!"

"Promise?"

"I promise!" she hissed.

The bag ripped one last time. George dug his back claws into the branch and lunged for the plummeting sack. He nabbed it with his long claws and pulled Whiskey up enough for her to dig her claws into the deep crevices of the tree bark. George bit her neck like a momma cat and pulled Whiskey to safety before the shredded bag floated down toward the dark water. It slapped against the surface and immediately sank. Whiskey shuddered. Her bones still ached and her muscles were sore, but she was grateful to be breathing and dry. George's hot, laboured breath flowed across the back of her neck.

"You can let go now, George."

"Mmurph?" George released Whiskey and stepped back. He started to groom himself. "Sorry, Whiskey, I-I guess I got scared."

"That's okay, George." Whiskey licked his soft cheek. "You're one of the bravest cats I've ever known."

George pawed his cheek. "Brave? You really think so?"

"I know so," she purred with calm assurance. "I mean, you seem to be surviving quite well out here all by yourself."

George beamed, and then head-butted Whiskey. "Can you keep a secret?"

Whiskey's ears moved forward. "What kind of a secret?"

"A secret that you would never tell anyone, not even Meagan."

For once in her long, cat life, Whiskey was tired of being the secret keeper. The one all the animals confided in, shared their hopes and dreams with. At times, her head ached with all the information stashed in there. She sighed. Oh well, what was one more.

"Okay, I'll keep your secret."

"Promise?"

Whiskey growled. "Do we have to go through this again?"

George flicked his tail and sauntered across the branch. Whiskey sighed. "I promise!"

George jumped around. "I've got a new family!"

"A new family?" Whiskey's eyes widened. "Where?"

"Over there, past those big trees by the creek, where the metal cave is. We live in it."

"We? Who exactly are *we*?"

George proceeded to climb down the tree. Whiskey watched the small, white cat with grey markings—and obviously no brains—jump to the base of the tree. He stretched a long stretch, and then rolled in the dirt. She followed, going slower than the younger cat, until she reached the tree's gnarled bottom. With a groan, Whiskey managed to land beside George, who was still enjoying his stretch, kneading the air above him.

"George, who are you living with?" Whiskey asked, in a wary tone.

George finished stretching, looked up at Whiskey, and with a slight purr, he said, "Why, with the lost cats, of course."

Whiskey's fur bristled. This wasn't good. This wasn't good at all.

16. Lost

"Don't worry, Meagan, Whiskey will turn up. You'll see."

Meagan didn't look at Nat. She kept staring at the scratched lottery ticket she'd found on the bathroom floor—a.k.a. Whiskey's room—this morning. The duct register had been put back in place, so she knew the old calico had returned from the dog floor sometime in the night. Nobel had told her that someone had come by late last night—someone who reeked of cigarette smoke. Her stomach rolled. Was it the same person who'd been poisoning the animals? Even if Meagan tried to tell her Aunt Izzy, or Bertie, or Gail, or Sadie that someone had entered the building last night, they'd want to know her source. Since her source was Nobel and she'd already been grounded for two weeks for yesterday's events, it was highly likely that Aunt Izzy would add another two weeks to her sentence. She thumbed the ticket. *Good Luck - Please Play Again*, she read. It appeared to have been scratched over and over again until there was no luck left in it.

Nat nudged her elbow. "She's okay, Meagan, just think positively."

Meagan's shoulders sagged. "Why wasn't Whiskey in her room? I know I was the first one to open the door to let her out this morning. She should've been in there."

"Are you sure she was put in before the shelter closed yesterday?" Nat asked.

"Both Gail and Sadie said she was." Meagan stood, stretching from sitting too long on the shelter entrance's stairs.

"Sometimes, I wish I could stand and do that," Nat murmured.

Meagan stopped stretching and looked down at Nat in her wheelchair. Today she wore a pink crew T-shirt and blue cotton pants. Nat's brown bangs were swept out of her face and held in place by a bejeweled barrette. Her head was down and hands severely interlocked as if wishing Meagan hadn't heard her. Meagan crumpled the ticket. "Well…I wish I could pull together an outfit like you do."

Nat released her hands and glanced up. She wrinkled her nose. "I don't know about that, Meagan, your choice of lime green scrubs and matching clogs bring out—"

"The ogre in me?" Meagan cut in.

Nat laughed. "I was going to say bring out the colour in your eyes."

Meagan grinned. Her eyes swept over Nat's shiny blue wheelchair and lingered on the embroidered knight's helmet on the back of the chair. "So, what's up with the knight headgear?"

"Knight is my last name."

"It's not Reynolds?"

Nat shook her head. "Mom and me moved up north to Fairy Falls from a town called White Pines when I was only three-years-old. There was an air force base near White Pines where my father trained soldiers to be firefighters—" Nat paused to take a deep breath "—but he died when a fire burned out of control and the building collapsed on him."

"Oh, I'm so sorry about your dad," Meagan said, patting Nat's shoulder.

Nat licked her lips. "Thanks, but that's okay. I never really knew him. I carry this around with me so I know he's always looking out for me." She reached into a small pouch sewn into the side of her wheelchair's arm and pulled out a creased photo to show Meagan.

She studied the image of a grinning man with light brown skin, hazel eyes, and soot smudges all over his face, wearing a firefighter's helmet. Meagan smiled. "You look a little like him, sans the grimy face. Bet you inherited his fearless attitude too."

Nat giggled as she stuffed the photo back into the pouch. "Thanks, I think. After some time passed, Mom met Kayla's dad, Ray Reynolds, at a parent-teacher meeting when Kayla and I were both in public school. It was a couple of years before my accident."

"Is that why you're in a wheelchair?"

Nat smirked. "No, silly, I'm in a wheelchair because I can't walk."

Meagan rolled her eyes. "Sorry. You don't have to tell me if you don't want to."

Nat grabbed the bottom of Meagan's scrub top. "It's okay, it's no big deal. I was hit by a car while crossing the road. I bounced off the windshield and I swear I felt myself fly at least thirty feet through the air." She released Meagan's top. "The flying part was an awesome feeling until I landed. Then the pain kicked in and I blacked out."

Meagan's eyes widened. Never in her life had she experienced the kind of pain and suffering Nat had gone through. True, she had lost her mom, but she still had her dad and her aunt. Meagan's eyes welled and she squeezed them tight. *And I still have the use of my legs.* She quickly wiped her face with the back of her hand before Nat noticed. The last thing Meagan wanted was for Nat to think she was pitying her.

The back of Meagan's throat throbbed as she said, "My mom was killed in a car accident." Her chin dropped to her chest. "A tractor trailer cut in front of Mom's car and she had nowhere to go but under the trailer."

Nat's fingers brushed across Meagan's knuckles like a butterfly's wings. "I'm sorry for your loss," she whispered. "It helps to believe everything happens for a reason and for the best." Nat withdrew her hand and squeezed the armrest of her wheelchair. "Even if we don't like it."

Meagan lifted her head and dropped to one knee. She locked eyes with Nat. "Did they catch the person who did this?"

"It was too dark," Nat replied, shaking her head, "but a witness thought it might have been a woman behind the wheel. The car was swerving as if the driver was drunk, or high, or both. All I know is that a dark green sedan was reported speeding out of town just after I was hit. The police thought the driver may have been a tourist."

Meagan knitted her raven brows. "When did this happen?"

"It will be three years next month. Screwed up my summer good, I can tell you."

"How do you stay so positive? I mean, it's gotta suck being in that chair sometimes."

"It sucks all the time. Morning, noon, night, but I have to deal with it, Meagan," she replied, shrugging. "My mom taught me to cope by showing me how to access the same healing energy you saw me use on the cats yesterday. Mom calls it Reiki energy. She also showed me how to use therapeutic touch to unblock stuck energy when I need to—which, living with Kayla, I'm constantly doing."

Meagan laughed. "I gotta get your mom to teach me that stuff!"

Beep, beep. The front door flew open. A wet nose pressed against Meagan's neck. "Me miss Meagan," Louis whined. He licked her ear.

Meagan flinched. Nat giggled. She gave the big, goofy dog a scratch on his chest.

"I miss you too, Louis," Meagan said.

"Stop pretending you can talk to animals, Meagan," Bertie said, pulling Louis's leash. "You've gotten Reid and yourself in enough trouble as it is. Just do your job and keep your nose clean."

"Keep my nose clean?" Meagan said, defensively.

"Nose clean, nose clean. Me do, Meagan!" Louis barked. He licked Meagan's nose.

"Ewww! Louis! I didn't mean that!"

Bertie shook her head. "You're a very strange girl. I don't get what Reid sees in you, other than you're pretty." She escorted Louis down the ramp and up toward the trial.

Meagan coughed. Her chest tightened. She curled her toes. *Pretty? Me?* She didn't feel pretty with Louis's drool all over her face. Meagan wiped her nose with the sleeve of her scrub top as she stood.

"With the exception of Reid, looks like you're in the dog house around here," Nat said. "Do you like him?"

Meagan's cheeks burned. "What's with you and Whiskey thinking that I like Reid?"

"What about me?"

Meagan jumped. She turned to find Reid standing at the bottom of the stairs. He wore a loose plaid shirt over a white T-shirt, faded jeans, and black canvas shoes. In his hand was a lunch bag. He jangled his keys in the other. Meagan's ears burned and a flush crept across her cheeks.

"N-N-Nothing," Meagan stammered. Nat stifled a giggle and Meagan smacked her arm. "Hey...I thought you were banned from here for a couple of weeks?"

"I am. Mom left her lunch in the fridge, so I thought I'd score points with her if I brought it over," Reid said. He nodded toward Nat. "Is Kayla here?"

Meagan crushed the scratched ticket in her hand until it was a ball. "She was, but we fed her to Boggart for breakfast."

Reid scowled. "Stop slamming her, Meagan! You don't even know her!"

"I know her enough to know she's not your type! Even Nobel says—"

"Zip it! I'm in enough trouble thanks to you!"

"Whiskey's missing," Nat blurted. "Did you happen to see her by the road, Reid?"

"Huh? No. How long's she been gone?" he asked.

"Nobel said someone came into the shelter late last night. Someone who has a key and smokes a lot. And whoever it was left this behind," Meagan replied, opening up her hand.

"A ball of paper?" Reid asked, frowning.

Meagan sighed. "No, wait." She flattened the ticket as best she could. "See, it's a lottery scratch ticket."

Reid gasped. "Katrina Smith!"

"Ms. Manager?" Meagan asked, arching her brows.

Reid pointed to the ticket. "Yeah, she buys that kind of ticket all the time. Her car's floor is littered with them."

Meagan stared at the wrinkled ticket before she stuffed it into her scrub pocket. "Does Smith smoke?"

Reid scratched his head. "I'm not sure, but I bet we could find out."

"Louis, get back here!"

Nat inclined her head. "Is that your mom, Reid?"

"Yeah, sounds like her. I wonder what's wrong?"

"I'd say something bad if she using her outdoor voice," Meagan replied. "I've never heard her yell like that before."

Reid smirked. "Oh, believe me, when mom wants to be heard, she finds her voice."

Suddenly, Louis ran around the corner, dragging his leash. He slid into the rail. *Bam!* Then he stood, shook, and headed for the three teens on the stoop. With his feathered tail wagging, Louis placed his front paws on the arm of the wheelchair to stand on his hind legs. There was something dangling in his slobbering mouth. He gently placed it on Nat's lap.

Nat cringed. "Ewww! Louis!"

"Me find, me find!" Louis barked.

Meagan looked down and gasped. "OMG! It's Whiskey's collar!"

Nat picked it up. The little bells on it jingled. "Are you sure?"

"It looks like hers," Reid said, flicking the bells with his fingers.

"Louis, is this Whiskey's collar?" Meagan asked, dreading the answer already.

Louis sniffed the collar. "Yup, smell like Whiskey, yup."

Meagan gulped. A sour taste exploded in her mouth. Her mind sought for a reasonable explanation why Whiskey's collar was outside. Did last night's intruder take her? Did Whiskey put up a fight? And why would someone steal an old cat? She balled her fists. It made no sense.

"L-L-Louis!" Bertie stammered, stumbling around the corner.

"He's here, Mom."

"R-Reid?" Bertie said, snapping her head back and panting. "Please...dear God...tell me…you're not doing…anything stupid again."

Reid's face twitched. "Gee thanks. Maybe I should give your lunch to Louis."

Bertie wrinkled her nose and placed a muddy hand on her heaving chest. Grass stains stretched across her light blue scrub pants and top. A few twigs stuck out of her long, red hair. Reid reached over to pull them out. She smacked her son's hand away.

"Oww! I was just trying to help!"

Bertie pursed her lips, trying to get her breathing under control. "You...can...help...by putting Louis back...in his kennel."

"Reid, wait," Meagan said. She snatched the collar from Nat and shook it in the big dog's mucky face. "Louis, where'd you find Whiskey's collar?"

"How do you know that's her collar?" Bertie asked, picking twigs from her hair.

"Louis told her," Nat replied.

Bertie wagged her finger. "Meagan, I thought I told you to stop—"

Louis whined. "By big stump, Meagan, big stump."

"Big stump? Where's that?" Meagan asked.

Bertie stopped wagging her finger. Her hand fell to her side. "How...did you know?"

"Because…Meagan can actually talk to animals, Mom!" Reid insisted. "It's not a magic trick, it's real!"

Bertie grasped her throat. "Are…are you sure the collar belongs to Whiskey?"

"Louis sniffed it good, Bertie. A dog's nose doesn't lie," Nat said.

Bertie's hand slipped away from her throat. Her lips thinned and her face changed to the colour of setting cement. "Oh dear, oh dear, oh dear," she muttered quietly.

"What's wrong?" Reid asked, placing a hand on his mother's shoulder.

"Fisher tracks," Bertie whispered. "There were fisher tracks all around the area where Louis found the collar."

17. The Lost Cats

"Wait up, George!" Whiskey hissed. "I'm not young anymore, you know!"

George stopped. He looked behind him, his eyes widening. "You used to be young?"

As if dodging swamp water and jumping over engorged roots weren't enough, Whiskey had to endure the younger cat's snide remarks. At least the various smells of the forest were more pleasing than what she was used to at the shelter. Fresh leaves, pungent moss, and clean air were a welcome relief for her sensitive nose. Then she sneezed. Warm snot bubbles shot through her nostrils and she pawed them away.

"That's odd," Whiskey meowed. "That's the second time my bells didn't jingle."

George's ears moved forward. "What bells?"

Whiskey's ear flattened. Was the younger cat blind as well as no-brained? "The bells on my collar."

"What collar?"

She growled, pawed at her neck, and then froze. Her ears rose. *Where's my collar? Did it fall off in my room? Or did I lose it in the forest?* Her pink nose flared. She'd had that collar on since the day she was received at the shelter. The Kind One had awarded it to her. The collar was her status, her rank as the only shelter cat, and now it was lost. Her chin trembled.

"Whiskey, is something wrong?" George mewed, rubbing up against her.

She sighed. "I lost my collar."

"Oh, is that all? Just ask the Chosen One for a new collar when you get back," George meowed.

Whiskey's yellow eyes widened. She'd never thought of that. Maybe George had more cat brains than she gave him credit for. She purred and rubbed up against George's chin. A sudden growl made both Whiskey and George jump. She instinctively jumped in front of George, her fur fluffed and back arched. A huge, grey and white cat stood in front of them, barring the way. His green eyes bore into her like she was nothing more than an insignificant rat. He arched his back, which made his head look too small for his fat body. He growled again, this time lower, and in a more intimidating manner.

"Wait, Brutus, it's me, George," the younger cat meowed, leaping over Whiskey.

"Brutus?" Whiskey's ears pricked up. "No, it can't be, can it?"

Brutus squinted and inclined his head. "You know of me, old cat?"

Whiskey ambled closer to the big tom. "Of course I do, you arrived at the shelter about the same time I did. The humans who care for us still speak of you with great respect. Why, you're a legend around the shelter."

"He is?" George asked. "'Cause me and Tess never heard—"

"You're too young to know," Whiskey hissed, swatting at George.

"Tell me more, old cat," Brutus said, now sprawling across the path. He started to lick himself.

Whiskey almost caterwauled. Brutus's legs were spread apart to reveal a generous roll of fat. He stuck one leg in the air to groom and she couldn't help but notice that he had been neutered. Then Brutus flinched and scratched one of his ears in a violent, uncontrollable manner.

"He does that all the time," George whispered to Whiskey.

Whiskey's ears moved forward. She approached him slowly, until she was a few whiskers away from him. Brutus paid her no heed. He was too busy scratching. Whiskey scanned the back of Brutus's head, and then gasped. The area behind his ears was a bloodied, raw mess. Wide sores oozed with thickening blood, like Brutus had torn his own skin open again and again. A piece of dried blood struck her across the face and she cringed.

"Itch bugs," Whiskey whispered. "You have itch bugs in your ears."

Brutus ceased scratching to stare at her. "Can you help me?"

"No, but I can lead you to the Chosen One. She'll give you special medicine that will kill the itch bugs and take care of those sores."

Brutus growled. "Chosen One? You mean that young human I saw you and the half-breed canine walking with?"

Whiskey's eyes widened. "You saw us on the path?"

Brutus grunted. "Yes. Humans are meddlers, old cat, and meddlers are trouble."

Whiskey's ears flattened. "My name is Whiskey, not old cat. Why don't you like humans? You were at the shelter. You must know how well they care for us."

"Like they cared for Tess?" George spat.

"You're not helping, George," Whiskey hissed.

"George speaks the truth!" Brutus roared. "The humans keep most of us in cages and don't allow us to be who we truly are. Out here we have choice, we have freedom."

Whiskey's tail flicked. "You also have itch bugs."

Brutus shrugged. "Humans don't understand us, they have too many rules. I couldn't live like that anymore. That's why I escaped from the outside cage."

George gasped. "You're the cat who broke the door to our play cage?"

Brutus nodded sharply. "I was tired of not feeling the grass under my paws, of not being able to hunt when I wanted, and of being poked at through my cage by taunting, human fingers. I wanted out and I got out."

"But the Chosen One is different from any human you've ever known, Brutus," Whiskey meowed. "She can understand us, talk to us, know what our needs are, and help us in ways your cat brain could never imagine."

"It's true," George mewed. "The Chosen One did find Tess for me. That's how we knew about the bad meat."

Brutus growled. "So what has this Chosen One done about the bad meat?"

George sighed. "Nothing, so far. The other Ones who care for us won't listen to her."

"Ha! See? If other humans won't listen to the Chosen One, then why should we?"

Whiskey growled. "Still not helping, George."

Suddenly, a long, sleek white cat lunged from the bushes. "I was hunting and heard growling. Do you need me, Brutus?"

Brutus waved the cat off. "No, Jules, it's nothing to concern yourself with."

Whiskey observed this male cat with renewed interest. He was definitely not neutered and both his ears were curled back as if they'd been bitten by the cold like she had been many years ago. His white fur was smooth, preened to perfection, and his long, thin tail whipped around his back end in a confident manner. Blue eyes stared back at Whiskey, sizing her up.

"Who's the old cat, Brutus?"

Whiskey growled. George tittered.

"She prefers to be called Whiskey," Brutus said, licking the drying blood off his front paw. "She's from the shelter."

"Mmph, shelter-smelter, I escaped that place when a human dumped me there many seasons ago. The box I was in wasn't strong enough to hold me. I pushed it open and ran toward the trees as fast as I could," Jules said with his chin held high. "Did you escape from there too, old...Whiskey?"

"No. I was stuffed in a bag, and then taken from my home at the shelter and hung in a tree over dark water," Whiskey explained.

"Home?" Jules meowed. "Brutus says the shelter is not a place for *true* cats."

Whiskey's ears moved forward. She was getting tired of this ignorant game. She knew of the lost cats, those like Jules, who were abandoned on the shelter's door step in boxes or cages, and had managed to break out. Many ran for the forest, some perished on the road, but most never came back, not knowing the warmth, the food, the clean water, and the care that the shelter had to offer. The lost cats may have had big cat dreams about being free, but they were little-minded when it came to what was best and safe for them. *Just warn them about the brown beast and move on before the light in the sky goes out,* the voice in her mind advised.

"Perhaps the shelter isn't a place for you, but it is for me, it's where I belong," Whiskey meowed, flicking her tail from side to side. "Now before I go, I must tell you—"

"You're not going anywhere," Brutus growled.

Startled, Whiskey's ears lay back. "Not go? But why—"

"Because you know about us!" Brutus snarled. "You'll tell this human Chosen One of yours and she'll come after us, try to capture us, and take us from our home."

"Why would you want to go back, Whiskey?" George asked, rubbing against her. "The human who stuffed you in the bag didn't want you there. What if it happens again?"

"The young cat makes sense, old...Whiskey," Jules added, stretching his long body. "As far as I'm concerned, humans are no better than dogs."

"Whiskey likes dogs," George blurted. "She talks to them all the time."

Whiskey glared at George. "You can shut your big cat mouth anytime, George."

Brutus grunted. "A cat that goes against her species is not to be trusted."

"But I'm the shelter's observer! It's my job to talk to the dogs, as it is the cats!"

"It's not your job anymore," Brutus growled. "Now you're under my laws and what I say will be done."

Whiskey's tail twitched as if it were on fire. She'd come here on good faith—followed George with the hope of talking him into coming back with her. Now this. Her bones ached from the damp ground, her stomach rumbled from no food. She'd been in worse spots before, but that was when she was younger, more agile, and had most of her teeth. She was too weak to fight and too old to take flight. Yet, Whiskey knew her weakness was also her strength, that her age was only a number the humans had given her. The culmination of her cat life experiences would help her get away from the lost cats and back to the shelter where she belonged.

"Jules, George, escort Whiskey back to our home," Brutus meowed in an overly loud tone. "I'm going to see if any of the females have caught a mouse for me."

George looked at Whiskey. His ears flattened and he looked away. She pawed his face to make eye contact again. "This isn't your fault, George. I followed you willingly."

"But...because of me, you're not allowed to go back to the shelter," George whispered.

Whiskey grinned. "Well, some cat has to look out for a no-brained cat like you."

"Enough talk!" Brutus snarled. "Move!"

George head-butted Whiskey's chin. "Come on, it's not far from here."

"Let's go, old...Whiskey," Jules meowed, "before Brutus decides another fate for you."

It seemed like an eternity for Whiskey, given the aches her body whispered to her as they walked through thick brush, climbed over bulging boulders, and slunk under fallen trees. Part of her wanted to escape back to the shelter, but another part wouldn't leave George behind. Not with a brown beast preying in these woods. It would only be a matter of time before that vile creature found the lost cats, and their world as they knew it would be forever changed. Any survivors would be fair game for the next night and the one after that.

Whiskey heard the brush rustle in front of them. Jules moved aside a branch to let Whiskey and George pass through. She immediately sneezed. Shaking her head, Whiskey gathered her wits and looked around. Her old, yellow eyes widened. *Cats!* Cats grooming each other, cats chasing and wrestling with each other, cats fighting over food, cats curled up, cats sleeping with each other; there must be more cats here than whiskers on her whole face. Her eye caught a movement on her left. A four-week-old kitten struggled to crawl out of the back end of what humans called a 'car'. It was the colour of dark, shiny leaves. All the doors were closed and all the windows rolled up. The only way in or out was through the open back end. *This must be the metal cave George spoke of,* she thought.

"Jules! Was your hunt successful?"

A black and white male cat pounced into their path. He seemed much older than most of the lost cats and wasn't as long as Jules, but he was taller. His tail appeared shorter, as if it had been cut off by something sharp, yet he flicked it about like nothing was missing. All four of his paws, his chest, and his belly were white. The rest of him was black. The most distinctive thing Whiskey observed about him was that one of his eyes was pulled back into its socket. A greenish liquid oozed from it, making Whiskey look away.

Jules ears pricked up. "No, Oscar. I was given a more important job to do."

Oscar looked from Jules to Whiskey. "Who's the old—"

"Stop calling me old, I am what I am!" she hissed. "Call me Whiskey!"

Oscar flinched. "She's a feisty one, Jules. Where'd you find her?"

"She's from the shelter, like me," George cut in, whipping his tail like the older cats.

"From the shelter? Did you escape too?" Oscar asked, inclining his head.

Trying not to look at his oozing eye, Whiskey decided to groom herself. "No. I was stolen."

Oscar howled with laughter. "Stolen? Who would steal such an old cat? You can't mouse anymore and you can't have kittens."

Whiskey's ears moved forward. "What of Brutus, then? He can't sire anymore and he gets others to hunt for him. That makes him no better than me."

"Whiskey's got a point, Oscar," George added. "He's got itch bugs, too."

Oscar growled. "You'll not speak ill of Brutus. He's our leader and gave us a home when we had none. We return his kindness by hunting for him."

Whiskey sighed. "But you could have a better home, a safer home, at the shelter. Just follow me and—"

"No!" Jules snarled. "We're free here. No human will ever abandon or hurt us again."

"You'll hurt yourselves if you continue to stay here," Whiskey hissed. "There's a brown—"

"Well, well, looked what the cat dragged in."

Whiskey arched her back. Her fur rippled across her body. "Shadow!" she hissed.

"The one and only," Shadow purred, rubbing herself against the closest male cat—a young, orange tabby. He let out a yowl and tried to sniff her. She swatted him away, and then went on to the next available male—a scrawny, black cat whose ears were too big for his head.

Whiskey knew she would have to use every whisker of her cat brain to fight Shadow. With no bars between them, she didn't stand a chance against her in paw to paw combat. Her tail flicked in thought. Back at the shelter, Shadow relied on her scent to control other cats, mostly males, into doing whatever she wanted. However, most of the females wanted nothing to do with her. Shadow used her female power for selfish, wicked reasons, and not for the good of the whole cat community. Female cats were supposed to pass on their teachings to the young, prepare them for independence, show them balance by playing and preying, not misuse their feline power like Shadow did. Everything was to be shared in the eyes of a well-balanced female. Whiskey's ears pricked up. Perhaps she could appeal to the lost cat females and show them Shadow's true, dark nature. Her nose twitched at Shadow's musky smell, and then she grinned a cat grin.

"Did you get that sickness taken care of yet, Shadow?" Whiskey asked.

Shadow's body jerked. "Sickness?" She moved away from the growing group of toms. "What are you up to, old calico?"

Whiskey glanced at a slender grey female, then another—a sleek, part Siamese with blue eyes. Both had recently had litters. It was time to use her cat mind like Shadow used her cat scent. She swished her tail. "Didn't Shadow tell you of her sickness? I do hope none of you have caught it. Especially the young ones, they're more prone to what she carries."

The two female's ears flattened at the same time. They glared at Shadow. "What have you brought to us, hell-cat?" the part Siamese growled.

"The old cat lies!" Shadow snarled. "And it is time I tear out her tongue!" She pounced at Whiskey, but Jules cut her off. He gave her a warning growl. His body arched, his head down in warning. Shadow's ears flattened and her tail wildly flicked. She retreated a few whiskers.

"The Chosen One will cure this sickness, but you must hurry before it spreads throughout the lost cats!" Whiskey meowed as loud as she could, trying to catch all the cat ears.

Some of the cats scattered into the forest. Some jumped into the open back end of the car. Kittens were gathered by their mothers and dragged underneath their metal sanctuary, hiding behind flattened rubber tubes. Even Oscar backed off. Jules, however, held his ground. "This is a serious crime, Shadow," Jules warned. "If one of us gets sick because of—"

Whiskey sneezed. Green goop exploded out of her nose and all over Jules. "See!" Whiskey cried. "Shadow has given me her sickness!"

"What goes on here?" Brutus roared, breaking through the bushes.

Shadow leapt over to the big cat to lie in front of him, her haunches up, while her hind feet moved back and forth seductively.

"Please help me, Brutus! I'm being unfairly accused by the old calico!"

"Whiskey claims that Shadow has brought a sickness to us," Jules explained, still holding his guarded position in front of Whiskey.

Brutus's ears moved forward. He flinched and pawed a red-raw ear. "What kind of a sickness?"

"I think it starts in the nose and spreads everywhere," Jules meowed.

"Look...it's already started in Whiskey," Oscar meowed.

Green liquid continued to bubble out of Whiskey's nose. Her eyes were damp with warm goo and a sudden tightness claimed her chest, but Whiskey chose to ignore these irritations. Dealing with Shadow was more important. She needed to stay focused and observe.

Meows and caterwauls rang out from the forest, "Save us, Brutus! Protect us!"

"This is very bad news," Brutus said, removing his paw from an ear.

"Surely you don't believe that feeble old feline over me?" Shadow purred, rubbing her slim body up against his fat one.

Brutus snarled, and swatted her away. Shadow rolled, screamed, and scrambled to duck behind the group of young males she seduced earlier.

"Daisy! Duchess!" Brutus roared. "Show the others what we have found!" Rustling leaves accompanied the sound of something being dragged across the forest floor. Two older female cats—one calico with diluted markings and a medium-haired tabby—pulled out a mutilated cat. Its belly had been ripped open, the innards severed and taken. An orange head was still intact as well as its striped legs and paws. Dark eyes were wide open, shock held within them. Dried blood had mixed with shredded fur and jagged puncture marks ran across its back.

Oscar gasped. "Is...is that Tiger?"

"It was Tiger," Brutus answered. "This is the reason he never came back last night."

"Did the sickness do this?" Jules asked, darting his eyes from Shadow to Whiskey.

Whiskey wretched. She knew what had happened to that poor cat, but to save herself she couldn't tell anyone a brown beast had done this horrible deed until Shadow no longer posed a threat to her and the lost cats.

"Yes," Whiskey lied, feeling her throat constrict. "The Chosen One is our only hope now."

18. Restraining Order

"What's a fisher?" Meagan asked, furrowing her brow.

Bertie wiped her mouth. "It's a cat killer, Meagan."

Cat killer, cat killer, cat killer, chanted through Meagan's mind until the words became real. Her throat tightened and her stomach twisted. Was Whiskey dead—no murdered—at the claws of this fisher? Someone had wanted Whiskey out of the shelter, someone who was hiding something big. Whatever the reasons, whatever the answers, Meagan knew that the blame would lead back to her. She swallowed hard, tasting a sour lump.

"Was there any sign that Whiskey had been attacked, Mom?" Reid asked.

Bertie shook her head. "No blood, no fur, no body, just the collar Louis found."

"Do you think Whiskey got away, then?" Nat asked, hopefully.

"Anything is possible," Bertie replied, shrugging. "I suppose Whiskey could have lost her collar at some point, snagged it on a bush, maybe, and the fisher found it first. Oh dear, I hope she's smart enough to stay put and hide in a safe place. Fishers usually hunt at night."

Louis whined. "Meagan sad. Me do bad?"

"No, Louis, you're a good boy," Meagan said, stroking Louis's head. "Meagan is bad. I should have kept my big mouth shut and never talked to Whiskey and the rest of you."

"Why would you tell Louis such a thing?" Reid asked. "He'd be dead if it wasn't for you."

"True, that," Nat added. "Do you know how much good you can do with your ability to talk to animals? How much you can help them? Think about that!"

Meagan's chin hit her chest. *What good is an ability if I have to constantly put up with being the butt of people's cruel jokes or made to feel like a freak because I'm different?* At least Meagan had felt somewhat normal winning the *Most Improved Student Award*, and for once she had finally fit in with the other kids at school. When Meagan found out that her mom had gotten killed that same night, nothing seemed important anymore. Not good grades. Not fitting in. And certainly not behaving like an 'improved' student. Things had changed when she met Cassie at grief counseling. They were both angry at the world and decided to be rebels without a cause together.

Meagan raised her head. "It didn't do Whiskey any good, did it?"

"We won't know until we start looking for her," Reid said, patting Meagan on the back.

A sudden heat radiated through Meagan's chest at the unexpected contact. "Uh, sure, um, I guess we'd better start by the big stump where Louis found the collar. Maybe he could help by picking up her scent."

Louis barked, and then wagged his tail. "Me help, Meagan, me help!"

His tail swatted Nat in the face. She giggled. "Hey, Louis, that's a lethal weapon!"

Bertie sighed, looking at Meagan. "You really can talk to him, can't you? This isn't just some attention-getting scheme. It's for real, isn't it?" She wiped her mouth again.

"News flash, Mom, duh. Yah!" Reid said.

Bertie smiled. "Well then, I guess you're never too old to believe in miracles."

The sound of tires grating across gravel made everyone on the porch jump. A forest green Jaguar was headed straight for the shelter. Following close behind was a black and white police cruiser. The lights and sirens weren't on, so Meagan figured the police car wasn't in pursuit. The car pulled into the shelter's parking lot and screeched to a halt. The police cruiser pulled off to the side of the sedan. Katrina Smith—a.k.a. Ms. Manager—emerged from the car. Dressed in a leopard print blouse, matching tan jacket and pants, and high heels, she squinted—which made her look constipated—and pointed at Meagan.

"That's her, Constable Wright." Smith smirked. "The girl in the puke green scrubs."

Louis growled. "Me help, Meagan."

"No, Louis," Meagan whispered. "Be a good boy. Stay."

Nat reached over and snatched his leash. She looked up at Meagan and winked. "And I'll make sure Louis stays a good boy."

"What's this about, Scotty?" Bertie asked, walking down the stairs.

The constable nodded. "Hey, Bertie, just doing my job."

Bertie crossed her muddied arms over her dirty top. "And that is?"

"This is none of your concern, Bertie," Ms. Manager cut in. "I suggest you get back to work before Constable Wright has to issue another restraining order to your son, who—if he's forgotten, then allow me to remind him—is not supposed to be here."

"FYI—I brought my mom's lunch in to her and I was just leaving," Reid said, squaring his shoulders. "But while you're here, maybe you could explain why one of your lottery tickets was found in the bathroom after Whiskey went missing?"

Ms. Manager inclined her head. "Whiskey's missing?"

"Restraining order?" Meagan said, frowning. "But...why?

Ms. Manager scowled. She held up her hand and started counting off of her fingers. "One, you had someone steal an employee's key to break into the shelter after hours—that's trespassing. Two, you interfered with a town employee by attacking him—that's assault causing bodily harm. Three—"

"Three?" Meagan asked, cutting in.

Ms. Manager continued to glare, holding up three fingers. "Apparently, Whiskey is missing. I'm sure you've had something to do with it—and that's theft."

Meagan's jaw dropped. "Are you crazy? Whiskey's likely missing because of you!"

"See, Constable, I told you she was prone to violent outbursts. Please escort her off the property before she attacks me," Ms. Manager said, in a demanding tone.

Constable Wright adjusted the black belt around his dark blue uniform, and then pushed the rim of his Stetson-style hat off his freckled forehead. His fair brows furrowed as he walked toward Meagan. "Come on, young lady, I'll take you home."

"But, Katrina," Bertie said, blocking the policeman's path, "Meagan's done nothing but help the animals since she's arrived, and gotten nothing but grief for it. I know it's hard to accept, but she understands them in ways you and I can't."

"Gail and Sadie have already informed me of the girl's idiotic claim that she talks to animals," Ms. Manager said, holding up a hand. "If you're going to tell me that you actually believe her, then I'll fire you on the spot!"

"You back-stabbing douche-bag!" Reid yelled, pitching his mother's lunch at Smith. It smacked her on the chest and whatever was in it exploded all over her clothes.

"Ugh!" Ms. Manager screamed. She stepped back, wiping lunch remains off her blouse. "That's it, you're fired, Bertie! If you can't control your son, then you definitely can't control the dogs! Pack up your things and take that ungrateful brat with you!"

Reid jumped off the stoop. His face was on fire. "Double douche-bag!"

"Reid, no!" Meagan yelled. She tried to stop him, but he easily passed her and stormed down the stairs.

Constable Wright grabbed Reid by the scruff of his plaid shirt and pulled him away. "Back off, Reid. That wasn't wise."

Beep, beep, the shelter door flew open. "What's going on?" Sadie asked, coming out with a cigarette in one hand and a bag of trash in the other.

"Negative energy," Nat mumbled, shaking her head. "Lots of negative energy."

"Huh?" Sadie asked, and then looked down at Ms. Manager. She dropped the garbage. "Katrina! What the hell happened to you?"

"Call Gail in, Sadie. Bertie's services are no longer required here," Ms. Manager replied flatly, shaking her blouse and jacket.

Leftover spaghetti clung to Ms. Manager like a parasite to a host. Meagan couldn't help smile, even for a moment. Louis's cold nose pressed against her palm and she shivered. Then, Meagan heard him sniff and snort, sniff and snort. "Mmm, me smell food, Meagan, food!" he barked. "Me hungry, me hungry!"

"Oh no, Louis, stay!" Nat shrieked as the leash snaked through her hands.

Meagan's stomach rolled. She reached for Louis's leash but it was too late. The big Rotti-mix knocked Ms. Manager to the ground and aggressively licked off the spaghetti bits, despite the slender woman's screams. Constable Wright withdrew his revolver.

"No, wait!" Meagan shouted, jumping in front of Louis. She grabbed his leash and dragged him off. "No, Louis, bad dog! You were told to stay!"

Louis whined. "Me bad, Meagan, me bad?"

Meagan rolled her eyes. It was like reasoning with a toddler. Spaghetti hung out of his mouth like helpless worms on a hook. "Yes and no, Louis," she whispered.

The policeman sheathed his gun. A wave of relief flowed through her.

"Isn't that dog supposed to be in quarantine?" Ms. Manager shrieked, as Constable Wright helped her to her feet.

"Yeah, and because of you he almost died!" Reid shouted, strutting toward Ms. Manager again. "So why don't you admit that you're the one who's poisoning the animals?"

Ms. Manager pressed a hand to her throat. "How dare you!"

"That's far enough, Reid!" Constable Wright warned.

"Reid, listen to Scotty," Bertie said. Her whole body trembled.

"No, Mom, you listen!" Reid ranted, raking his wavy, red hair. "Smith's got money problems, and guess what, so does the shelter! Don't you find it weird that cash has been missing lately? Betcha Gail's not the one to blame for that either!"

"Get in your car and leave now, Reid, before I have to resort to using these," Constable Wright said, pulling out his handcuffs.

"Reid, stop putting out negative thoughts and words and just walk away," Nat said, rolling her wheelchair around the porch's walkway and down to the parking lot. "Karma will catch up to whoever's responsible, you'll see."

Reid balled his fists. "Karma-smarma, that witch just fired my mom for no good reason!"

"I fired your mother for insubordination—for not doing her job—and from where I stand, it looks like you've failed your co-op course this semester!"

Reid's brown eyes bugged. "Y-You can't do that! I need those credits!"

"The way I see it, you've made your bed, now lie in it," Ms. Manager replied, sneering. "You're done here."

"But..." Reid's voice caught in his throat. He looked at Bertie. "Say something!"

Bertie's lips were thin, white lines. She pointed to his red Neon. "Calm down, get into your car, and go home. We'll talk later."

Feeling her cheeks burn, Meagan held Louis's leash tight, hoping he wouldn't pick up on her angry thoughts. Reid could blame Ms. Manager all he wanted, but without any hardcore evidence, he had nothing on her. Nada, zero, zip. Now their hunt for Whiskey had been compromised by a restraining order and a very pissed seventeen-year-old with a chip on his shoulder. Life was getting more complicated by the second.

Then, it got even more complicated as Kayla Reynolds pulled up in a burgundy Dodge mini-van. Suddenly, Reid turned and pounced at Ms. Manager. "Admit it! You're an animal murderer and thief!"

"Reid!" Bertie yelled, finding her voice.

"Louis, jump on Reid, stop him from getting to the Bossy One," Meagan whispered in his ear. "Go!" She dropped his leash.

Louis barked. "Me do, Meagan, me do!" He raced after Reid, bowled him over, and sat on him. He licked his face.

"Umph, Louis!" Reid yelled. "Bad dog! Get off!"

Meagan ran over. "Good dog, Louis, good dog."

Louis whined. "Good dog, bad dog, me confused!"

Meagan pulled him off Reid. "So am I, Louis, so am I."

"That's it, Reid, you're coming with me," Constable Wright said, grasping Reid by the arm and yanking him off the ground. He spun Reid around and slapped handcuffs on him. "Maybe some quality time in the station will cool your jets. Let's go."

"But...my car," Reid muttered, red-faced.

"I'm afraid you'll have to make other arrangements. Now move," Constable Wright said in a no-nonsense manner.

He guided Reid into the back of the cruiser. Reid's body slumped in defeat. Bertie walked over, said something to her son, and then left to go up the stairs and into the shelter. Beep, beep, went the door.

"What'd you do now, Meagan?" Kayla asked, coming up from behind her. "Must have been something good if the police are here. Did you sucker Reid into fighting your pathetic battles for you? Couldn't you have asked the dogs or cats to do that for you?"

Happy thoughts, happy thoughts, happy thoughts, hummed through Meagan's mind. She balled her fists anyway.

"Stay out of this, Kayla," Nat said, rolling her wheelchair over to park beside Meagan. "It's none of your business."

Kayla puckered her pink-glossed lips to one side and crossed her bare arms over her tight-fitting purple T-shirt. "Whatever. But sooner or later I'll find out what happened and Meagan will still be a freak of nature."

Meagan took a step toward her, but Nat pivoted her chair in Meagan's way. "What you think about, you bring about," Nat muttered.

"Your beliefs are bang on, Nat—like does attract like," Kayla said, laughing. "The more you hang out with this loser, the more you become one."

"Sticks and stones, Kayla," Nat said, smirking.

"Oh, Kayla," Ms. Manager said in a sickly-sweet voice. "Would you be a dear and take Louis down to his kennel? He's still under quarantine and I wouldn't want any of the public to endure what I have just experienced."

"Sure, Katrina, anything to help," Kayla replied, grinning.

"And as for you, Ms. Walsh," Ms. Manager glared at Meagan. "I suggest you gather your belongings and join that psychotic

Robertson boy in the cruiser before we have any more incidents. From now on, you're not to come within one hundred feet of this place. Is that understood?"

Meagan's jaw dropped. "One hundred feet? But...what about looking for Whiskey?"

"Whiskey and any of the other shelter animals are none of your concern anymore. For all the trouble you've caused, you're lucky your aunt still has a job here." Then, Katrina Smith removed her jacket and shook the rest of the spaghetti off. She clicked open her trunk and threw her jacket inside. Meagan spied a yellow jug of antifreeze. Her mouth fell open as Smith slammed the trunk shut, got into her car, and drove away, spinning the tires in the process.

"OMG, I can't wait to tell my friends about this!" Kayla roared with laughter and yanked the leash from Meagan's hand.

Louis growled. "Me stay, me stay."

Meagan sighed. "No, Louis, go with Kayla. She'll put you in your kennel and give you a big bowl of kibble. Right, Kayla?"

Kayla shrugged. "Sure, whatever, freak." She looked down at Nat. "Roll over to the van. Your mom wants you home by noon. I've got the van for the rest of the day."

"Why?" Nat asked, straightening in her chair.

Kayla smirked. "I'd tell you I have a date, but it's none of your business."

"A date?" Meagan furrowed her brows. "But I thought you had a thing for Reid?"

"Reid Robertson and me?" Kayla clutched her stomach as if her insides had exploded, and burst out laughing. "Not in this lifetime, douche-bag!"

"So Nobel was right, you're just using Reid!" Meagan spat.

"Is that what Nobel said? Now that's harsh, even for a dog. Besides, Reid's a big boy. He doesn't have to do anything he doesn't want to do." She walked toward the stairs. "Come on, Louis, before Miss Crazy-Kitty starts a conversation with you."

Louis whined, licked Meagan's fingers, then obeyed and went with Kayla up the stairs and into the shelter. Beep, beep.

"I-I don't freaking believe it. That's cruel, even for that witch," Meagan mumbled.

"Well, seeing is believing, and Reid will just have to believe it once he sees this—" Nat flashed Meagan her pink metallic cell phone and played back Kayla's video recorded response "—she's so busted."

Meagan's eyes bugged. She covered her mouth. "Isn't that some kind of bad energy?"

Nat smiled. "No. That's karma." She rolled toward the van. "Text me later. We'll need to come up with a search and rescue plan."

Meagan dropped her hand. "A search and rescue plan?"

Nat stopped, and then pivoted on her back wheels. "Yeah. Somebody has to organize a rescue plan for Whiskey. It might as well be me. I'll download a map of the area around the shelter to help with the search. Don't worry, Meagan, we'll find her before that fisher does." Nat turned around and proceeded to roll to the van.

"But, Nat, how's that supposed to happen?" Meagan asked, dumbfounded. "I'm grounded, you're in a wheelchair, and Reid's going to jail."

"Just live in the now, girl, just live in the now," Nat replied, without turning.

Meagan grunted. *Now* wasn't where she wanted to be—there was too much uncertainty, too much stress. *Now* promised a restraining order for her, a lost job for Bertie, and possible jail time for Reid. *Now* sucked big time.

19. The Sickness

"The old calico lies!" Shadow hissed from behind her sanctuary of toms. "Look closer at the cat's body—there are teeth marks all over his back! No sickness did this!"

Whiskey's head felt soggy, but she was coherent enough for a battle of wits with Shadow. "The sickness looks like teeth marks, but acts like what itch bugs do in cat ears, only it starts deeper inside us—chewing, biting, eating, until there's nothing left," Whiskey yowled.

"The old cat makes sense," Daisy meowed. "Most of Tiger's insides are eaten away."

"Idiot!" Shadow howled. "An animal could do that!"

"In all my cat years, I've never seen an animal attack a cat with such fierceness, such savagery," Brutus said, staring at Tiger's remains. Then he glared at Shadow, his ears lowered. "What animal is capable of doing such horrible things?"

"It was probably one of the shelter dogs!" Shadow hissed. "No doubt a friend of the old feline's!"

"But, Shadow," George mewed, "you know shelter dogs are always on a leash, it's a rule. Even I know that."

"The young cat makes sense," Jules meowed. "Besides, I've never seen a dog do that to a cat."

"Do you have another animal in mind, Shadow?" Brutus growled impatiently. "Or are you just guessing?"

Shadow's eyes widened. Huge black dots stared at Brutus. She whipped her tail side to side. Whiskey grinned. She knew Shadow had no clue, no idea what did this. Only she did. Most cats never lived to tell of how a brown beast attacks, how it tears into cat flesh, and how it severs the cat body to take what it wants. Whiskey sneezed again. Her nose gushed and her eyes watered.

"The sickness has taken over Whiskey!" Oscar meowed. "Soon she will be eaten from the inside-out, like Tiger! We must listen to her before it's too late! We must find the Chosen One!"

"Nooo!" Brutus snarled. "This is our place, our problem! Humans are meddlers!"

"Then, what do you suggest we do about this sickness, Brutus?" Jules asked, glaring at him. "Have you got a better idea?"

"Are you challenging me, Jules?" Brutus growled. His ears flattened.

Jules arched and turned his head to one side. "Do you want what happened to Tiger to happen to you or any of us?"

Brutus's ears moved forward. He winced in pain from his itch bugs. "We've managed hardships before, Jules. Why do you doubt me now?"

Jules relaxed. "This isn't the white cold stuff on the ground that freezes us, or fire from the sky that booms and brings pounding water with it. This is different. We can't hide from it, and we can't fight it."

"Jules is right!" Oscar meowed. "Tiger was one of our strongest, best fighters! If he couldn't protect himself from this sickness, how are we supposed to protect ourselves?"

Whiskey, weak from the illness her body was fighting, sat down and observed. Most of the mother cats seemed to side with Jules and Oscar. However, the younger toms and females wanted Brutus to make the final decision. This was going to get ugly if she didn't step in. Whiskey pushed up on all fours and then collapsed to the ground. Her head spun as a grogginess invaded her body.

"Whiskey!" George cried. He rushed up to nudge her. "What's wrong?"

"I'll tell you what's wrong!" Shadow hissed, slinking out from behind the pack of younger males. "The old calico has lied to you all! The Ones at the shelter have never treated any cat for a sickness that eats cats, but they have cared for the sickness that she has. I've seen this myself! Cats sneezing, feeling dizzy, water in their eyes, sticky stuff in their noses—oh, here's the best part—any cat can catch this sickness. Just go near her, let her sneeze on you if you want to get sick like her."

Jules's jaw dropped. "She...she sneezed on me!"

George's ears moved forward. "Is that true, Whiskey? Can we get sick from you?"

Whiskey weakly lifted her head and nodded. "Need white pills, George," she mewed weakly. "Tell Chosen One. She'll help." Her head dropped from its heaviness.

"See!" Shadow meowed. "The old feline admits it! Kill her, before she infects all of us!"

Brutus struck the ground with a paw. "You'll not give orders around here, Shadow! Whiskey is safe until I say so."

Duchess rubbed up against Brutus. "But what if the old cat sneezes on you? Who will lead us if you get the sickness?"

"If it wasn't a sickness that did this to Tiger, then what did?" Oscar asked, pawing at the severed tom.

Whiskey heard meows, yowls, and snarling all around her. The lost cats seemed divided, either out of fear or ignorance, or both. She sighed. Perhaps she had let her problems get in the way of what was best for the lost cats. Perhaps Shadow was darker than she thought and would do anything to ensure her survival. She took a deep, painful breath, and looked up. George continued to stand over her, not moving a whisker, whipping his tail from side to side in staunch vigilance. Whiskey forced a smile. Perhaps this battle wasn't over yet. It was time for a new plan. It was time for the truth.

Whiskey meowed faintly to George. "Tell them...a brown beast did."

The younger cat's grey ears pricked up. He looked down and pawed her face. "What's a brown beast, Whiskey?"

"A...monster with...claws and...fangs that…" Whiskey stopped to catch her breath. "...tears, rips, kills, eats...us."

"Another lie!" Shadow shrieked. "I tell you a new breed of dog killed him!"

"Yes," Jules meowed. "That makes more sense than a sickness or a brown beast."

Whiskey rolled to her side. "No...brown beast…not dog," she stammered out, and then sneezed.

All the cats scattered away from Whiskey. All but George. He stayed with her, by her side. Whiskey was sorry she had called George a no-brained cat earlier. If anything, she was the cat who was no-brained for taking him for granted. She struggled to sit up; her chest ached more than her bones and her head was fuzzy. For the first time in her life she was unable to think like a shelter cat thinks.

George rubbed up against her. "I believe you, Whiskey."

"Isn't that sweet?" Shadow purred in mockery. "But the old calico's already lied once. She can't help herself. She's feeble, weak-minded, and is dying before our eyes. She has nothing to lose, so let's do her a favour and put this ancient cat out of her misery."

Shadow advanced toward Whiskey, her head low, ears back, and tail cracking as if it was a lethal whip.

"Nooo!" George growled, swatting the air between them. "She needs her white pills!"

"Enough!" Brutus snarled, pouncing in between them. "I can't risk any of us getting the sickness Whiskey has, so I've made a decision!"

"It's about time," Jules said, as he preened himself, trying to get Whiskey's sneeze off his shiny white coat.

Brutus glowered at him. "Thank you for volunteering, Jules."

Jules stopped grooming. "For what?"

"To go to the shelter with George. If Whiskey needs her white pills to stop this sickness, then George will ask the Chosen One for them." Brutus glared at George. "I warn you, the human is not to return with you, or Whiskey will suffer at my paws. Understood?"

George shuddered. He nodded many times over.

Jules's ears moved forward. "So why do I need to go?"

Brutus sneered at the white cat. "To protect him, make sure this brown beast or new breed of dog doesn't attack him. I'm sure you can manage that, Jules. The future of the lost cats is in your paws, so you'd better make sure George returns safely with those pills."

Jules's blue eyes widened. "What if I'm attacked?"

Brutus snorted. "Use your instincts. Run and hide until it gives up, but don't let it follow you back here. And, Jules, the next time you challenge me, I'll make you sorry that you did."

George's grey ears moved forward, his tail swished. "What will you do with Whiskey while I'm gone?"

Brutus grunted. "She is to be confined so her sneezes can't reach us. Follow me, and bring her over to the front of our home."

Brutus sauntered toward the dark car. Shadow tried to sneak around him and he gave her a warning hiss. She backed off and headed into the forest. Whiskey observed in silence, staring up at the car, wondering how it got to such a remote area. There weren't any dents or scratches on it like the Kind One's and it didn't have lots of brown holes in it like the Loud One's car had. Her whiskers twitched. Seemed a silly waste to put this car where a human couldn't use it. Silly and stupid.

"Sorry, Whiskey," George mewed.

Roused from her thoughts, Whiskey's ears pricked up. "For...what?"

"For this," George replied, grabbing the scruff of her neck with his mouth.

The little white cat with grey markings on his ears and tail began to drag Whiskey. She wheezed, but tried to help him the best she could, even though the ground felt spongy and uneven. Guiding her, George moved past the shiny side of the lost cats' home to the front. Whiskey glanced up. Round, glassy eyes gleamed in a macabre, uneasy manner. Grass and brush stuck out from the slats of its metal mouth as if silencing its secrets. At the highest point, a statue of a gold cat peered down at her in an intimidating manner. Chills crawled along her spine.

"Here," Brutus said, pointing. "Whiskey will stay in there until you return."

Whiskey's yellow eyes widened. It was a cat carrier like those she'd seen used at the shelter. Weather-worn and covered with green slime, its rusted steel door was half open and inside, a moldy, pink blanket was its only source of comfort. Whiskey cringed and glanced at Brutus. It took all of her strength to say, "You...don't...expect me—"

"I do," Brutus growled. "If you sneeze again, you'll do it on yourself. I can't risk this sickness spreading to the rest of the colony."

"But, Brutus," George meowed, "Whiskey's too—"

Whiskey placed a paw over George's mouth. "It's...okay, George. I'm old...sick...tired." she huffed, struggling to take a breath. "You go...be safe...I need...rest."

"Enough talk," Brutus grumbled. "Get in before I change my mind and let Shadow have her way with you."

Whiskey crawled into the moldy carrier, turned around, wobbled, and then collapsed onto the damp blanket. Brutus pushed the door closed with both front paws, and then extracted one of his claws to pull the latch to lock the door. *Snap!* The noise went through her, rattling her old bones like the boom of a summer storm.

George placed a paw on the barred door. "Don't worry, Whiskey, I'll get your white pills, I promise."

Whiskey mewed weakly. "Wait...George." She reached over to touch his paw through the bars. "Promise...me that...you'll be...back...by dark."

George nodded. "I'll sure try."

"Not...try. Do," Whiskey wheezed. Then, she crawled closer to George and whispered, "Bring...Meagan...or...the...brown beast...will...come, will...kill. Go...do."

"How much farther?" Jules huffed, racing beside George.

George stopped, gasping. He thought his heart would pop out of his mouth. "Not...far...now," he stammered.

Jules sat down to groom himself. "I think I've finally gotten the sneeze off me."

George's ears flattened. "Don't you care about Whiskey or any of the other cats that might get sick?"

Jules snorted. "Kid, out here, it's every cat for himself."

George's jaw dropped. "That's selfish! We don't think that way in the shelter!"

Jules caterwauled. "That's because you're not allowed to think there. You eat and sleep when you're told to, have to use those disgusting litter boxes, and you don't get to choose your human family—they choose you."

"What's wrong with that?"

"Everything!" Jules yowled. "Being a cat is about being independent, not answering to anyone, sleeping when I want to sleep, and hunting when I want to hunt. Humans have too many rules for us. They'll never understand what it is to be a cat."

George wiggled his nose. "Brutus has rules and you answer to him."

Jules blue eyes narrowed. "Not for long. I've got a plan." Then the white cat with the shiny, sleek coat bounded toward the row of trees bordering the trail.

What kind of a plan? George's cat brain wondered. He shook his head to clear it like Tess had taught him. A sudden stillness surrounded him. The air had become heavier since their journey began. When the trees allowed a peek at the sky, George noticed it had turned the colour of fresh litter. A slight breeze whipped up and rustled the leaves and bushes. George's whiskers twitched. Chills rolled in his small stomach. *Boom!* The sky rumbled above him.

Startled, George darted after Jules, pushing himself, until he felt safe from the scary noises, heavy air, and brown beasts. He growled. This would have never happened in the shelter. He should never have followed Shadow out the window. At the shelter, he would have been cuddling with Tess in a basket, with a full tummy and a warm blanket. Now, his world had changed. Now, Tess was gone. If only she hadn't eaten that bad meat.

Slamming into the back of Jules, George rolled a few feet until he smacked into a big, hard stump. *Whump!* Tiny bright lights pinged and bounced inside his head.

"Whoa, kid, slow down! You've messed up my fur!" Jules roared.

George shook his head to get the fuzziness out. "W-What was that noise?"

Jules looked up. Another boom sounded from the sky. His ears flattened. "The sky is getting ready to drown us. We'd best hurry and get those white pills. My fur hates water."

Trying to stand, George staggered until the ground felt stable. He shook his head again. "Okay, which way to the shelter?"

"Are you all right, kid?"

"Huh? S-Sure," George mewed. Then, he did a double take. "Who's your friend, Jules?"

Jules inclined his head. "What friend? It's just me here."

George squinted. "Nope. I see two cats."

"Fantastic," Jules grumbled. "Look down the path. How many do you see?"

George obeyed and looked. "Two, no maybe three, no wait, two paths."

Jules pawed his head. "Looks like I'm going to have to kitty-sit a little longer. Come on, kid, let's find this Chosen One of yours."

George teetered from side to side. His brain felt mushy. Suddenly, Jules sunk his teeth into the scuff of George's neck and started dragging him down the dirt path. George's nose flared. Smells of dog droppings and dog pee marked most of the trail, while the odd whiff of cat spray lingered in certain spots. The sky boomed again and he flinched, closing his eyes, hoping the water wouldn't shower down yet. Jules released George and he dropped to the ground.

George opened his eyes and glanced around. "Hey, look—"

"I know, kid, two shelters."

"No. Two dishes of meat." He licked his cat lips.

"Where?" Jules meowed, his ears moving forward. "I'm starving!"

George pointed. "Over there, in those two caves."

Jules's stomach rumbled. "There's only one cave and one dish. Sorry, kid, but like I said, every cat for himself!"

Jules bounded across the gravel lot to where the cave with the dish of meat was. George grunted. Boscoe would have put that selfish, white cat in his place if they had been in the shelter and Poppy, being so fat, probably would have sat on him till his fur matted. George shook his head, trying to get the cloudiness out. He stood up, stretched, and then attempted to walk toward Jules, hoping that maybe he might have left him a morsel.

Snap! George jumped.

"George, help me! I'm trapped!"

Still wonky on his paws, George managed to stagger over to the cave. He noticed his eyes were working better, focusing on just one thing instead of two. Reaching the cave, he peered in, his ears moved back in a haughty manner. "Serves you right for hogging all the meat."

"Just get me out of here, George," Jules growled. "You can have what's left."

George snorted. "There's probably nothing left."

Jules's blue eyes widened. "George...behind you!"

A strong hand grabbed the scruff of George's neck before he had a chance to turn around. "Gotcha, George," the Quick One said. "Gail, need some help out here! I think we've got Shadow too!"

"Hold your Ps and Qs, Momma's coming!" Gail yelled, strutting around the corner.

The sky boomed again and George tried to wiggle away from the Quick One's grasp.

"Settle down, George, it's just thunder," the Quick One said. Only, to the younger cat, it sounded like a mish-mash of garble.

Then George floated through the air until the Quick One opened the mouth of another cave, similar to the one Whiskey was put in, and dropped him in it. She shut the opening and placed him on the ground. "No, wait!" he meowed as loudly as he could. "Whiskey's sick! She needs her white pills! I must talk to the Chosen One! Let me out!"

"What's with George?" the Loud One asked. "I've never seen him freak out like that."

"Beats me," the Quick One said. "I'm just glad we got them before the storm hits."

"Uh, Sadie. We got a problem. This ain't Shadow."

George could hear Jules growl, hiss, and spit. "Go away, humans, go away!" he snarled.

"That's not helping, Jules," George meowed, but Jules didn't listen. He continued to rant and howl as if he were being neutered while awake.

George slumped against the cave wall. He had let Whiskey down terribly. She was right, he had no cat brains. He squeezed his eyes shut, then opened, squeezed, and then opened again. There. His vision had fully returned and his head seemed clearer. He took a deep breath. Maybe Meagan was inside the shelter. Maybe there was still hope in saving Whiskey from her sickness and the lost cats from the brown beast. A shuffling noise made him look up. George gasped. There, behind the bright metal bin overflowing with garbage, sat Shadow. Her tail whipped back and forth, her eyes alert and glowering.

"Shadow!" George meowed loudly. "Find the Chosen One before it's too late!"

Shadow's cat lips curled. "It's already too late, George. Too late for Whiskey and too late for you," she yowled. "You've made your choice. Live with it."

Then, Shadow darted up the path just as the sky ripped out a terrible boom.

20. Lucky

"Are you feeling lucky?" Meagan whispered.

Reid slumped in his seat. He pulled at his plaid shirt. "Yeah. About as lucky as a mouse in the cat room at the shelter."

Meagan rolled her eyes. "Sometimes you're such a douche. Look on the bright side, at least Constable Wright removed the handcuffs."

Reid sat up. He rubbed his wrists. "Look around you, Meagan. We're sitting in a police station waiting for my mom and your aunt to pick us up. We're both probably gonna be grounded until we're eighteen, I've just failed my entire co-op semester, and my mom has no job. If this is your idea of luck, then I'll need a few extra horseshoes shoved up my—"

"I was talking about this kind of luck," Meagan said, cutting in. She laid a long firecracker across Reid's lap.

Reid's eyes bugged. "Where'd you get that?"

"It was a leftover from the May long weekend firework celebration. I bought it at the Fairy Falls General Store and stashed it in my bag in case something came up. Well, something's definitely up. What d'ya think? It's called a

Screaming Midnight Cluster," Meagan replied, scooping the long firecracker up and waving it in the air like a magic wand. "I have some lady-fingers too."

"Have you lost it? We're on police turf. Put that away," Reid muttered through clenched teeth.

Meagan pursed her lips. "How else are we supposed to escape and rescue Whiskey? We need a diversion to slip past the front desk. This will work brilliantly."

Suddenly, loud thunder rumbled all around them. The lights flickered off, then on.

Reid looked up. "Mmm, by the sounds of it, looks like there's another firework show in the making. Now put that Screaming-whatever-it-is away before someone sees you with it!"

Meagan smiled. "Okay. Bend down."

Reid shook his head. "Ever thought of getting therapy?"

Before Meagan had a chance to offer Reid a pithy comeback, her phone vibrated. She scowled at him anyway, shoved the firecracker back into her red canvas bag, and then pulled out her cell phone. "Hello?"

"It's Nat, and you won't believe what I found out," she said over the phone. "It was way too much to text."

Meagan looked at Reid. "It's Nat. She's got some info for us. Go on, Nat."

Meagan heard her sigh. "I downloaded a map of the area behind the shelter like I said I would. It's quite a big parcel of land by the looks of it, and it backs onto the Vista River. There's an old road that comes out behind the back part of the shelter's property, near the shed. It's blocked off, but looks like it might still be used by local hunters. Anyway, I did some digging and found out that the land was once owned by none other than Katrina Smith."

"Wait…Katrina Smith owned the land behind the shelter?"

"What's going on?" Reid asked, tugging at Meagan's green scrub top.

She waved him off. "So who owns the property now?"

"Oh, you're gonna love this! Matt Moody bought it almost three years ago."

Meagan frowned. "Moody? The animal control officer, slash control freak?"

"What about Moody?" Reid asked, poking Meagan's arm.

"Stop it." Meagan elbowed Reid. "I'll catch you up in a sec."

"Hello?" Nat asked. "Stop what?"

Meagan puffed out her cheeks. "Not you. Reid. How did you find all this out?"

Nat laughed. "My stepfather, Ray Reynolds, a.k.a. Kayla's dad, is a real estate agent with Karen Bean. I asked, he told. In fact, it was Ray who did the deal between Smith and Moody."

"I wonder why Smith would still have money problems after she sold that property." Meagan scratched her nose. "It must have been worth a good chunk of change."

"Not as much as you'd think," Nat said. "At least that's what Ray told me. The only thing going for Moody's property is that there's plenty of waterfront on it. Ray said his land would be worth big bucks if it had a serviced public road leading to it."

Meagan strummed her knee. Reid nudged her. She placed the phone to her chest and glared at him. "You'd better wrap it up. My mom is talking to your aunt out in the parking lot," Reid said, pointing at the glass doors.

Meagan nodded. *It's showtime.* She put the phone back to her ear. "Nat? Quick, can you send me that map? Reid and I gotta bust out of here if we're ever gonna find Whiskey. Bertie and Aunt Izzy are standing in the parking lot, so we don't have much time."

Silence hovered between them for a moment. Nat cleared her throat. "I've got a better idea. Do what you have to do. I'll meet you behind the arena in fifteen minutes. It should take you guys about that long to walk there from the police station. Okay?"

Meagan's chest tingled. "How are you gonna—"

"Never mind. Just meet me there. Bye."

Dead air replaced Nat's voice. Meagan pocketed her red phone.

Boom! Crack! Both Meagan and Reid jumped. The lights flickered off and on again. Another boom sounded close behind. This time the lights dimmed and went out.

Meagan reached for her bag, pulled out the firecracker, and then fished around for her lighter. "You're still serious?" Reid asked, holding out his hand. "They'll be in here in a minute, Meagan. We have no time!"

"Dead serious." She dropped the string of lady-fingers in Reid's palm. "We have plenty of time, and you're helping." Meagan flicked her lighter. It lit up their faces in an eerie way as she ignited the lady-fingers.

"Meagan! Crap! W-What are you doing?"

"Creating an opportunity. You'd better throw that somewhere. I suggest the washroom."

Reid jumped up. "You're freaking psychotic!" He ran for the bathroom around the corner, exit signs fueled by an emergency generator lighting his way.

Meagan heard the door open, then shut. *Bam, bam, bam, bam, bam, bam, bam, bam, bam, bam, bam, bam!* echoed in rapid succession. "What the hell?" Constable Wright yelled. "Sara! Help me check out the washroom!"

Reid returned, taking his seat, his breathing raspy, and his body shaking. He wiped his mouth with the back of his hand.

Meagan shook her head. "You're such a pussy. Get up. We're going out the back door."

Then, she flicked her lighter one last time and lit the Screaming Midnight Cluster. "To freedom!" She pitched the firecracker toward the front double doors.

"Let's go!" Meagan jumped from her seat, slung her bag over one shoulder, and made a bee-line for the back section of the station.

"Wait for me!" Reid pushed his chair so hard it clattered to the floor.

Screams and whistles reverberated in the hallway as it lit up with the most brilliant hues of greens, reds, and blues. Cracking and popping followed the star-bursts, flaring and dancing against the walls and ceiling, like it was creating new life. The explosive display seemed to go on forever, but Meagan knew she had only about thirty seconds. Running past the officer's lounge, she turned and headed for the back door. *Finally,* Meagan thought before she pushed the door open. Only, the door wouldn't budge. It was locked. They were screwed.

"You're kidding me!" Reid shouted, catching up. He huffed, holding his chest. "It's...it's freaking locked?"

"Don't worry, I've got this. I know how to pick locks." Meagan patted down her scrub top in search of her nail clippers.

Her eyes widened. *Crap! Must have left them in Aunt Izzy's apartment.* Meagan's face, neck, and ears heated up. "Quick! Back to that lounge we passed. Maybe there's a way out in there!"

Reid groaned. "You'd better hope so!"

On their way there, Meagan heard yelling, shrieking, and some juicy vulgar cursing coming from the front of the station. Thankfully the lights hadn't come back on yet. Slipping into the lounge, the pair of fugitives closed the door and locked it. Meagan looked around the dim room. A brown leather couch was placed up against one wall. A newspaper lay draped over its cushions. A metal lunch table with pulled out mismatched vinyl chairs stood in the opposite corner, near a full-size almond-coloured fridge and small white stove. A tiny countertop with an ancient microwave completed the retro look. Beige walls complimented the equally beige floor tiles. Meagan cringed. It was a designer's worst nightmare.

Reid leaned up against the door and scowled at Meagan. "So, you wanna tell me where you learned how to pick locks?"

"Uh, my friend Cassie taught me," Meagan replied, pursing her lips.

Reid snorted. "Some friend. She sounds more like a trouble-maker to me."

"Trouble-maker?" Meagan balled her fists. "FYI—I met Cassie in grief counseling and she's been there for me ever since I lost my mom."

"Look around, Meagan. Is Cassie here for you now?" Reid asked, pushing away from the door. "More important, has she even bothered to phone or text you since you've moved here?"

Meagan's cheek twitched. *When was the last time Cassie sent me a text?* Her brow furrowed. Cassie hadn't even answered the text Meagan had sent her after getting caught by Aunt Izzy's superintendent. Meagan's chest tightened. Had Cassie found another BFF to confide in? Meagan stared at the beige tiles and found an image of a cat in the vague design on one. Strangely, the cat resembled Whiskey.

"There," Reid said, breaking Meagan's thoughts. He pointed to the only window in the room. "Let's see if it's open."

Meagan raised her head and nodded. "Okay, last one there's a—"

"—rotten egg!" Reid pushed Meagan out of his way. She stumbled and landed on the leather couch, bouncing to the floor.

Meagan shook her head. "Nice manners, Robertson!"

"My bad, but from what I've witnessed today, you're worse," Reid said, trying to wiggle the window open. "Crap! It's not budging! Now what?"

Meagan stood, smoothed out her scrubs, adjusted her canvas bag, and raked her raven hair out of her face. "Now, we get badder than bad. We get nasty."

"Huh?"

"Move!"

"What?"

"I said, *move!*" Meagan replied, picking up one of the chairs. "Now!"

Reid jumped out of the way just in time as Meagan heaved the chair with its metal legs facing the window. *Smash!* The chair landed outside in the bushes, bending limbs and crushing foliage. She peered outside. The sky had turned grey and the air had gotten sticky. There was a greenish hue to the clouds Meagan had never seen before. Thunder rumbled across the sky, startling her. She backed away from the window.

"I need something to cover the opening so we don't cut ourselves," she said, looking around the room.

"What you need is a good shrink," Reid muttered. "Here, use this." He tossed Meagan a winter coat hanging on the wall.

"Grab a couple of those rain coats. I think we're gonna need them too." Meagan draped the coat over the broken glass of the window frame. "All set."

Suddenly, the doorknob jiggled. It jiggled again, and again. Then, it stopped. *Bang, bang, bang!* "Open this door immediately!" Constable Wright demanded. "Reid? Meagan? Are you in there?"

"Nooo," Reid said in a high-pitched girly voice. He yanked the raincoats off their hooks.

"It's your turn to move, Meagan," Reid said as he sailed out the wide window.

She grunted. "Whatever happened to ladies first?"

Meagan jumped out the window and rolled across the uneven ground.

"Let's go before Constable Wright figures out we're gone," Reid said, pulling Meagan up. He dragged her around the side and headed toward the row of bushy cedars that led back to the road.

"Oh, I'm sure he'll be too busy cleaning up after the Screaming Midnight Cluster show," she said, waving a hand. "Admit it. It was pure genius."

"Okay, genius, any thoughts on how we're gonna make it to the arena without the police catching us?" Reid asked, leading her through the cedars and down a well-trodden path.

Suddenly, a buck with five points on his antlers broke through a line of bushes bordering the edge of the road and headed directly for them. A dog barked madly in pursuit. "Skoka! Skoka! Git back here, dang it!" a man yelled in the distance.

"Holy crap, move, Meagan!" Reid said, pulling her down with him. They rolled off the path, into a small ditch filled with dead leaves and pine needles. The sky yawned a loud, long rumble.

"If you go that way, you'll be trapped!" Meagan yelled at the deer, pointing. "Go around those trees, there's no fence there."

The buck slowed down, blinked, and struck the ground with a hoof. "Much obliged, human, much obliged." Then he reared, and sprinted for the trees.

"Did you just talk to that deer?" Reid asked, standing. He helped Meagan to her feet.

"Sure. I just don't chat to cats and dogs, you know," Meagan replied, brushing dirt from her scrubs.

The dog's barking was getting louder and Meagan could feel the ground vibrating beneath them. "Skoka! Come!" the same man yelled again. His voice sounded strained.

The bushes rustled and branches snapped as a yellow Labrador galloped toward them. He skidded to a stop, sniffed the air, whined, and then sniffed the air again. His tail wagged. He looked toward the trees Meagan had pointed at a few moments earlier, and then growled and let out a high-pitched bark. He bounded in that direction.

"Wait!" Meagan yelled. "I-I need your help, Skoka!"

The big yellow dog froze. His broad head turned to stare at Meagan. "Help?" he whined. What fer?"

Think, think, think, stumbled through Meagan's mind. Then her eyes widened and she glanced at Skoka. "I'm lost and I need you to lead me to the road."

Skoka turned and sat down. He stared at Reid. "Can't cha ask him ta lead ya?"

She shook her head. "You're stronger, smarter, and more reliable than he is."

"Uh, did you just insult me?" Reid asked, arching his red brows.

Meagan ignored him. She focused all her energy on Skoka. His brows bobbed up and down, left and right, trying to choose between the deer or her. Then, he sighed, stood up, and padded over to Meagan. "Hold me collar," he barked gruffly. "I'll go slow fer ya."

Skoka led Meagan, who gestured for Reid to follow, down the path, past a rock cliff, and then down through a muddy ditch leading up to the road. She patted his big, solid head. "Thanks, Skoka. I wouldn't have made it without you."

Reid rolled his eyes. "Unbelievable."

"Skoka! There ya be, ya dang dog!" a man called out, as he pulled up in a blue Dodge pick-up truck. He looked at Meagan and Reid. "Thanks fer findin' Skoka. He's a handful at times, 'specially when the critters come out of hibernatin'."

Meagan's eyes raked over the old man. Metal-rimmed glasses framed a clean-shaven, tan face full of wrinkles, and short silver hair and a hawk-like nose made him resemble a beat-up bald eagle. His red plaid bush jacket was done up all the way to his thick neck. The name 'Pete' was embroidered in black thread above the breast pocket. She gulped, and then grinned, silently hoping Pete wasn't packing a sawed-off shotgun.

"Hey, Mr. Ellis," Reid said. "I didn't realize this was *your* dog."

Grey eyes squinted at Reid. "Oh, yer Bertie's son," he said, his eyes widening while smacking the steering wheel. "Yer ma helped Gertie and me adopt Skoka." Then he grinned, showing off his straight yellow teeth. "I guess it's too late for a trade-in, eh?"

Reid laughed. Meagan looked down at Skoka. "You came from the Fairy Falls Animal Shelter?"

"Yup, got me a nice home now," Skoka barked. "Is Nobel still there?"

"You know Nobel?"

"Course, he's a dang good pack leader from what I 'member," Skoka yipped.

Meagan giggled. "Yes, he's still there, and he's still a dang good pack leader."

"Young lady, if I didn't know any better, I'd swear you was conversing with me dog."

Reid cleared his throat. "Stop playing around, Meagan, we've got to get you to the arena to meet your Aunt Nat."

"Huh? Oh, yeah, right, my Aunt Nat," Meagan said, cluing in.

The sky rumbled, unleashing its pent-up angry sounds. A flash of lightning streaked across the grey clouds in ominous pursuit. A sharp, wicked wind kicked up.

"Dang," Mr. Ellis grumbled. "Storm's a coming. You two best jump in. I'll take ya to the arena. Put Skoka in the back fer me."

"Gee, thanks, Mr. Ellis," Reid said, throwing one of the stolen raincoats over his shoulders. He passed the other yellow coat to Meagan. She quickly shrugged into it.

"Yeah, thanks," Meagan added, rolling up the long sleeves. Then she slapped her thigh. "Come on, Skoka, in the back of the truck. And, promise me, from now on no more chasing deer."

Skoka cocked his ears. "No chasing deer? But that ain't natural!"

Meagan arched a brow. "And I say better to die a natural death than get hit by a car on the road or lost in the woods."

Skoka whined, wagged his tail, and licked Meagan's fingers. "I'll promise only if ya ride in the back with me. I hate the loud booms."

She stroked his head. "Deal." Meagan walked to the back of the truck and pulled the gate down. "Hey, Mr. Ellis, I'll ride with Skoka. He's afraid of thunder. Oh, and you shouldn't have any problems with him running after deer again. I made him promise me he'd stop."

Mr. Ellis shook his head. "That there's a strange little gal. Must be touched in the head."

Reid laughed as another clap of thunder sounded. Seconds later, the sky lit up.

21. Life Lessons

"There's gotta be a way out. Whiskey's counting on me!" George meowed. He looked over all the windows in the shelter again, but none were open, not even a crack. The Quick One and the Loud One had locked them up tight before they left.

"What's this I hear about Whiskey, George?" Boscoe asked. He stretched his long body across the blue tiled floor.

George hung his head. "Whiskey's sick. She needs her white pills. Brutus and the lost cats won't let her go because she'll tell the Chosen One about them. There's a brown beast in the forest that eats cats. Jules is trapped in the other room where the new cats go, and I'm stupid, stupid, stupid," tumbled out of his mouth in rapid succession. Dizzy with worry, his head drooped.

Boscoe stared at George. "I got: Whiskey sick, white pills, Brutus, lost cats, Chosen One, brown beast that eats cats, Jules trapped, stupid, stupid, stupid. Is that about right?"

George pulled his ears back. Whiskey was right. Dogs weren't the only ones who were thick-headed. "Are your ears stuffed with itch bugs?"

"Did I hear you mention the name Brutus?" Poppy asked, swinging her fat behind around like she owned the place. She swatted away one of the young males trying to sniff her.

George nodded. "Brutus won't let Whiskey go. He sent me back here to get her white pills 'cause she's sick."

Poppy scrunched her pushed-in face, which made it look even more pushed in. "How sick?"

"She's sneezing lots, goop comes out of her nose, and she's having trouble breathing."

"Oh dear, oh dear, that's not good, not good at all," Poppy meowed, cringing. "Boscoe, remember that older tabby named Helga? She got sick like that. Sneezing, wheezing, coughing, and choking. Poor dear. The Kind One took her out of her cage and she's never returned since. Between me and you, I think she got the sleep needle."

George's eyes widened.

"Now don't go telling the boy cat horror stories, Poppy," Boscoe said, grooming his front paws. "You'll put the wrong notion in his cat brain. We don't know what really happened to Helga. Maybe she got adopted."

Poppy let out a yowl. "And maybe cat kibble will start pouring out of my butt!"

Boscoe stopped grooming. "With the amount you eat, I'm surprised it hasn't already happened."

Poppy growled and then swatted at Boscoe. He jumped up onto the closest cage, avoiding the fat Persian's wrath.

"Did George say something about Brutus?" Carol, a calico, asked. She was one of Poppy's tough girls—she liked to be called 'the enforcer'. No cat in their right cat mind would mess with her.

George nodded. "Do you know him?"

Carol lifted her chin. "Every cat who's any cat knows of Brutus. He's the handsome tom who broke the door to our play cage. A work of art, that was. Brilliant!"

"My dear, you sound like you had a thing for that big boy," Poppy said, preening her fat, white face with a paw.

Carol swaggered. "I don't like to brag, but I knew him before he got neutered, if you catch my meaning." She winked at Poppy.

The two females caterwauled.

George's ears flattened. No cat seemed to care about Whiskey—the shelter's observer. They just wanted to gossip about how sick Helga was and how strong and tough Brutus was. A growl, originating from the back of his throat, let loose in a way the little white cat with grey markings on his ears and tail had never experienced before in his life. He pounced on Carol, growling, hissing, scratching, biting, and snarling. His fur fluffed out to three times its size. Carol never saw it coming. She screamed and lashed out in defense.

"Get him off! Get him off!" Carol hissed.

"I can't get to him, he's too fast!" Poppy huffed.

"No, *you're* too fat!" Boscoe said, jumping down from the cage. "Step aside and watch a real leader in action!" He waited for his chance, lunged for the cats rolling on the floor, and sunk his teeth into the back of what he thought was George's neck.

"Oww! Idiot!" Carol hissed. "That's my head!"

George rolled into the closest cage. *Whump!* He felt a warm paw caress his face. He looked up to find a single, white young female who hadn't been spayed yet. "That was the bravest thing I've ever seen any cat do," she purred.

"It was also the stupidest!" Olivia growled from behind.

George's eyes bugged. Uh-oh. Olivia—the other half of Poppy's pesky posse. He twisted his body around so all four paws were on the floor. "W-Wait, Olivia, I-I made a mistake."

Olivia growled. Her black tail twitched back and forth. "You certainly did. Now it's time to pay for it." She lunged at him.

George jumped up and onto the adjacent table. He turned and ran for the metal cage where Shadow had been kept before she escaped. His cat brain hummed. Maybe he was small enough to fit underneath? At least, he hoped he was. He leapt over another cage, and then onto the floor. Unfortunately for George, Poppy cut him off. She swatted at him, but missed.

"Leave him alone, Poppy!" Boscoe roared, leaping from behind. "He's been through enough with losing Tess and running away with Shadow."

"He needs to learn some respect!" Poppy snarled.

Boscoe's ears flattened. His back arched. "What he needs is a little support from us."

George heard growling and hissing approaching from the back of the room. Carol and Olivia were closing in, stalking him like a mouse. Carol situated herself high up on a cage above him, while Olivia positioned herself behind Boscoe. George gulped.

Boscoe growled. "Call your girls off, Poppy, or..."

"Or what?" Poppy asked indignantly.

Boscoe slunk closer until he was a whisker away from her ear. "Or I'll tell them where you keep your secret stash of catnip," he whispered.

Poppy's eyes widened. "You...you wouldn't?"

Boscoe grinned. "I would. Now tell them to back off or the nip's out of the bag."

"What's he saying?" Olivia asked Carol.

Carol shook her head. "Not sure. Poppy, what are your orders?"

Poppy glared at Boscoe. "Stand down, girls. Let him go."

"What?" Olivia caterwauled. "But he attacked Carol!"

"Carol's a big girl. She'll get over it!" Poppy hissed.

"I knew you'd see it my way, Poppy," Boscoe meowed.

"This isn't over, Boscoe," Poppy spat. "Sooner or later you'll need a catnap and George will be left to fend for himself."

Poppy waddled away with Olivia at her side. Carol shot him a warning hiss, and then jumped down to join Poppy and Olivia. He vaguely overheard them discussing Brutus again. The felines caterwauled in unison as they rounded the corner leading into the back room.

George sighed. "Thanks, Boscoe. I owe you."

"The way I see it, you owe me most of your nine lives, George, but I'd settle for busting you out of here to help Whiskey instead."

"Huh? How?"

Boscoe smiled a black cat's smile—white, shiny teeth with a touch of mischief—then said, "Follow me."

He led George to the back of the room, next to the door that led downstairs to the dog floor. He could hear one of the dogs howling, no doubt from all the booming and flashing in the sky. Around him, some of the cats were meowing morosely and hiding under their blankets. Boscoe stopped by the metal cover stuck in the floor that brought up hot or cold air depending on the season. Its metal mouth grinned at George. Boscoe extracted his claws, hooked them into the cover, and yanked it up and off. It clattered to the floor.

"There ya go, George. Get in and follow the tunnel out."

George stuck his head in the hole. His nostrils flared as a blast of cold air went up his nose. He sneezed and pulled his head out. "You want me to go in there?"

Boscoe's ears moved forward. "That's the plan."

George looked down. "That's a stupid plan."

"Whiskey does it all the time. What's the problem?"

"What if I get stuck?"

"Whiskey never got stuck and you're about her size."

George frowned as best as his cat face would allow. "Whiskey's not getting any bigger. I'm still growing. What if I grow while I'm in there?"

Boscoe yawned. "Suit yourself. But it's almost time for my catnap, so that leaves you with a choice: escape through the tunnel, or face Poppy and her girls while I'm curled up with the cute orange feline in the next room."

George sighed. He glanced behind him and spotted Poppy, Carol, and Olivia rolling around on the floor. Carol's eyes locked on his. She extracted a claw, pointed at him, and then ran it underneath her throat. George's eyes bugged. He peered into the hole in the floor and swallowed hard. It was a cat no-brainer.

"I choose saving Whiskey," he said, crawling into the tunnel.

"Good call," George heard Boscoe meow before the sly black cat slid the metal cover over the hole and pushed it down. *Clunk!*

"Where am I?" George meowed. Then he sneezed.

There was so much dust in the tunnel he couldn't breathe properly. He rounded one corner, then another, and there was still more tunnel in front of him. Why would Whiskey do this every night? Was being the shelter's observer that important? He was at an impasse. Three tunnels forked out in front of him. One went straight ahead, the second veered to his left, and the third to his right. He growled. It was a guessing game now. Then he heard cat noises. Faint at first, but George moved his ears around until he picked up a clearer sound and locked onto it. There, the noise was coming from his right side, so that was the tunnel George chose.

As George got closer, he realized it was Jules making all that fuss. He was still snarling and growling. George followed the tunnel, turning once more until it headed upwards. He looked up. A metal cover resembling the one Boscoe had removed stared down at him. The open slats let in just enough light for George to see it was another room—the room where the new cats go. He smiled a haughty cat smile and with his head, pushed against the cover. Off it popped with a clang.

"Who's that?" Jules hissed.

"It's George," he replied with a sneeze.

A loud rumble from outside seemed to shake the shelter. It was followed by a bright flash that lit up the room. Another rumble, this one louder, pierced George's ears and he flattened them. A streak of light from the sky flashed again. *Boom! Zap! Crack!* George's skin prickled as if thousands of fleas were crawling all over his body. His fur and tail fluffed out, his ears started ringing, and he sensed the entire floor around him come alive. Panicking, George squeezed out of the hole just as something crashed through the window above him.

"George, move!" Jules yowled.

Grunting, George flew across the room and landed by the row of metal cages stacked on top of each other. He shook his head, then looked up. A huge, gnarly tree branch now lay inside the window, jagged glass hung from the frame like the fangs of a wild cat. George immediately thought of Carol. Another boom and flash rippled through the sky. Some of the cats in the new cat room yowled fearfully.

Then a high-pitched sound echoed throughout the shelter.

"Kid? You okay?"

George glanced up at the cages. His head was jumbled, but his fur had flattened. He'd never felt anything like that before. His hearing seemed off, too. Did Jules just speak to him? Or was it one of the other cats? He pawed his head, trying to get the fuzziness out of it.

"George, dear, are you hurt?" an older feline meowed.

"Who said that?"

"Up here, dear."

George looked up to the right. A huge metal cage with an old tabby cat peered down at him. "Who are you?"

"I'm Helga. I used to be in the large cat room in a cage at the back."

George's eyes widened. "You were sick!"

She nodded. "That's right. I'm better now."

"Did the Kind One give you some white pills?" George asked.

"Why yes, she did."

"Do you know where those pills are?"

Helga scratched her white chin. "I think they're over there." She pointed to a corner table piled high with multi-coloured towels. "The Kind One kept them in a small brown bottle."

George whipped his tail back and forth like an older cat. "Thanks, Helga. Whiskey needs those pills to get better like you." He bounded for the table with renewed strength.

"Uh, George? Have you forgotten about me?" Jules called after him.

"No, but I need to bring Whiskey her white pills so she can get better."

"Fine, kid, but let me out first. I don't do small spaces well."

George skidded to a stop, mindful of the broken glass all over the floor. He sighed and then turned around. Hooking his paws into the bars, George managed to climb up the empty bottom cage to reach Jules's cage in the middle. He peered in. Jules was right. He didn't do small spaces well. His litter box had been upturned, his food dish emptied, and the water dish was filled with cat poop and litter. George scrunched his face. *Doesn't Jules have any manners?*

"How you gonna get me out, kid?"

George wondered that too. He looked at the door's latch. There was only one way to do this. The hard way. George took a deep breath and looped a paw through the round handle of the latch. He shut his eyes tight, pushed off the cage with both his back paws, and yanked the handle toward the opposite wall. He yanked and yanked and yanked. *Clink!* It opened with George swinging in mid-air.

"All right! Freedom! Now that's what I'm talking about!" Jules jumped down, landing on all fours. "Come on, kid! That open window is calling our names!"

"Uh, Jules, a little help here!" George meowed, still swinging.

"Just let go, kid. Consider it a life lesson."

George growled. "Easy for you to say, you're not the one left dangling!"

"Let go, dear!" Helga meowed. "You're not going anywhere doing that."

"Okay, okay, okay!" George loosened his grip, and then timing his swings carefully, he let go and landed on Jules's smooth, preened back. Jule's legs collapsed from underneath him. "Umph! Get off, kid! You're mussing my fur!"

"Consider that a life lesson, Jules."

George jumped off the flattened cat and headed for the table where the white pills in the brown bottle were kept. He sidestepped broken glass, leapt onto the table, and stuffed the small bottle into his equally small mouth. It was a perfect fit.

Jules shook his head, and then stared up at George. "And what lesson would that be?"

George leapt from the table to the tree branch, and then gently pushed the pill bottle between his two front paws. He looked back down at Jules and said, "Be prepared for whatever life drops on you!"

22. Ruffling Feathers

"**Y**our chariot awaits," Nat said, pulling up in an army green, eight-wheeled, all-terrain vehicle.

Meagan's mouth fell open. "How can you drive—"

"Hand controls," Nat said, cutting in. "It's Ray's Argo. He uses it for hunting in the fall and showing potential clients hard to reach properties, like the one we'll be combing for Whiskey. I'm sure he won't mind me borrowing it just this once."

Reid raked his hair. "You mean you didn't ask to use it?"

Nat shrugged, making the navy poncho she wore crease. "It's for a good cause. Now get in. We've gotta move before this storm turns nasty."

The sky let out a horrendous boom. Lightning forked across the belly of a grey cloud.

Meagan pulled her rain coat tighter around her shoulders. "Too late. I think nasty is here."

"Shotgun!" Reid jumped in next to Nat.

Meagan sighed. She didn't care where she sat as long as this vehicle could navigate through the woods to help them find Whiskey before the fisher found her. Meagan climbed into the back seat behind Reid. Nat's folded wheelchair was shoved in behind the driver's seat. Meagan was impressed at Nat's self-sufficiency. She unzipped the stolen rain coat, removed her canvas bag from her shoulder, and tossed it on the floor next to her feet. The sky clapped again and again, and the wind had picked up since Pete Ellis had dropped them off at the arena. Meagan forced a smile. She was glad she'd talked the old man into letting Skoka ride in the cab with him.

"Hold on," Nat said as she engaged the Argo.

Meagan bounced and slid back in her seat. She reached out to grab something to hold onto and ended up with a fistful of Reid's hair. "Oww! Meagan! Do you mind? I'd like to keep my hair as long as possible."

"S-Sorry, Reid. No seatbelts back here," she said, releasing his red locks.

Nat left the big grey building behind them and pulled out into the road, heading for the northwest end of Fairy Falls toward the animal shelter. It was a bouncy ride, but better than walking. They passed a public school on the right with a small playground decked out with a new swing set, merry-go-round, monkey bars, and some picnic tables. As Nat drove around a bend, Meagan's cell phone vibrated and she pulled it out of her scrub pocket. Her eyes widened. *Finally, a text from Cassie!* But as Meagan read the message, it became all too clear why Cassie hadn't bothered contacting Meagan since she moved to Fairy Falls. *Counselor says UR a bad influence. Stop texting me.*

Meagan's stomach fluttered. Reid was right. Cassie had never been there for her. Cassie only cared about herself. *It's time to start seeing with your heart, Meagan,* Whiskey had advised. Meagan's eyes teared-up and she placed a hand on her chest, thinking of Nat and Reid and even Whiskey and the lengths all three would go to for her. She knew now who her true friends were. She smiled, wiped her eyes, and pocketed her phone.

Then Nat jerked, squeezed the hand brake, and skidded to a stop. Meagan's butt went airborne, her head banged against the back of Reid's seat, and her body fell to the floor. *Thud!*

"Oh, crap!" Nat yelled.

"What?" Meagan asked, careful to avoid the rusty fish hooks, dried fries, and the red pocket knife that littered the floor next to her bag.

"Big bad stepsister at twelve o'clock."

"What the hell do you think you're doing driving dad's Argo?" Kayla demanded from the middle of the street. "Are you brain damaged?"

Meagan peered over the seat. Kayla had strategically blocked the road with her van. Behind her stood two teens roughly Kayla's age. One, a guy—cute, hockey sweater, jeans, blonde, and easy on the eyes. The other, a girl—tall, skinny, short dark hair, shorter skirt, and scary looking.

Scary girl nudged Kayla. "See, I told you I saw Nat riding around in your dad's Argo. You owe me, girlfriend."

"I'll handle this," Reid said. "After all, Kayla's got a thing for me."

"I say run the witch over," Meagan muttered, planting her throbbing behind in her seat.

"Get over yourself, Meagan," Reid said, standing. "You don't know her like I do."

Nat passed Reid her phone before he jumped out. "And you don't know her like I do. Enjoy the show."

Nat's phone replayed the video of Kayla's cruel confession. *"Me and Reid Robertson? Not in this lifetime, douche-bag. Not in this lifetime, douche-bag. Not in this lifetime, douche-bag."* Reid played it three times. His shoulders slumped and his chin dropped to his chest. He sat down and handed Nat her phone back.

"I'm sorry, Reid," Meagan said, patting his shoulder. "I know how much you like—"

"You heard Meagan, Nat," Reid cut in. There was a rough edge to his voice now. "Release the flying monkeys and run the wicked witch over!"

Nat revved up the Argo. "Fine by me." Then she let the green machine loose.

"Natalie!" Kayla screamed, running to the front of the van. "Are you freaking crazy?"

The guy and girl dove into the van's open side door, cursing all the way.

"Reid!" Kayla yelled. "Please help me! Stop my psycho stepsister!"

"Not in this lifetime, douche-bag!" Reid shouted, as they passed Kayla where she squatted beside the van.

Nat barreled up the road. Thunder roared, and then lightning forked to her right, hitting a nearby tree. It cracked and fell onto the road, blocking them. She veered left, heading for the Fairy Fall's quarry pit and passed through the open gate. The rocky landscape was nothing but a dead end. No trails led out. Unearthed quartz glittered back, like the devil winking at them. Meagan frantically looked around for another way out. Heaps of sand and crushed gravel were piled by the front, blocking off any other exit but the way they came in. A long blue and white trailer was tucked in a corner with no car in sight. Big, black birds were perched across the top of the trailer's roof—huddled and hunched— as they prepared to wait out the storm. Suddenly, the van pulled up to the front gate and skidded to a gravel-crushing stop. Hockey sweater guy jumped out of the back and closed the gate behind them.

Kayla killed the engine and rolled down the window. "You freaks are so busted! I'm phoning dad, and your mom, to deal with you, Nat! I'm also gonna phone the police to come and arrest your two psychopath friends!"

"Quick, Nat, drive over there," Meagan said, pointing.

"To the trailer? But, why? There's no way out—"

"Just do it. I've got an idea."

"I hope it's a good one," Reid said, wiping sweat from his brow.

Meagan smiled. "Nope. It's a *great* idea! Have you guys ever heard of the movie *Birds*?"

Nat and Reid glanced at each other. "Yes," they said in unison.

"Okay, then get prepared for the remake." Meagan jumped out of the Argo.

"Who's in charge here?" Meagan asked the line of black birds.

They all looked at each other. Some ruffled their feathers. Others started preening. The biggest of the flock took a step forward and inclined his head. "Yo-yo, what's it to ya, human?"

"My name's Meagan and I need your flock's help."

The black bird cawed. "Why should Blackie and his crew help a human?"

"Uh-huh, you tell her, Blackie! You da bird!" the bird at the end of the line squawked.

Meagan clenched her fists. Being a diplomat for human-animal relations was new to her. She sighed. "If you don't help us, the Animal Shelter will lose their observer. We need to find her before it gets dark."

"Don't be gettin' all up in my beak, girl," Blackie cawed, and then inclined his head to the other side. "What's in it for me and my gang?"

Meagan rolled her eyes. *Fantastic. I'm dealing with Snoop Bird and his feathered flock of homies.* Suddenly, an ear-splitting boom sliced through her. The birds flinched and huddled closer together, squawking nervously. Meagan smirked. Her eyes went from the birds to the trailer, and back to the birds. "How would you and your flock like a dry, safe crib to hang in until the storm passes?"

Blackie flapped his wings. "Now you're talking our talk, home-girl!"

"I thought that might tickle your tail-feathers," Meagan said. She pointed. "See that van?"

Blackie looked, and then bobbed his head. "You want we should pimp that ride?"

Meagan smiled. "Oh yeah, pimp it good, and make sure those humans don't follow us. In return, I'll open the door to this trailer for you and your crew. Do we have a deal?"

"Hell, yeah!" Blackie cawed. "Come on, boys, it's time to jam and bam!"

Blackie flew off. The rest of his gang followed, leaving small, black feathers spiraling down toward her. The birds regrouped in the air to form a V-shape with Blackie out front. They flew higher, twisted, and descended, heading for hockey sweater guy guarding the gate. He didn't stand a chance. There were too many of them. Some clung to his sweater, some pecked at his curly blonde hair. Blackie circled around him, cawing again and again, urging his flock on like a demented little league hockey coach.

"Get'em off! Get'em off! Get'em off!" he screamed, flapping his arms, mimicking the birds surrounding him.

Scary girl pulled a beach towel from her bag and tried to flick the birds away with it. Suddenly, they turned on her, pecking and pulling at her short hair and shorter skirt. One of them even managed to fly up it. She let out a murderous scream, wrapped the towel around her body, and did an awkward sprint for the open side door. She jumped in and slammed it shut. Blackie's squad pummeled hockey sweater guy until he was on his knees, crawling for the security of the van. Kayla panicked, closing all the van's windows before any of the birds could fly in.

Hockey sweater guy banged on the side door. "Let me in! Let me in!"

But scary girl wouldn't open the door for him. He swore, crawled over to the driver's door, reached up, opened it, and then grabbed Kayla, pulled her out, and jumped in. "She's your freaking stepsister! You deal with this crap!" He slammed the door and locked it.

Kayla started to do the bird dance. Not the one you do at weddings—the one you do when a battalion of birds swoop down on you over and over again. "Stop it! Stop it! Stop it!" she screamed as if razor blades were slashing her skin. Then, out of desperation, Kayla covered her head, dropped to the ground and rolled underneath the van.

The black birds turned their attention from the humans to the van. Some started pulling at the windshield wipers, while others went for the side decals and tried to peel them off. Few were successful. Caws, squawks, croaks, and cackles flooded the air.

Meagan cupped her hands around her mouth. "Reid! Throw me that pocket knife on the floor in the back!"

It took all of five seconds for Reid to respond. Meagan nabbed the knife in mid-air, opened it, and jimmied the trailer door's lock until she heard a small click. *There. Victory is mine.* She pushed it open for the birds and grimaced. The smell of stinky work boots, stale cigarette butts, and decaying fast food wavered in the air. Her nose wrinkled. Blackie and his fine feathered friends would love it.

"Do this kinda thing much?" Reid asked, coming from behind.

"Only in emergencies," Meagan said, grinning. "I'd say this counts as one."

Reid laughed. "No doubt."

"Come on, guys! It's starting to rain!" Nat yelled, driving up to the trailer. She slipped her poncho's hood over her head. "Hurry!"

"Shotgun!" Meagan shouted, running for the front seat.

Reid groaned and jumped in the back.

As they passed the van, Meagan cringed. White bird poop ran down the van's front and side, smearing the windows and settling on the door handles. Hanging decals flapped in the wind, and she was sure a new pair of windshield wipers would be needed.

"Hey, Blackie!" Meagan shouted. "Thanks! The crib's all yours!"

"No probs, home-girl!" Blackie cawed. "You can chill with us anytime!"

Nat gunned the eight-wheeled Argo toward the gate and busted through it. She maneuvered around the fallen tree, and then headed up the road that led to the Animal Shelter. It was bumpy and rutted, but Meagan didn't care. She just wanted to find Whiskey safe and sound. A sudden vibration went off in her pocket. *Uh-oh. Someone is trying to get a hold of me.* It wasn't Nat and it wasn't Reid.

Meagan checked her phone. "Crap."

"Double crap," Reid said.

Meagan looked over her shoulder to find Reid checking his black cell phone. She frowned. "Your mom?"

"Yeah. Your aunt?"

Meagan nodded. "If Kayla phoned the police and your mom and my aunt are still there, then—"

"Then we might as well change our names and move out of the country," Reid said, cutting in. "I wonder if we can get into a witness protection program?"

"Come on, you guys, I...uh-oh, my phone's vibrating too," Nat said. She reached in her pocket and pulled it out. "Great. My mom knows, too. Kayla sucks!"

"We've already established that," Reid muttered. "So what are we gonna do?"

"Stick to the plan. Find Whiskey first, deal with angry relatives later," Meagan said, just as the sky opened up and poured down on them.

Thunder roared, lightning flashed, and the rain pummeled them. Reid and Meagan flipped on their hoods. Nat pulled up into the Animal Shelter's parking lot, passed Reid's red Neon, then drove down toward the dog runs and parked behind the shed. The sky seemed darker than normal. Meagan checked the time on her phone. It was almost six p.m.

"Reid, unroll the convertible top at the back. It'll give us some shelter," Nat said. "I'll go over the map and see where that blocked road leads."

Reid nodded. He jumped out, pulled the black top forward, and started snapping it into place. Through the pounding rain, Meagan thought she heard an alarm going off. Hugging the side of the soaked Argo, she swung a leg over, then got out. The piercing noise sounded like it was coming from inside the shelter. Meagan peered around the corner. A burgundy van pulled up into the parking lot with its headlights on. It looked a lot like Kayla's van, without the bird poop make-over. *Could the rain have washed it off that quickly?* She clenched her teeth. *How did Kayla and her bird-beaten friends manage to escape from Blackie and his gang so soon? And how did they get around that tree?* Her stomach bunched, feeling like they were being hunted by a relentless bounty hunter.

The van door flew open. Her jaw dropped. It was Matt Moody—the animal control officer, not Kayla. The van's lights remained on, its engine running. Windshield wipers worked hard to fight off the pelting rain, but it seemed a losing battle.

"What's he doing here?"

"Who?" Reid asked, finishing the last snap.

"Moody. He just pulled up in the animal control van."

Reid peeked around the shed. "Hmm. Maybe he found a lost dog in the storm. He usually puts strays in a cage in the garage after hours." He walked toward Nat.

"Is Sadie usually with him?" Meagan asked.

Reid stopped. He turned around. "Not that I'm aware of."

Meagan chewed her bottom lip while she watched Sadie get out of the van. A black trench coat covered her slim body. She ran up the stairs to the main door. Meagan barely heard the beep, beep through the downpour. Then, the alarm was killed. Thunder clapped again, trailed by brilliant flashes of light. Next, Moody got out. His blue uniform was almost soaked through. In his hands were two red gas cans. He carried them up and into the shelter, then closed the door, leaving his van still running.

"I don't get it. Why would Moody and Sadie come here without a stray dog? And why did he just bring gas cans into the shelter?"

"Gas cans?" Reid asked.

"What's going on?" Nat yelled.

"Something's not right, guys," Meagan said. "We've got to check this out."

"But…what about Whiskey?" Nat asked.

Meagan's mind went into overdrive. She had to make a decision, and fast. What would Whiskey say to her if she were here? Meagan struggled with her thoughts until she had a breakthrough—*A good pack leader does what's best for the whole, not the one.* Her heart instantly warmed. The choice was clear. Save the animals, and then save Whiskey.

"We have to make sure the shelter is safe. Whiskey will understand."

"How are we gonna get in? I've got no key," Reid said.

Meagan smiled under her hood. "Yeah, but I still have this." She pulled out the pen knife she used at the trailer.

"Atta, girl," Reid said. "Come on, we'll go in through the dog runs."

"Hey! What about me?" Nat yelled. "You're not leaving me behind!"

"Wouldn't think of it," Meagan said. "Help Nat with her wheelchair, Reid, while I use my expertise in breaking and entering."

"Okay, but don't do anything stupid," Reid warned.

She thumped a hand to her chest. "Who, me?"

Before Reid had a chance to respond, Meagan darted to the back gate of the closest dog run, lifted the latch, and pushed the gate open. *Good. One down.* She ran for the door, then knelt down. Opening the pocket knife, Meagan jiggled the lock until it clicked. *Good. That's two for two.* She pushed the door open and looked behind her. Reid was negotiating Nat's wheelchair around some ruts, and then over the cement pad into the run. He picked up speed until he reached Meagan. Nat was hunched over, trying to cover as much of her wheelchair as possible with her poncho. *Good. We're all home free.*

Reid rolled Nat into the hallway adjacent to the dog runs. "Now what?"

Meagan shrugged. "I guess I'll sneak upstairs—"

"No, I'll sneak upstairs," Reid said, cutting in. "I've worked here longer than you. Stay here and watch Nat."

She flicked his forehead. "No. You watch Nat."

"Oww!" Reid rubbed his head. "No, you watch...Nat? Where ya going?"

Nat rolled to the bottom of the stairs. "If I stay with you two any longer I'll probably end up running you both over."

Meagan closed the pen knife and shoved it in her pocket. "Sorry. It's just...I'm better equipped for the job than you or Reid. At least I can ask the animals what's going on."

"Fine, but once you find out, report back to us," Reid said, wagging his finger.

Click. Creak. Slam. Meagan heard voices coming from the landing at the top of the stairs. "Are you sure no one else will check on the shelter?" Moody said. "The security company monitoring the shelter alerts all of the staff when an alarm goes off."

"Positive!" Sadie snapped. "Izzy and Bertie are too busy looking for their brats and Gail's at the Court Jester probably downing her third beer. I phoned Katrina and told her I'd check it out personally. She trusts me."

Startled, Nat looked up the stairs. She pointed and mouthed, "They're coming."

Reid gave Meagan and Nat the 'come along' sign with his finger, and then opened the door to the storeroom underneath the stairs. Meagan tip-toed and Nat rolled over. Footsteps echoed down the stairs. Reid pulled the door until it was only slightly open, just as Sadie and Matt Moody hit the bottom. Meagan let out the breath she was holding onto, and then sat on the floor, crossed her legs, and peered through the tiny crack in the door. Reid stood above her and stared out, too.

"Here," Nat whispered. She passed Meagan her cell phone. "Make them overnight *YouTube* stars."

Meagan reached for her phone and positioned it through the opening. She heard Moody clear his throat and she started recording.

Matt laughed. "Little does Smith know, you're the last one she should trust, baby-buns." He grabbed Sadie, tweaked her behind, and planted a hard, sloppy kiss on her open lips.

Both Meagan and Reid glanced at each other and grimaced.

Sadie pulled away and smacked his chest. "Save it for later, sweet-cheeks. We've got work to do."

"Good thing that tree branch went through the window in the cat isolation room. Now we can blame the storm for the fire we're going to set. Our plan's all coming together now, baby."

Meagan's eyes bugged. Reid covered his mouth. However, Nat was a little more vocal. "Fire?!"

Moody jerked. "Who in the hell?"

"The storage room under the stairs!" Sadie yelled.

Reid slammed the door. He fumbled for the doorknob. Unfortunately, there was no lock. Meagan turned Nat's phone around, stopped recording, and punched in 911. Nothing happened. There were no bars displayed on the screen. It was a dead zone. And now, they were dead meat.

23. The Brown Beast

"Wait up, kid!" Jules huffed. "It's not a race!"

George ignored Jules. He ignored the drowning sky. He ignored the booms. He ignored the scary flashes. Jules was wrong. This was a race. A race to get Whiskey her white pills. They had managed to make it deep into the forest before the sky poured water down on them. Now, George's fur was soaked through and all Jules could do was complain how unmanageable his fur would be. Suddenly, another boom sent one of those scary flashes tearing through the sky. It hit a huge tree ahead of them. George's whiskers tingled, feeling the ground come alive.

Crack! Snap! The old, grey leafless tree broke apart in the middle. Half crashed down into the forest while the rest of the tree fell across the trodden path, splintering in several places. George and Jules braked to avoid the fallen tree. They skidded off the path, tumbled down an incline, and landed in a deep pool of fresh rainwater at the bottom. *Splash!*

"Ugh! Help, kid, I can't swim!" Jules meowed, splashing wildly in the water.

George rolled his eyes. Careful not to get Whiskey's pills wet, he tilted his head back, and then stood up. He walked out of the water and headed toward the nearest boulder. Jules stopped sloshing about. His ears flattened. "Thanks for the heads-up, kid."

George delicately placed the brown bottle on the flattest part of the rock. "Sometimes, you're more work than a newborn kitten, Jules. If I'd listened to you about 'every cat for himself', then you'd still be in that stinky cage at the shelter, whining and complaining like a sissy cat!"

Jules crawled out of the pool. His white fur was flat and soggy and his usually preened whiskers drooped down the sides of his face. He shook his entire body, sprinkling George in the process. Then Jules stared at the young cat, his blue eyes devouring George like darkness swallowing the light. His wet tail flicked back and forth until it was almost fluffed out.

"How dare you judge me!" he hissed. "You know nothing of being a true cat! It's survival of the fittest out here and you wouldn't stand a chance if I left—"

A brown animal with ratty fur and a black tail jumped Jules from behind. Five claws dug into his back. Jules let out a pained yowl. The creature sunk its fangs into the back of Jules's neck while clawing at his back. Streams of thin, red lines appeared on Jules's white fur as he frantically raced around, trying to knock off his attacker.

"Food, food, food!" George heard the brown animal screech.

"Get off! Get off! Get off!" Jules roared in pain.

George crouched. His ears flattened and moved back.

"Oww! Do something, George, anything!" Jules screamed.

Something? Anything? Truth be told, George had never seen an animal like this before in his life. It was hideous, vicious, and smelled like it had rolled around in a used litter box. His yellow eyes widened. *This must be the brown beast Whiskey was trying to warn the lost cats about! A monster with claws and fangs that tears, rips, kills, and eats cats!* He shuddered. What could a little white cat with grey markings on his head and tail do against such a beast?

Panicking, George retreated slowly up the hill toward the path, looking to the left, then to the right, for anything he could use to help save Jules. Then George winced. *Oh, no, I've just been bitten by one of those yellow and black stinging bugs.* He gritted his teeth and twisted around, hoping there wasn't a nest of stinging bugs behind him. There wasn't. Instead, a sharp, pointed stick lodged in the ground between two rocks had stabbed into him. His cat brain hummed, his ears moved forward and without a second thought, George lunged for the stick.

Grasping it between his teeth, he waited for his chance, and then charged the brown beast with the sharp end out. The beast never saw it coming because George pierced it in the eye. It screeched and immediately released Jules. Screaming, hissing, and striking the air, the brown beast howled a terrible howl as it tried to pry the stick from its bloodied eye.

"Come on, Jules, you're free!"

Disoriented and shaking, Jules searched around for George. Blood stained his wet, white fur, and he appeared to have trouble breathing. "Jules! Over here!" George meowed.

Jules wasn't responding. George would have to move fast before the brown beast pulled the stick out of his eye and went for Jules again. George rushed to the white cat's side. Jules lashed out, hissing and spitting, "No, get away, get away!"

"Jules, it's me, George!"

Startled, Jules withdrew his claws. "S-Sorry, kid. Don't know what came over me."

"It's the brown beast," George whispered so the monster wouldn't know their whereabouts. "Now, quick, run up the hill. You go first. I have to get Whiskey's pills."

Growling and snarling, the brown beast continued to flail and thrash across the ground in an attempt to pull the stick from its eye with its back claws. Finally, it succeeded. Out popped the stick.

It bellowed, matching the ferocious, loud booms in the sky, then it hissed and struck the ground. "You'll regret that!"

"Watch out, Jules!" George wrapped his paws around Jules neck and pulled him backward as the brown beast charged the two cats.

They somersaulted over each other at least three times. The brown beast tripped on a protruding root, sailed over the rolling cats and toward the flat boulder where Whiskey's pills sat. It careened through the air, its black tail whipping back and forth. The tail struck the brown bottle and knocking its lid off, sending it and its contents into the shallow pool. The open bottle gurgled and then sank. The brown beast landed on top of the boulder, still snapping its jaws and flailing its claws.

George's jaw dropped. "Nooo!"

"Come on, George, before the brown beast comes to his senses!" Jules sunk his teeth into the scruff of George's neck, pulled him onto the path, and dragged him until they reached a dead tree with a hollowed out trunk.

Jules let go of George and nudged him in. Another boom sounded and another flash streaked across the tops of the trees. Both cats shrunk in fear of the great power in the sky—bowing to the drowning water, the scary rumbles, and the crooked light. George trembled. He'd lost the pills that would help Whiskey. Pills that would save her life and set her free. George hung his head. He'd failed her. He'd failed the lost cats. He'd failed himself.

Both cats remained silent, taking in what had happened, and what could have happened. Jules's breathing slowly eased up, sounding more like a cat should—calm, relaxed, content. "You're mighty brave for a little cat," Jules meowed softly, head-butting George.

George shrugged. He looked up at Jules. The white cat's wounds were deep. The gouges glistened at George like sinister smiles. Fang marks circled the top of his neck and ended below his ears. Claw marks ran across Jules's back, making his fur appear the colour of a kitten's tongue. Yet, despite everything, Jules was grinning at George. The biggest cat grin he had ever seen to date.

George moved one ear forward. "Are...are you okay, Jules?"

"Never better, kid. Well, except for the brown beast's bites and scratches."

"Yeah. I guess that wasn't part of your plan, was it?"

Jules stopped grinning. "What plan?"

George sighed. The water from the sky was slowing down now, the rumbles getting farther apart. "On the way to the shelter, you said you had a plan."

"Oh, *that* plan. That...that plan's old, kid. Things change. I got me a new plan now."

George scrunched his cat face. "What's your new plan?"

Jules started grooming his dirty, wet paws. "We go back."

George's ears pricked up. "Back to the shelter to get more white pills?"

Jules stopped licking his paws. "No. Back to the lost cats. We have to warn them about the brown beast. We have to tell them they're all in danger. We have to tell Brutus that Whiskey is telling the truth. He'll let her go—forget about her sickness—when he sees me, sees the gashes on my back, the fang marks on my neck. Then I'll help you take her back to the shelter."

George's ears flattened. "But...what if Brutus doesn't let her go? Then what?"

Jules was silent for the moment. The sky gasped out a less-than-scary rumble, followed by a flicker of light. He smiled and looked into George's desperate yellow eyes. "Then, my brave cat friend, we challenge him."

George's ears moved back. "When you say 'we', don't you mean—"

"I mean you."

"Me!"

"You're the one who rescued me. You're the hero. I'm living proof that you're the lost cats' new champion! Don't you get it, kid?"

"No. No, I don't. I'm not fighting Brutus. I'd never stand a chance."

"Trust me, George, when he sees what that brown beast has done to me, and I tell him you fought it in paw-to-paw combat, all you'll see is his fat behind waddling away from you."

"I don't know, Jules, I—"

"Look, it's a win-win situation, kid," Jules cut in. "Nobody will challenge you. You'll have the lost cats' respect, and free Whiskey at the same time."

George sighed. Him, a hero? Respected? Revered? The little white cat with grey markings on his ears and tail that no cat at the shelter had paid particular attention to? It was hard to imagine.

Jules nudged George. "So what d'ya think, kid? Are you up for the challenge?"

George licked his pink nose. It was a plan. A new and improved plan. At least he could help Whiskey this way, seeing as her white pills were gone. The sky was sprinkling now. He glanced at Jules with renewed hope and said, "Okay, Jules, but promise me if something goes wrong, if something happens to me, you'll take care of Whiskey."

"That's a promise, kid. I got your back." Then Jules sprang out of the hollow tree and headed for the bushes across the path.

George grinned. "Better you got my back than that mean brown beast."

George bolted after Jules and they disappeared into the lush greenery of the forest.

As the two cats broke new ground, a wet, ratty brown animal staggered about the forest floor. It moaned and whined, sniffing, trying to catch a scent, any scent that would lead it to some food. Hunger overrode its pain. It needed meat, and soon. Smelling fresh blood on an adjacent tree trunk, it stopped to sniff the blood deeply, inhaling its smell, almost tasting flesh. There. It had its scent, and soon would be sooner.

Whiskey shivered. How much longer would she have to wait in this damp, moldy cage? George and Jules should have been back by now. What was keeping them? The storm? A stray dog? Or maybe George was too late and couldn't get to Meagan before the shelter closed? She sneezed and then pawed her sore nose. Her breathing had calmed, but only because she wasn't moving around. At least it gave her a reprieve, a break from what was to come.

The pounding water from the sky—what humans call rain—had subsided, if only a little. Now a fine mist covered the ground and fogged the air. Half of the pink blanket that lined the crate was soaked, so she huddled at the back where it was drier and cleaner, curling her head into the crook of a paw. Throughout the storm, Whiskey heard snippets of cat talk coming from behind her, inside the car—the lost cats' metal cave. Some were terrified of the booms and flashes and caterwauled constantly, making it hard for her old eyes to close.

Suddenly, Whiskey heard crunching through the wet leaves. She opened one eye. A beady-eyed mouse stopped by her cage to peer inside. Her stomach rumbled. She could go for a nice, juicy mouse-morsel. She licked her lips. Her tail flicked. The mouse poked its head through the bars. It sniffed, twitching its tiny whiskers like crawly bugs moving their many legs. Whiskey remained still, inanimate, just one eye on the prize. It squeaked once and then tried to squeeze the rest of its body into the cage.

"Got'cha!" Shadow hissed, clamping her jaws down on its tail. The mouse squealed.

Whiskey watched, mouth agape, as Shadow tugged on its tail until the mouse popped out of the cage. She juggled it between her paws, poking it, prodding it, jabbing it. Then Shadow tossed the mouse in the air and batted it against Whiskey's cage. It slammed head-first into the door. It squeaked and squealed, pleading for mercy in its own rodent language.

"Just eat the poor thing!" Whiskey snarled. At least this short rest had given her back her voice.

Shadow caterwauled. "I see you're feeling better. Wanna come out and play?"

Whiskey's ears flattened. "Over my dead body."

"Now we're talking," Shadow mewed, as she scooped up the half-dead mouse with a paw and shoved the whole mouse into her open jaws.

"Mmm, Whiskey, this is to die for!" Shadow belched.

Whiskey's tail flicked. "Be careful what you say, Shadow. It just might happen."

Rustling leaves and snapping branches made Shadow arch her back and fluff her tail. Whiskey could feel something heading toward them, feel it through the ground. She closed her eyes and hoped it was George.

"Jules is back!" Oscar announced. "And George is with him."

Whiskey opened her eyes as she heard the big hatch on the back of the car groan open. Something heavy—most likely Brutus—hit the ground. She could tell that other cats followed him as she could feel every vibration through her cage. The fine rain had almost ceased, yet the dampness remained—the part that

Whiskey hated the most about water from the sky. Ignoring her aching bones, Whiskey crawled closer to the barred door and craned her neck to see if she could spot George. She pushed her head up against the door and instantly felt the sting of a claw scratch at one of her eyes. She balked, then hissed, retreating to the back of the cage.

"Stay back, old calico!" Shadow hissed. "I don't see any white pills with them, so you're still a threat to all of us."

Whiskey lay back down. Now her eye throbbed. She gently placed her paw over it and turned her head in the direction George and Jules had come from. She cocked her ears. At least she could still hear what was going on.

"Jules!" Brutus roared. "What happened to you?"

"Did a dog attack you?" Oscar asked. "Was it big? Was it mean?"

Whiskey's uninjured eye widened. *What happened?*

"It was the brown beast!" Jules meowed so that all of the lost cats could hear him. "It did this to me! It almost killed me!"

"Why isn't George hurt?" Brutus asked suspiciously.

Whiskey held her breath and waited for his answer. Her heart pounded. Why wasn't George hurt? How could that be? She knew what that horrible creature was capable of. She knew unless there was a human present to beat it off, there would be no escape for a cat. The beast was relentless, persisted until there were no meows left in a cat, no light in its eyes. She shivered. This was a real conundrum indeed.

"George attacked the brown beast!" Jules meowed with pride. "He saved me!"

"Did he, now?" Brutus asked. "And how did George do this to a beast that rips, tears, kills, and eats us? A beast that Tiger—our best fighter—had no chance against."

Whiskey didn't like his tone. He sounded doubtful.

"George poked the brown beast's eye with a sharp stick! Didn't you, kid?"

"That's right, I hurt it bad! But I..." George paused, as if reliving the moment. "...I lost Whiskey's white pills while saving Jules."

Whiskey detected a maturity in George's voice she'd never heard before.

"My, isn't that unfortunate," Brutus said. Whiskey heard him sigh. "Well, I guess there's no choice but to—"

"Free Whiskey!" Jules growled. "That's an order, Brutus, not a request."

Whiskey's jaw dropped. Had the brown beast pierced Jules's cat brain? He was no match for Brutus in a fight. None of the cats were. Her nose twitched. *What is that slick, white tom up to?*

"Are you challenging me, Jules?" Brutus snarled. Whiskey heard him strike the ground.

There was a moment of silence, followed by a distant rumble in the sky.

"No. I am."

Whiskey blinked. That sounded like...but, no, it couldn't be. Could it?

"George?" Brutus asked as if his hearing was off. "Are *you* challenging *me*?"

"Yes I am," George meowed loudly.

Suddenly, caterwauling the likes Whiskey had never heard before filled her cage and ears. She sagged. No cat was taking George seriously. Even she doubted him. George was slender, gentle, not a fighter. He would never be a smart fighter like Boscoe, a heavy-weight scrapper like Poppy, or even a devious one like Shadow. He didn't have the experience or the skills to take on Brutus, who was one of the biggest and meanest cats she had ever known. Whiskey sneezed, making her eye throb all the more.

"Silence!" Brutus roared over the catty laughter. "Let George make it official."

"Oh, he makes it official, all right," Jules cut in. "If he can fight off the vicious brown beast with just a little stick, think of what he could do to you with his claws and teeth, fat-cat!"

Whiskey heard a lot of ohhs and ahhs, a few snickers, and some gasps.

"I wasn't talking to you, traitor!" Brutus roared.

Whiskey envisioned Jules shrinking to the size of a little white mouse.

"You shouldn't have to deal with this lowly shelter cat, Brutus," Shadow purred.

Startled, Whiskey looked out the cage door. Shadow wasn't there.

"I don't recall you being challenged, Shadow," Brutus growled.

Shadow meowed loudly. Whiskey could smell her manipulating scent from her cage. She reeked of pure malice. "Let me prove my loyalty to you, Brutus. Let me take on your challenger. Let me fight George for you. A fight to the death."

"Nooo!" Whiskey caterwauled, sounding more like a croaking frog. She coughed.

Shadow let out a loud, seductive yowl. "If I win, then I want to be the queen of the lost cats, and my first order will be to put that old calico out of her agony forever."

"And if you lose?" Brutus asked.

There was a short pause as Whiskey waited for that hell-cat's reply. No more rumbles came from the sky, no more flashes lit up the dark spots. It was scary quiet and Whiskey silently wished she could trade places with George.

Finally, Shadow hissed profoundly and said, "I won't."

24. Dark Confessions

"We're doomed."

Meagan rolled her eyes. "Stop talking like that, Reid."

Both Meagan and Reid jumped at the sudden, successive knocks. "Meagan? Reid? I know it's you two hiding in there," Sadie said from the other side of the door. "Haven't you both been banished from the shelter?"

"It's not just them!" Nat shouted.

"Natalie!" Meagan and Reid yelled in unison.

Sadie coughed. "Natalie? The girl in the wheelchair?"

"The one and only," Nat replied in a snotty tone.

"You kids are in a heap of trouble," Sadie said and Meagan envisioned her wagging a spindly finger at them.

"And you're in a heaper heap of trouble!" Reid yelled, reaching over Meagan's shoulder to switch on the light. She blinked.

"A heaper heap?" Nat whispered, wincing at the sudden brightness.

"Am I now?" Sadie asked. Her tone had changed from cloudy to stormy. "So, how much did you kids hear, then?"

Meagan scraped her teeth across her bottom lip. This would take some diplomacy. And a little lying. "Only that you and Moody are here to check on the shelter. We were out searching for Whiskey in the backwoods when we heard the alarm going and decided to check it out."

"So why hide?" Sadie asked. Suspicion dripped from her tongue.

Meagan's chest tightened. This was starting to feel like an interrogation. She cleared her throat, and said, "We thought you were either my aunt or Reid's mom. They're really pissed with us right now. We figured we'd get into more trouble if we were found, so we ducked in here."

Sadie coughed nervously. "I see. Then why would you think *I* would be in trouble?"

Think. Think. Think. Why? Why? Why? Meagan's eyes widened. "'Cause…we caught you and Moody making out. Don't deny it. Reid and I saw you."

"Yeah, we captured it all on Nat's phone too," Reid added. "You'll be viral throughout cyberspace in no time!"

Meagan elbowed Reid. "Not helping!"

"Do you know what I think, Meagan?" Sadie asked. Meagan heard something heavy scraping across the floor.

"Uh, what?" she asked.

"I think that somehow, someway, you actually can talk to animals. I've been watching you, listening in. I've noticed that the cats and dogs seem very responsive to you."

Meagan shrugged. "So?"

"So here's the rub, missy. You've either got a better imagination than a five-year old, or you know more about what's going on at the shelter than anyone else. The question is what do you know and what have the animals told you?"

"That's two questions," Reid pointed out.

The door knob wiggled as if an object was being jammed underneath it. Reid glanced at Meagan and then tried to open the door, but he couldn't. So Reid threw his body into it. It didn't budge. The door was braced. They were locked in.

"I'll ask you again," Sadie warned, "how much do you know?"

Meagan balled her fists, and then stretched her fingers. "I know Katrina Smith is poisoning the animals with antifreeze—I saw the jug in her trunk. I know the shelter is running out of money. I also know Ms. Manager's strapped for cash. You do the math. Smith is trying to destroy this shelter for some reason. What I want to know is why you're helping her."

"True, Smith is in lots of doggy-do with the bank," Sadie said, laughing. "Her little gambling addiction doesn't help much. That's what made it so easy to set her up. You see, it's not Smith trying to destroy the shelter, it's me. It was me who wrote those bogus receipts then blamed whoever I wanted, knowing all fingers would be pointing back at the manager. It was me who poisoned the animals, and then planted a jug of antifreeze in Smith's car. I needed a patsy to take the fall. She was a perfect fit."

Reid hit the door. "So why destroy the shelter? What's in it for you, Holmes?"

"I've got my reasons."

"Moody's land!" Nat snapped her fingers. "It all makes sense now! They're planning on burning the shelter to the ground so they can buy this property cheap, knowing that with lack of funds, the shelter can't afford to rebuild here. Then Moody's waterfront land backing onto the shelter's property will finally have road access, making it worth millions."

"Kudos to the girl in the wheelchair," Sadie said, snickering.

Meagan's face burned. She balled her fists again. "Y-You're going to kill innocent animals just so you and Moody can buy this stupid piece of land?"

"Correction, so we can get lots and lots of money," Sadie replied haughtily. "Buying this land is just a stepping stone. Why do you think I got rid of Whiskey? She was your confidant, your lifeline to this place. You didn't even suspect me, did you? All I had to do was plant a used scratch and win ticket at the scene. Again, Smith's addiction proved to be my diversion, my little magic trick, if you will."

Meagan's eyes bugged. "You took Whiskey?" She pounded the door several times, ignoring the pain running down her arm. "Where is she, you demented witch?"

Sadie let out a throaty chuckle. "Oh, she's hanging around in the forest, probably drowned, eaten, or dead by now. I took off her collar so you'd never be able to hear her."

Meagan threw her body at the door again and again. Reid wrapped his arms around her waist and pulled her away from the door. "Stop, Meagan, you're only hurting yourself," he whispered.

"Upstairs is ready, baby-buns. I'll sprinkle some gas around in a few empty kennels and we'll be good to go," Moody said, heavy footsteps announcing his arrival. He let out a sinister chuckle. "Say buh-bye to your little furry friends, kiddies."

"Nooo!" Meagan screamed. "You can't kill them! They're innocent!"

Sadie snorted. "Innocent? Have you ever been lunged at by a vicious cat? Bitten by an unpredictable dog? Gotten pissed, puked, or pooped on by flea-bitten strays? The way I see it, I'm doing these abandoned animals a favour. I'm putting them out of their misery. Face it, Meagan, most of these mangy fur-balls won't get adopted. No one wants them. They're a burden to the shelter, they're a burden on the community. I say good riddance to all of them!"

"What about us?" Reid asked, still holding onto Meagan. "We're kids, not burdens!"

Moody chuckled again. "You are to us, punk!"

Sadie tried to laugh, but ended up coughing instead. She recouped her voice, and said, "I wouldn't worry about being roasted alive. The smoke will get you long before the flames!"

"Come on, baby, let's finish what we started," Moody muttered, as he walked Sadie away from the storage room, their footsteps leading toward the kennels. The door creaked opened, then slammed.

Meagan's whole body trembled. Reid still held her. He was shaking too. She glanced over at Nat. Her eyes were closed, her hands were palms up on her lap, and she was still. Tears streamed down Nat's cheeks, but she seemed to ignore them, breathing deeply, consciously, in and out, in and out. Nat was doing that feel good energy thing she does, only this time it was for them and not for the cats. Unfortunately, Meagan couldn't feel a thing.

Meagan set her teeth, grinding her back molars till they ached. Her throat felt raw, hot, as if acid had erupted from her stomach and burned its way up. Meagan's eyes welled as she continued to stare at Nat, trying as hard as she could to suck in some of that positive power in order to gain an unfathomable high. It wasn't working, though. Nothing was working. She broke out of Reid's grasp, turned, and pushed him away. He lost balance and fell back, his head kissing the cement floor. *Smack!*

"Stop it, stop it, stop it!" Meagan screamed, shucking her stolen raincoat and throwing it aside. "Don't you two get it? We're toast! Burnt toast! Whiskey's probably dead! All the shelter animals are about to be barbequed, and by the sounds of it, we're gonna become beef jerky!"

A loud squeak from the top of the nearest shelf startled Meagan. She looked up. A brown rat with beady black eyes peered down at her. Its whiskers twitched incessantly. "Ock! Would ye humans be so kind as to keep it down a wee bit? It's me nap time, doncha know!"

Meagan dropped her jaw. "I-I'm sorry."

"You'd better be!" Reid snapped, cradling the back of his head as he stood. He wormed out of his rain coat and tossed it to the floor. "I was only trying to—"

"Not you," Meagan cut in. She pointed toward the shelf. "The rat."

"Huh? What rat?"

Nat opened her eyes. She wiped her cheeks, then looked up. "That rat, Reid. See? Next to the box of dog biscuits."

Reid shook his head, then blinked. "Oh, so you're the bugger who's been chewing the bottom of the food boxes."

Meagan took a deep breath and stretched her fingers. *Time to make that rat earn its keep around the shelter.* "Umm, excuse me, rat, but do you think you could help us get out of here?"

"Ock, not now, human, me nap comes first. And it's Miss Minerva to ye."

Meagan could have sworn the rat sounded like an old Scottish woman berating her.

"Look, Miss Minerva, in a few minutes, two human douche-bags are gonna set fire to the shelter. You'll lose your home and most likely your life if you don't help us," Meagan explained as quickly as she could.

"Miss Minerva? The rat's got a name?" Reid asked, frowning.

Miss Minerva's nose twitched. "What's that human saying about me?"

"He wants to know why you have a name," Meagan answered.

"Ock, I was named by me human companion. He could'na keep me, so he put me in a box and left me on the steps of this place. I chewed me way out and found me way inside here where there's warmth and food. It's been me home ever since."

Meagan nodded and turned to Reid. "Said she was dumped on the steps, like most of the animals, chewed out of her box, and now this is her home. Got it?"

"Ask Miss Minerva if there's another way out of here," Nat asked, pulling off her rain poncho. She threw it next to Reid's discarded jacket.

Reid scoffed. "Don't you think I'd know that, Nat?"

Nat rolled her eyes. "Just ask, Meagan."

"Miss Minerva, do you know another way out of here, other than this door?"

The rat started preening her whiskers. Beady eyes darted back and forth as if in deep thought. Then she squeaked, "Ock, there's the big hole in the far wall behind the end shelf. It might be big enough for one of ye to go through."

"A hole in the wall?" Meagan muttered. "Behind the end shelf?"

Reid shot by Meagan and wiggled by Nat to get to the back of the storage room. It was shaped like an 'L', veering to the left. Meagan heard some grunting, groaning, and scraping.

"A little help?" Reid pleaded.

Meagan dashed by Nat, followed the small hallway until it ended where Reid was trying to push a steel shelf away from the wall. Thankfully it wasn't loaded down with boxes. She put her shoulder into it and pushed with Reid. It moved about two feet. Reid crouched down and pulled a sheet of half-chewed plywood away from the wall, revealing a huge hole in the cement blocks. The hole was concealed by an upright plastic pallet usually used for a dog's bed. Reid gently pushed the pallet aside and winced.

He plugged his nose. Meagan stepped back. All she could smell was gas fumes.

"It's an empty kennel. The one closest to the door," Reid said, sounding muffled. "If one of us can squeeze through it and then go around and remove whatever's bracing the storage room door, then maybe we can still save the shelter."

Meagan covered her nose and mouth. "Okay. Can you get through?"

Reid studied the opening, and shook his head. "Too small. You?"

Meagan stared at the hole. It looked to be about fifteen inches wide by a little over a foot. She peered at her chest. If parts of her weren't so well-endowed then she might have been able to pull it off.

"I can squeeze through that."

Both Reid and Meagan jumped and looked behind them. Nat had managed to maneuver her wheelchair around the corner. Her fists were balled, not opened, as if she was ready for the fight of her life.

"But how—" Meagan started to say.

"I can crawl," Nat interrupted. "I did it when I was a baby and it got me to where I wanted to be, so my mom tells me."

"But Nat, how ya gonna open the kennel door without alerting Moody?" Meagan asked. "You'd have to pull yourself up, squeeze your hand through, and unlatch it. Then you're gonna have to go through another door to get to the storeroom."

"Yeah, and don't forget about the gas all over the floor," Reid added.

Nat's face turned somber. "I'll manage."

"Ock! Have faith, humans," Miss Minerva said, as she scurried up Nat's wheelchair. "When something is taken away from us, we don't give in, we adapt. We find ways to make things work for us. If we don't, we stagnate or perish. It's as simple as that, doncha know."

Meagan smiled. She reached out and stroked the rat, who was sitting on the wheelchair's armrest. "Can you help Nat adapt?"

Miss Minerva squeaked loudly, "Ock! Of course I can. Besides, I'm getting too old to look for another home. This is a bonny place to live."

Meagan nodded. "Okay, Nat, you're up. Miss Minerva's gonna help you."

"How?" Nat asked, lifting her feet to the floor. Reid went over to help.

"Just have faith," Meagan replied, patting Nat's knee. "She'll know what to do."

Nat smiled, and then held up her hand. "Wait, Reid, I'm gonna need some extra help from above." She reached into the pouch sewn under her wheelchair's arm, grabbed the photo of her father, and tucked it into her back pocket. "Okay, let's do this."

Guiding Nat to the hole, Reid gently lowered her to the ground. She wiggled through the wall, moving like a winged serpent. Miss Minerva squeaked, and then followed Nat into the empty kennel. She leapt on her back and scampered across to sit on Nat's shoulder. Meagan stuck her head through the gap. She covered her mouth. The gas fumes were overwhelming. Using her elbows to power her, Nat crawled over to the cage door, getting close enough for Miss Minerva to jump and climb up the door. She reached the latch, pulled on it, and Nat pushed it open. Meagan smiled. That was one door. The next would be more difficult.

Craning her head as far as it would go, Meagan watched Nat push herself onward to the door leading to the runs. She reached up, straining, huffing and puffing, to grab onto the door knob. Miss Minerva crawled up Nat's arm, balancing as best she could. There was a leash tied to the knob that Bertie often used to hold the door open when she was rotating the dogs. Using her teeth, Miss Minerva latched onto the leash and raced down Nat's arm. *Click.* Nat opened the door, then grasped the leash before it closed on her. She groaned, pulling as if she were the anchor in a tug-o-war contest. The door opened wide enough for Nat to wiggle her body through. Good. Second door done. One more to go.

Meagan pushed away from the hole and looked up at Reid. "She's through the main dog floor and heading toward us."

Reid nodded and helped Meagan up. "Great. I'll get Nat's wheelchair ready."

Meagan raced around the corner and skidded at the door. She pressed an ear against it. Hearing huffing and puffing, she knew Nat was near Then, the doorknob jiggled as Nat grunted.

"What is it, Nat?" Meagan asked.

"It's a chair. It's shoved in there good." Nat's breathing got heavier. Then Meagan heard a scrape, a thud, and a clatter. "Oww! Crap! That'll leave a mark!" Nat groaned. "Okay, you guys can come out."

Meagan took a deep breath, turned the knob and pushed the door open. She looked down. Nat wasn't there. She looked from side to side. Nope. "Nat?"

"Over here, by the hose."

Meagan looked up. Nat was spraying herself down. Miss Minerva was hunched by her feet, nibbling on a broken dog biscuit. A large bump was forming on Nat's forehead. Bloodied elbows attested to her journey. She glanced over at Meagan, and grinned. "My clothes stink, my elbows sting, and that damn chair hit my head. Hey, I earned this."

Meagan giggled. "You did good, BFF!"

Nat slid her father's photo out from her pocket, and winked. "We did good."

"Coming through, move aside," Reid said, rolling the wheelchair past Meagan.

While Reid helped Nat into her chair, Meagan pulled out her phone. She walked around till she saw enough bars. "We've got to alert the fire station."

"And the police. I'll do it," Nat said. "You two go stop Tweedle-douche and Twiddle-dumbass."

Meagan nodded, put away her phone, picked up Miss Minerva and placed her on Nat's knee. "Thank you for helping us. You're a credit to your race."

"Yeah, the rat race," Nat added, as she scratched the rodent's back.

"Ock, ye are most welcome, but I must insist, I do need me nap." Miss Minerva yawned, squeezed herself into the side of the chair next to Nat's leg, and closed her beady eyes. "Helping humans is but a tiring business, doncha know."

Reid nudged Meagan. "Come on, we're running out of time."

"Go. I'm calling now," Nat said, as she fiddled with her phone.

Meagan and Reid stole down the hall and back through the main dog floor. The smell of gas now permeated the air. "We need to open some windows," Meagan said, waving her hand in front of her nose.

Suddenly, they heard someone whistling. Moody was headed their way.

"Quick, hide in there," Reid whispered, pointing to an adjacent kennel. "If I can get in the next room, I'll let the dogs out."

Reid ran down the hall, past the mop and bucket, and ducked behind the furnace. Meagan opened the kennel, jumped in, dodged a couple of tennis balls, and hid behind a pallet leaning against the wall. The door flew open and Moody strutted in. Dogs were barking wildly behind him. Meagan made out a few pieces of dog talk—most were complaining about the gas fumes. She balled her fists and then stretched out her fingers. *I've only got one shot at this.* She waited, waited, waited until she saw the tops of Moody's grungy boots, then threw one of the balls across the room. It bounced off another kennel and rolled into the middle of the hall.

Moody stepped on the ball and it popped. "What the—?"

"Woof, woof," Meagan barked in a high-pitched voice.

Meagan heard Moody backtracking, opening, and searching each kennel. Soon he'd be up to hers. Meagan's fingers curled around the pallet. She readied herself. As soon as her kennel door swung open, she poked her head up over the pallet. "Miss me, sweet-cheeks?"

Moody stepped into the kennel. "How did you—"

Meagan didn't let him finish his sentence. She lifted the pallet and ran toward him full steam ahead. The impact sent him flying backward into the hallway, his head hitting the opposite cage. Moody grasped the back of his head, rolled to the floor, and assumed the fetal position.

The sound of howling filled the air. The first dog out was Nobel, who bounded toward Moody, his tongue hanging out and his hackles raised like he was on a mission. Next was Louis, followed by Boggart. The remaining dogs—a lab mix, a hound, and what looked like a poodle with a bad haircut, brought up the rear.

"Oh, no, no, no," Moody yelled, backpedaling his legs.

"Sick him, boys!" Meagan commanded.

"Hey, I'm a female," the poodle barked.

Meagan arched a brow. "Er, sorry. My bad."

Nobel stood on Moody's chest and growled into his face. Louis decided to mark his territory by peeing all over the animal control officer's head. Boggart pulled on one of his boots, while the other dogs each shared a pant leg, tearing at it, ripping it. Moody screamed and flailed his free left arm. That motion didn't last long as the poodle chomped on it.

"Get off, get off, get freaking off me...ummmm!"

Reid stuffed the dirty mop head into Moody's mouth. "There's some duct tape on the table by the door. Fetch it, Meagan."

She scowled at Reid. "Bite me."

The dogs all looked up at her in unison. She puckered her lips. "Er, never mind."

Suddenly, the back door by the runs burst open. Sadie stood behind Nat's wheelchair. She had one hand on the chair's handle while her other hand held something to Nat's neck. Meagan squinted. It looked like a gun, but it was thicker, bulkier, and all black.

"Is that a BB gun?" Reid asked, inclining his head.

Sadie shook her head. "No. It's a Taser. If you want to see how well wheelchair girl tolerates pain, then I dare one of you to step forward."

"Mmm, mmm," Moody mumbled.

"Get that damn mop out of his mouth!" Sadie commanded, pushing the Taser harder into Nat's neck. Nat clenched her teeth, wincing.

"Back off, Reid, she's serious," Meagan said, squeezing his shoulder.

Reid nodded and pulled the mop out. He tossed it to the side and crossed his arms over his chest. His face hardened.

"Very good. Now get those mutts off of him and put them in the kennels," Sadie said with a pinched face. "Do it, now!"

Nobel looked up at Meagan, his brows bobbing up and down. "What's wrong with the Quick One? Why do I feel so much anger from her?"

"She's sick, Nobel. Sick in the head. She and Moody were gonna torch this place. Kill every animal in it, even me, Reid, and Nat. All so they could buy this stupid piece of land."

Nobel's blue eyes widened. He let out a bone splitting howl.

"Quick One bad!" Louis barked and spun around. "Me pee on her too, Meagan?"

Boggart growled. "What Meagan want Boggart to do? Protect?"

Meagan put her hand out. "No, wait, boys, uh... and girl. Be patient. I can hear the sirens."

"Enough talk!" Sadie pulled the trigger. Nat screamed. Her fingers curled around the armrest, while her pretty face contorted with the electrical current. Sadie stopped her assault.

"Okay, okay, Sadie, you win. Reid, come on, let's get the dogs in the kennels."

Louis snorted. "Stinky, me not like smell, Meagan. Bad smell, bad smell."

Meagan sighed. "I know, Louis. Just try to put up with it."

Moody coughed up mop water. "Sadie's right, you are some kind of freak."

A surge of anger swept through Meagan's body. Her throat tightened. Nobel growled, baring his teeth. She grabbed for his collar before he snapped at Moody. Meagan swallowed hard and then looked over her shoulder to check on Natalie. Her jaw dropped. Miss Minerva had roused from her nap and was slowly crawling up Nat's arm. The side of Meagan's mouth curled. All she had to do was make sure Moody didn't notice. *It's lie time.*

"You might think I'm a freak, sweet-cheeks, but I know something you don't," Meagan said with all the confidence she could muster.

He stopped wiping his mouth. Meagan smiled. She had his full attention. "I was told by a reliable furry source that Sadie's got the hots for someone else."

Moody scowled. "What the hell...who?"

"For Christ's sake, she's lying, Matt!" Sadie yelled. "Now get up and get over here!"

Miss Minerva had almost reached Nat's shoulder. "All I can say is cats don't lie about details like that," Meagan said, smirking. "Wake-up and smell the gas fumes, Moody, she's just using you to get your money."

"I'm warning you, you smart-mouthed freak!" Sadie spat. "If one more word comes out of your mouth, I'll...ahhhh! Owww, owww! Something's biting me!"

Sadie dropped the Taser, backed away from Nat, and started smacking herself down. Miss Minerva had successfully crawled up one of her sleeves. Before Sadie knew what bit her, Nat backed her wheelchair up and ran over her feet. Sadie lurched, grabbing for her toes. Reid raced over, scooped up the Taser, plucked Sadie off the floor, then shoved her up against the wall, holding the weapon to her throat.

"How's your pain tolerance, Holmes?" he asked, grinning.

Sadie coughed. "No, wait, there's...there's something crawling all over me, biting me!"

Nat clicked her tongue a few times. "Miss Minerva, here, Miss Minerva." She held out an open palm.

An urgent squeak startled Sadie. A furry brown head popped out from between Sadie's bosom. Sadie screamed and her eyes rolled back into her head. The rat squealed, jumped out of Sadie's bra, and scurried across Sadie's shoulder and down the length of her arm. Miss Minerva jumped into Nat's hand. Sadie fainted and Reid let her go. *Thud!* She crumpled to the floor like a dollar store rag doll.

"Are you all right, Nat?" Meagan asked.

Nat gave her the thumbs up. "I'm a little sore, but I'll survive. I'm not so sure about baby-buns and sweet-cheeks, though. By the sounds of it, the fire department and police should be here any minute."

Meagan listened. Nat was right. They'd be here soon. She licked her bottom lip. It was time for her to be a pack leader. A *real* pack leader. The animals were safe. Now it was Whiskey's turn.

"Louis, Boggart, protect Reid and Nat! Make sure this slime-bucket doesn't move!" Meagan ordered.

"Me do, Meagan, me do!" Louis barked, spun around in a circle, and planted his butt on Moody's chest.

"Boggart protect Reid! Boggart protect Nat!" The big, black dog snarled.

Moody groaned. "I-I f-freaking h-hate…dogs."

Meagan released Nobel's collar. "Nobel, you're coming with me."

Nobel whined. "Coming? Where?"

Meagan rummaged around her scrub top's pocket and pulled out Whiskey's red collar. The bells jingled. "To the backwoods. To find Whiskey."

25. Double Challenge

Whiskey couldn't believe her old cat ears. Shadow had challenged George to a fight to the death. *George. Fight. Death.* Together, those three words made absolutely no sense. George was a free spirit, got along with every cat that came into the shelter, minded his business, and stayed out of trouble. The little white cat with grey markings on his ears and tail barely let out a meow when annoyed. So how was he going to pull this off? Whiskey scrunched her half-masked face. *What does George have up his paws?*

"Very well, Shadow," Brutus said. "The challenge is yours."

"B-B-But," George stammered. "That wasn't the plan. The plan was to fight you. Jules, say something."

"Plans change, kid," Jules meowed. "You'd better come up with a new one, fast."

Whiskey heard George groan. She knew he had no clue what to do.

"I object! I object!" Whiskey meowed loudly. She coughed and then sneezed.

"I may be wrong, but you're not in a position to object, old calico," Shadow warned.

George growled as best he could. "If I have to fight Shadow, then I want Whiskey out of that cage, Brutus. I'm fighting for her life, too."

"I agree with George. It would save me the trip of walking all the way over there to rip her to shreds after I'm finished with him," Shadow mused.

"Shut up, Shadow! Cut the kid some slack!" Jules growled. "At least he's braver than most of the cats around here."

"Don't worry, Jules, you'll get your chance to show just how brave you are," Brutus said.

Whiskey's ears pricked up. *Uh oh. That doesn't sound good for Jules.*

"What chance?" Jules asked.

Brutus let out a catty snicker. "Why, a chance to fight me, Jules. You see, while Shadow and George are scratching and spitting it to the death, you and I are going to be doing much the same. Call it a double challenge."

Jules gasped. "A double challenge? You...you can't be serious, Brutus?"

"Dead serious, Jules," Brutus growled. "I told you you'd be sorry. You've been a thorn in my paw for too long. It's time to show you how a real leader acts. Oscar, release the old calico, and bring her to the fighting pit."

Whiskey heard pawsteps heading her way. At least the air smelled fresher after the boom storm. The throb in her eye had lessened, but she still felt weak from the sickness inside her. She closed her eyes for the moment, and laid some cat thoughts out. The only chance George or Jules had was if a human stepped in and broke up the fight, scattering the cats. It would have to be a special human, a brave human. Whiskey smiled a cat smile. It would have to be Meagan Walsh—the Chosen One.

Whiskey's thoughts deepened. Humans searched for their lost animal companions all the time. Some were successful. Some were not. What would be the difference if an animal companion was to search for their lost human? So Whiskey focused on Meagan. She imagined Meagan looking for her, searching the forest, trying to find her. She didn't think of the brown beast, or George's fight, or of her sickness. She just thought of being found. As Whiskey's thoughts grew bigger, more real, she thought of being hugged by Meagan, of being scratched behind the ears, and of being back with her pack leader once again. *I'm here, Meagan, I'm here.*

"Wake up, Whiskey, it's time to come out," Oscar meowed.

Whiskey's eyes opened. "I am awake, thank you."

Oscar grunted as he pulled on the latch. *Creak.* He yanked the cage door open. Whiskey stood up. She cringed. Her bones felt hot, as if fire stones were rattling around inside of them. She moved slowly, limping to get outside. The pink blanket squished when she walked over it. Whiskey blinked. The crate had been dim inside. Its only source of light came through the small holes at the sides and from the door. She heard a low mew and turned around. Oscar was waiting, his stubby tail flicking apprehensively.

Oscar's eye oozed. Some of the goop had trickled down his face. She reached over to wipe his black, furry cheek. Startled, Oscar turned away. "Is it sore?" Whiskey asked.

Oscar sighed. "Sometimes. I know it looks scary. I see it in the water every time I take a drink."

Whiskey purred. "Promise me the next time you take a drink, look at your good side. That's what I see inside of you."

Oscar flashed a toothy grin. "Would you care to tell the young females that?"

The walk to the fighting pit felt long and arduous for Whiskey. It didn't help that the ground was uneven and mucky in some places. Dodging dips filled with murky water and climbing over a slick, mossy boulder played havoc with her aches. Whiskey could feel her chest tightening again. She knew the sickness was beginning to stir inside of her, rousing, making her feel groggy and weak.

"How much farther?" Whiskey asked, panting.

Oscar swished his short tail. "Not much. Just through those bushes ahead."

As Whiskey broke through the dripping foliage, she felt herself stumbling. Oscar grabbed the back of her neck and gently pulled her up. He released her. "Careful, unless you plan on taking George's place." He inclined his head down toward the fighting pit.

She sighed. "I wish I could, Oscar."

Whiskey peered over the ridge. The fighting pit appeared to be dug out of the side of a hill, as if humans had purposely shoveled here for shelter in order to set up camp. Chunks of charred wood and misplaced round rocks were scattered about. An old rubber boot and some broken long-necked bottles littered one of the sloped sides. Her yellow eyes squinted, trying to make out something she didn't recognize by a huge, grey rock jutting up from the ground. It looked like an assortment of white sticks stuck together.

"What's by that rock?" Whiskey pointed.

"Cat bones," Oscar said, twitching his nose. "I believe that was Ghost."

Whiskey's tail flicked. "Who did he fight?"

"Brutus," Oscar replied with a heavy sigh.

Suddenly, caterwauling commenced. Whiskey searched for the source. It was Daisy and Duchess—Brutus's females. They were rubbing against him, marking him with their scent. Not far from Brutus, Shadow was rolling on the ground, sharing her scent with a few scrawny males. Whiskey noticed many of the lost cats had arrived to line the top of the fighting pit. Most were meowing, yodeling, cat calling, scratching the ground, and swishing their tails in anticipation of the double challenge. The rowdy felines were mostly made up of young males and females. Whiskey let out a grateful breath. Thankfully, there were no kittens.

George and Jules were huddled next to each other at the farthest corner. They looked nervous and scared, like they were in a cage with no way out. Then Whiskey glanced up at the sky. The light was beginning to fade. Soon it would be dark. Whiskey shuddered. She hoped George had hurt the brown beast enough so it wouldn't hunt tonight. A sharp sneeze jolted Whiskey out of her thoughts. Hot liquid gushed from her nose. The sickness was taking hold of her again.

"Are you all right?" Oscar asked. He sounded genuinely concerned.

She pawed her nose, her ears flattening. "No. I'm here and George has to face Shadow. He shouldn't have to. This is my fault."

Oscar nudged her. "No, it's not. George made his own decision. There's a time to run and a time to fight, and this time he chose to fight. You can't fight another cat's battles, only your own, Whiskey. You can't live another cat's life for them. It's not natural. That's something I learned from my mother."

Whiskey stared at George. "Your mother sounds like a wise cat, Oscar."

A loud cat scream startled both Whiskey and Oscar. Duchess had sauntered into the middle of the fighting pit. She scratched a long line across the length of the pit, then sat down. "One pair of challengers must fight on this side of the line," Duchess announced, pointing. "The other two challengers are to fight on the other side of the pit. No cat shall cross this line. The challenge is to the death. Only one cat on each side will survive. Is that accepted and understood by all four challengers?"

"Accepted and understood," Brutus growled, as Daisy kneaded his back.

"Yes, yes, yes—one cat dies and the other cat survives—accepted and understood!" Shadow hissed. "Let's get on with it!" She swaggered over to her side of the pit.

"What was that middle thing?" Jules asked, his whiskers drooping

Duchess glared at him. Jules's ears flattened. "Accepted, understood."

"Accepted and understood, as long as I can use my cat brain to fight," George meowed.

Duchess's face scrunched. Daisy tittered.

"I'm good with that, Brutus," Shadow hissed. "After all, it doesn't matter what George uses to fight with, his cat brain will end up being splattered all over this fighting pit."

Brutus grunted. "Fine. On Duchess's yowl, the challenge begins. May the best cats win!"

George moved to his side of the pit to face Shadow, while Jules stayed where he was. The sleek, white tom shook in his paws, and Whiskey doubted it was from the brown beast's bites and scratches. His fear went deeper, past his hurts, and spiraled into the uncertainty of not knowing how he was going to get out of the box he had put himself in. Whiskey sighed. All Jules needed was a little shove to set him free.

Duchess pawed the ground. She pawed it again, then again. She tilted her head and let out a loud, cantankerous yowl. Brutus made the first move. He arched his back, his flabby belly rubbed up against his knees. With his massive head turned to the side, Brutus took a swipe at Jules, hitting him in the face with dead-aim accuracy. Jules flinched, reared, then rolled backward. He curled up and covered his head with his paws. He seemed to be still in that box. The same box, Whiskey guessed, that had imprisoned him when he was dumped on the shelter's steps many seasons ago. Her limbs tingled and her whiskers twitched. *It's time to set you free, Jules.*

"Stand your ground, Jules!" Whiskey meowed. "Don't let Brutus trap you like a human once did! Look for his weaknesses!" She sputtered, and then coughed.

As if awakening from a long catnap, Jules uncovered his head and looked up at Brutus. His long, white tail twitched. In that moment, Brutus flinched. He pawed one of his sore, raw ears and scratched it. Jules's blue eyes widened. Before Brutus knew what happened, Jules had jumped onto the huge cat's back and sunk his teeth into one of Brutus's tender ears. He clawed the other ear, tearing at the open flesh, ripping it until blood stained both his white paws.

"Owww! My ears!" Brutus caterwauled, spinning, jumping, trying to knock Jules off.

Shadow hissed. "I'm afraid things won't go that easy for you!" She lunged at George.

George rolled away in time. He got up and backed away.

Shadow's tail whipped from side to side. She dropped to her hunches, preparing for her next attack just as George spit at her. "You know, Shadow, you're nothing like a *true* cat."

Shadow stopped swishing her tail. "Is that so?" Shadow crept closer. "And what should a true cat be like?"

George dug a paw into the ground. "Like Whiskey!" He flung a pawful of sand into Shadow's face.

Shadow flinched. She pawed her eyes to wipe the sand away, then hissed a terrible hiss. "When I'm finished with you, George, you're going to wish you'd never been weaned!"

George meowed, and then turned and raced toward the rubber boot. He wiggled his small body into the open end. Whiskey smiled. *That's using your cat brain, George!* He knew Shadow would never fit inside there. Angry yowls answered George as

Shadow struck the boot again and again, hissing, spitting, and lunging, but he remained safe. Whiskey snatched a peek across the pit. Jules was still riding Brutus, holding on, nipping, biting, scratching the backs of his itch bug infested ears. Between Brutus's high-pitched whines and Shadow's screeching, Jules and George appeared to have the upper paw in this challenge.

Suddenly, what sounded like a human child screaming made Whiskey's ears flatten. She looked toward the rock jutting out of the ground, close to where Shadow had George trapped. Her yellow eyes widened. There, sitting on top of the rock was the brown beast. It stood on its haunches and sniffed. One of its eyes was bloodied, a useless mess, so it used its other beady one to scan the area. Its black tail whipped back and forth, back and forth, back and forth, as if watching, waiting for the most opportune moment.

Panicking, Whiskey looked down into the pit. "Shadow! Get out of there! It's the brown—" She coughed, sputtered, and sneezed. Her front legs gave out from under her.

Shadow stopped attacking the boot and glanced up at Whiskey. Her ears were pushed back against her head. She hissed and snapped her tail. "Don't worry, old calico, I'll be done with George soon enough! Then it will be your turn!"

The brown beast pounced on Shadow's back. The surprised grey tabby snarled and spat before she knew what was happening to her. The beast dug into her with its claws and fangs, shredding her fur, gnawing at her face. It wasn't about to let go. Shadow screamed just as the brown beast flipped her over and burrowed into her belly like an over-sized flea, chewing, biting, and ripping as she managed to gurgle out a last hiss. Then Shadow went limp.

Yowls, cat screeches, and fearful meows filled the fighting pit. Jules let go of Brutus and jumped off his back. "It's the brown beast! It's the brown beast! Run, hide, don't let it get you!" Jules meowed as loudly as he could. "Tell the mothers, keep the kittens safe!"

Trembling, Whiskey stood up. Her whole body ached, but she didn't care. She had to get George out of there while the brown beast was still busy with Shadow. Or die trying.

"Where do you think you're going?" Oscar jumped in front of her.

"To help George. Now move aside."

Oscar's ears flattened. "You don't understand. You can't fight it. We have to run. It's the only way to be safe."

"I know what the brown beast is capable of. Let me pass."

He shook his head. "My entire family was destroyed because of it. I lost part of my tail and the use of my eye running from it. My mother saved me that day, told me to run, to keep running until I was safe. That's what I did, and that's what we're going to do."

Stunned by his story, Whiskey slumped down and stared up at Oscar. There was a familiar ring to his tale, a truth she hadn't realized until now. She stared at him, searched his face, lingering over his injured eye for an answer to why she felt connected to him. Then her old eyes widened. Whiskey grunted to stand.

"Why, Oscar," she purred, nuzzling his cheek. "I do believe that you're my son."

26. Found

"Take this." Reid handed Meagan a black walkie-talkie he had retrieved from the store room. "In case your cell phone doesn't pick up a signal. Nat and I will join you as soon as we can."

Meagan nodded, then switched it on. "Thanks, Reid, I owe you...*umph!*"

Reid kissed her full on the lips. Meagan's body tingled all over as he pulled away. "No. I owe you," he said, smiling. "Now go, before it gets too dark."

Flushed, Meagan turned to catch Nat smirking at her. Miss Minerva was curled up in her lap, sleeping. "Here, take this too—" Nat passed her a flashlight hanging by the leashes "—and forgive me if I don't pay you back the way Reid just did. We'll do lunch instead. My treat."

The sirens were getting louder and louder. The firefighters and police would be there any moment. Meagan slipped the flashlight into the deep side pocket of her scrub pants, then hooked the walkie-talkie in her waist-band. She winked at Nat. "I'll hold you to that lunch."

Nat giggled. "You'd better. In the meantime, I'll send you and Nobel some positive energy to help you find Whiskey."

Meagan stroked Nobel's head. "Thanks. We'll need all the positive energy you can muster. Come on, Nobel, you've got a cat to find!"

Nobel barked. "You can count on my nose, Meagan!"

"Be careful, Meagan!" Reid shouted after her. "Now, you owe me!"

Meagan's cheeks were still aflame as she followed Nobel toward the blocked road. She glanced at the Argo parked behind the shed. It was tempting, but better to leave the ATV for Nat and Reid. Besides, it would be easier to track Whiskey on foot. Nobel put his nose to the ground. He sniffed around, tail wagging, ears alert, until he found a scent. She pulled Whiskey's collar out of her scrub top pocket and held it out for him. The bells jingled.

"Does it smell like this?" she asked.

Nobel sniffed the collar, then the ground all around him. He whined. "Nope. It's a cat smell, though. It's leading my nose up the rocky road."

Meagan followed the road with her eyes. It led over a hill into a heavily forested area. The storm had washed some of the gravel away, exposing logs and rocks. Broken branches and overflowing puddles attested to the recent high winds and pounding rain. Meagan looked down at her feet. Her lime green clogs now resembled the colour of a toad.

"Here, Meagan, here!" Nobel howled. She looked up. He was waiting on the crest of the hill. "The cat smell's getting stronger. My nose says there's more than one cat smell, too."

Meagan thumbed Whiskey's collar. If there were feral cats living in the forest, maybe she could get close enough to ask them if they knew about Whiskey's whereabouts. It was worth a try. Meagan closed her eyes, squeezed the collar and made a wish. She hoped Whiskey was still alive. She wished that Whiskey would be protected from the cat-killing fisher. She asked that Nobel would find her. The bells tinkled in response. Then, she heard a faint whisper, *I'm here, Meagan, I'm here,* and knew without a doubt her wish would come true. Whiskey was out there. All Nobel had to do was find her.

Nobel howled. "Come on, Meagan, the cat smells are getting stronger!"

Meagan raced over the pitted road, dodging ruts and mud. She pushed on, following Nobel into the canopy of green. The clean, damp air sent a chill through her body, and she shuddered. The road narrowed and turned into a trail wide enough for a four-wheeler to pass through. Long grass had grown between the furrows tires had once made and low hanging branches created an annoying obstacle for her. Ducking became a skill.

"Caw! Go away, human, go away! This is Brutus's forest!"

Meagan froze. She looked up. A huge raven was perched on a gnarly limb. There was something shiny stuffed in between one of its claws.

"Who's Brutus?"

"Caw! Leader of the lost cats. He doesn't like humans. Humans are meddlers! Go away!"

"Meagan!" Nobel yipped, returning. "The cat smells are confounding me! There are too darned many!"

Startled, the raven flapped his wings, causing it to drop the shiny thing it held. It floated down and Meagan snatched it up in mid-air. Her mouth opened. It was a scratch ticket—the same kind Katrina Smith played. *This raven may know something.*

"Caw! Give, human, give!"

Meagan pursed her lips. "First, it's Meagan. Second, where'd you get this?"

"Caw! From Brutus. He knows I like shiny things. Gave me it to watch over the lost cats. Caw! Give!"

"The lost cats? Where do they live?"

"Caw! Not telling, not telling!"

Meagan smirked. If she had learned one thing about bird behaviour it was that she could talk a bird out of giving up its tail feathers for something it really wanted, and she had just the ticket that would turn this raven into a stool pigeon. Rummaging around in a pocket, Meagan pulled out the crinkled scratch and win ticket that she found on the bathroom floor that morning. She held it up.

"Would you tell me if I gave you another one of these?"

The raven twisted its inky black head, mulling over Meagan's offer. She frowned. *Hmm, I need to sweeten the pot.* "Tell me where the lost cats are and I promise I'll give you more of these shiny things. Do we have a deal?"

The raven flapped its wings. "Caw! Deal! Follow me, Meagan!" It flew up, circled them twice, then soared up the trail where Nobel had come from.

Nobel barked and dashed after the big, black bird. Meagan followed, dodging, jumping and sidestepping potholes, ruts, and rocks. The raven led them deeper into the forest. The trail curved around thick trees and weather-beaten boulders. Meagan felt like she was following a snake instead of a bird. Suddenly, the wide path veered off to the right, but the raven flew left. Meagan heard branches snapping ahead. Nobel yelped.

"Nobel? Don't worry, boy, I'm right behind...umph!"

Meagan slammed into something metal and rolled over it. *Whump!* She hit the damp ground hard, cringing at all the pains her body had acquired lately. Dizzy, Meagan shook her head and brushed the hair out of her face to search for what she'd smacked into.

"A car?" Meagan frowned. "What's that doing way out here?"

Nobel whined. "My nose is broke."

Meagan crawled over to Nobel. The soaked ground squirted and squelched. She cupped his snout. There was a chunk out of his nose, and it was bleeding. "How bad does it hurt?"

"Not bad enough to stop smelling for Whiskey!" Nobel barked.

Meagan scratched Nobel under his chin. "Atta, boy!"

"Caw! Here it is! Lost cats' home! Give me shiny things!"

"But this is a car. It belongs to a human."

"Caw! Belongs to Brutus. Give!"

Meagan rolled her eyes. The bird was persistent. She stood up and placed the two tickets on top of the car's dark green roof. The raven landed, scooped up the tickets with its beak, then flew to the highest branch above them. Meagan waved. "Thanks. Fly by the Animal Shelter tomorrow morning and I'll give you more of those shiny things."

Nobel whined, and then sniffed. "Meagan, my nose says there are cats in there."

"Where?"

Nobel jumped up on the side of the car and sniffed again. "In there."

Meagan pressed her face against the driver's side window. A cat lunged at her from the inside, hissing, and striking at the foggy window. Meagan backed off. Nobel snarled.

"Whoa. Maybe I should try another approach," Meagan said, scratching her head.

"Want me to go fetch Louis? He loves cats with attitudes."

Meagan rolled her eyes. "I can handle this, thank you very much."

Meagan crept closer to the same window. She noticed that this abandoned car looked exactly like the car Ms. Manager drove. Its colour blended in well with the forest, hiding it from anyone who wandered by. Flattened tires and rusted rims gave it a forlorn appearance. Meagan shook her head. Other than its dented hood and cracked windshield, she wondered why someone would dump a perfectly fixable car here. *Seems such a waste,* Meagan thought, shaking her head.

Stopping a foot away from the window, Meagan cleared her throat, and said. "Hi, I'm Meagan. I'm not here to hurt you. I just want to ask you something."

Hisses emerged from the car. "Go away, we don't talk to humans!"

"But, I want to talk to Brutus. Is he in there?"

More hisses and a few spits answered her.

Meagan sighed. The time for diplomacy had passed. It was time for another strategy—face to furry face. She reached over to open the door. It didn't budge. *Great. It's locked.* Meagan tried the other doors. They were all locked.

Nobel yipped softly. "The back part's open. Want me to—"

"No, I'll do it," Meagan said, wagging a finger. "That is, unless you'd like more chunks out of your nose?"

Nobel's ears drooped.

"I thought not. Move aside and watch the master."

She pulled out the flashlight Nat gave her, switched it on, and then lifted the trunk gently. "Listen up cats! Where's Brutus?"

Meooow! Hissss! Multiple eyes eerily glowed back at her. Then, one, two, five, eight, twelve, Meagan lost count of the cats jumping out of the trunk. She danced around them, avoiding their claws. Most ran into the forest behind them, some wiggled underneath the car.

Nobel wagged his tail. "Want me to get Louis now, *master*?"

Suddenly, screeches and meows flooded the air.

"Brown beast, brown breast!" a skinny tabby meowed, heading for the car. It skidded to a stop when it saw Meagan and Nobel. "Human! Dog! Human! Dog!"

More cats exploded through the greenery. There were too many to count, and all meowing wildly about a brown beast. When the cats saw Meagan and Nobel, they detoured around them and headed toward the path on the other side.

"What's a brown beast?" Nobel yipped.

"I have no clue, but the cats seemed to be terrified of it."

Meagan hunkered down and directed the flashlight under the car. "Where's Brutus? If you don't tell me, I'll bring the brown beast here."

A mother cat—half Siamese, Meagan guessed, came forward. "Brutus is at the fighting pit. Go past those trees where the other cats came from and go over a big rock."

Meagan nodded, then stood and looked down at Nobel. "Let's find this Brutus and ask him if he knows where Whiskey is."

The half-Siamese poked her head out. "Whiskey? The old calico?"

Stunned, Meagan looked down. "Yes. Do you know where she is?"

"Are...are you the Chosen One?"

Nobel barked. "Yes. Meagan is our new pack leader."

"I have heard of you. Whiskey and George say—"

"George is here too?" Meagan asked, cutting in. "Where is he?"

The mother cat stared at Meagan. "At the fighting pit. Shadow challenged George to a fight to the death."

Meagan's eyes bugged. She dropped her flashlight. "Shadow! Death? Come on, Nobel, we've got a fight to stop and a cat to find!"

Nobel howled as they ran in the direction the cats had come from. Branches whipped Meagan's face and twigs beat against her legs. Cat yowls and caterwauling seemed to be coming from the other side of the moss-covered boulder ahead. Seeing a ledge at the far end he could climb up on, Nobel sprinted toward it, while Meagan scaled the boulder. She caught the setting sun twinkling through the forest, lighting up the brush as if it were on fire.

Reaching the pinnacle, Meagan jumped up, broke through the bushes, and stumbled down into a shallow pit. Cat wailing surrounded her. She propped herself up on an elbow, and glanced around. A big grey and white cat with bloody ears was cowering behind a rock. Strange screeching and hissing made her look across the pit. A ratty, brown animal, roughly the size of a big cat was trying to work its way inside a rubber boot. Beside the boot lay a mutilated cat. Her jaw dropped. It was Shadow—or what was left of Shadow. Her insides had been torn out and her eyes and mouth were wide open. Death masked her face.

"Meagan!"

Startled, Meagan twisted around, searching for the cat who called her name.

"Over here! Look up!"

A black and white cat with a disfigured left eye and a short tail waved a paw at her. Then, she spied a familiar calico cat lying next to this cat. Her chin trembled as she cried, "Whiskey!"

Whiskey pointed to the boot. "G-George," she gasped. Her voice sounded strained, crippled. "George...is in...boot!"

Meagan maneuvered around the sand to stare at the boot. She balled her fists, then flinched, her fingers catching on something sharp. Meagan looked down and spied a beer bottle. She reached for it and threw it at what must be the fisher—the dreaded brown beast the cats were so afraid of. The bottle exploded across its back. It jumped and glared at Meagan. It whipped its tail and screeched at her, sounding more like the scream of a ranting child than of a wild animal.

"Me hungry, human, me hungry!" It snarled, fresh blood dripping from its snout.

"The Chosen One will save us from the brown beast!" the black and white cat sitting next to Whiskey meowed.

The brown beast twisted its shaggy body and glared at the two cats huddled on the hill.

"More food, more food!" It snarled, bounding toward them.

"Noooo!" Meagan screamed, trying to stand. A chunk of wood tripped her up.

The brown beast was almost upon Whiskey and the black and white cat. For whatever reason, Whiskey's companion crawled on top of her to protect her from what was about to happen. Suddenly, from out of the bushes, Nobel sprang forward and intercepted the brown beast in his powerful jaws. He shook, and shook, and shook, then let it go. It hit the closest boulder. *Crack!* Its body crumpled to the ground. No sound, no movement, no life emanated from it. Nobel pounced over and sniffed. He howled victoriously. The brown beast was dead.

"C-Can I come out now?" George asked, poking his head out of the boot.

Meagan smiled. "Sure, George, but you missed all the action." She stood and brushed off the sand.

"Meagan! You came for us!" George wiggled out of the boot. "Whiskey needs her white pills! Did you bring them?"

"White pills? What are you talking about, George?"

His ears moved forward. "Whiskey has the sickness. Can you make her better?"

"Sickness?" Meagan looked at Whiskey. Something was wrong with her. She was lying on the ground—still—not even a tail flicker, while her vigilant friend sat next to her.

Panicking, Meagan pulled out her walkie-talkie and pushed the button. "Reid? Nat? I need you! Whiskey's sick! She needs her white pills!"

The walkie-talkie squelched. "Meagan? It's Aunt Izzy. Dear, where are you?"

Meagan's stomach tensed. Part of her was glad to hear her aunt's voice; the other part of her knew she didn't want to face Aunt Izzy. After all, lighting fireworks and breaking a window in a police station was probably going to cost Meagan her freedom somewhere down the line. Meagan's eyes widened and she raised her chin. But this wasn't about her. This was bigger than her. This was about Whiskey.

She pushed the button. "Take the Argo, drive up the dirt road, and follow it into the forest until there's a sharp turn on the right. Nobel will be waiting for you there. Follow him. I'll meet you next to the abandoned car in the clearing. Please hurry!"

Meagan released the button. She glanced at Nobel. Their eyes locked. *A good pack leader follows through. A great pack leader gets the job done.* Meagan realized then that since her mother's death, she'd run away from her problems, blamed others, shirked responsibility, and hid from the truth. She needed to set her old life aside. That was then, this was now. No more running, no more hiding. She was who she was, and if it was good enough for Whiskey and Nobel, then it was good enough for her.

"Wait for the Kind One at the bend, and then meet me by the car."

Nobel wagged his tail. "Glad to see you've finally decided."

Meagan scrunched her brow. "Decided what?"

"To become our pack leader," he barked, then bolted for the ridge and disappeared into the forest.

Meagan stuffed the walkie-talkie into her scrubs. She sprinted over to Whiskey and knelt down. Meagan's chest ached. Whiskey didn't look well. Her eyes were closed and her breathing harsh, as if she were fighting something foreign inside of her. Meagan ran a hand across her frail body. Her eyes opened and she started to purr.

"I'm here, Whiskey, I'm here," Meagan said softly.

"I'm here too, mother," the black and white cat said.

Meagan balked. "Mother?"

"Yes. I'm Oscar, Whiskey's son. Don't you see the resemblance?"

Meagan inclined her head. "Can't say that I do."

Oscar grunted. "Humans are so stupid."

"Oh, now I see it," Meagan said, smirking.

George bounded up and rubbed against Meagan's leg. "How's Whiskey?"

Meagan stroked him. "Don't worry, George, she's a fighter."

"M-Meagan...I'm...so...tired," Whiskey wheezed.

Carefully, Meagan picked Whiskey up, and cuddled her to her chest. She weighed next to nothing. "Don't worry, Whiskey, Aunt Izzy's coming. She'll make you better."

Standing, Meagan turned and ran toward the forest. "Come on, boys!"

Trampling saplings and crushing twigs, Meagan headed for the clearing, trying not to bounce Whiskey around too much. She heard Nobel barking in the distance and knew her aunt was nearing. Rounding a tree, Meagan, George, and Oscar arrived at the opening. There was a white cat waiting by the car. Meagan squinted. It looked like he'd been attacked recently.

"Jules!" George meowed. "Your new plan worked!"

"I'd like to take the credit, kid, but it was Whiskey's plan. She's the one who made me remember who I was. She's the one who really saved me."

Meagan smiled, then looked down at Whiskey. Her eyes were half-closed. Green stuff oozed out of her nose and her mouth was open. Her breathing was raspy and troubled. Suddenly, the Argo crashed through a small opening in the clearing, missing the car by a few feet. The all-terrain vehicle jerked to a stop, while its headlights illuminated the open area. Aunt Izzy had brought some reinforcements with her. Reid, Nat, and Bertie were in the middle seats. Nobel had the whole back to himself. Meagan's aunt rode shotgun to Constable Wright. She gulped when he honed in on her. Meagan looked away.

"Meagan, bring Whiskey here," Aunt Izzy said, waving her over.

"What's with the car out here?" Reid asked, hopping out. "It looks too new for a junker."

"I don't get it either, but the lost cats use it as their home." Meagan said, rushing over. She placed Whiskey on her aunt's lap.

"The lost cats?" Nat asked, pulling at the red fleece blanket draped around her shoulders.

"Cats!" Miss Minerva squeaked, peeping out from under Nat's blanket "Ock. Forgive me, but I think I'll stay in here."

"Stay as long as you want, Miss Minerva," Meagan said, grinning. "I don't think Nat will mind one bit."

"Yeah, and I don't think mom will object to adopting Miss Minerva, seeing as she saved our lives and all," Nat added with a smile.

Meagan winked at Nat, and then looked back at her aunt. Her fingers gently combed Whiskey's body, checking her over, sweeping for injuries. She wiped her face and chin with damp cloth, paying attention to her stuffed nose, cleaning her and caring for her. Meagan's skin tingled all over. Now she knew why her aunt was called the Kind One. It was a no-brainer, and Meagan should have figured it out earlier. Aunt Izzy pulled a vial from her coat pocket containing a pink liquid. Using a syringe, she sucked some of the liquid up, nudged Whiskey's mouth open, and shot it down her throat. Whiskey wretched, then sneezed.

"You know that car looks awfully familiar," Bertie said, getting out of her seat.

"I think I know why," Reid said, as he rummaged around the open trunk. "Look what I found wedged under the spare tire." He held up something shiny.

Curious, Meagan looked. She blinked a few times, making sure she was seeing what she was seeing. "A scratch and win ticket?"

Reid nodded. "There's a couple more lodged behind the back seats. This car must have belonged to Katrina Smith at one time. It's a Jaguar. Same kind she drives now."

Constable Wright jumped out of the Argo to join Reid. He walked around the car, once, twice, three times, then glanced at Nat and said, "I do believe we've finally found the car that hit you. It fits the description perfectly."

Reid's jaw dropped. "Are you telling us that Katrina Smith was Nat's hit and run?"

"It all makes sense now," Bertie piped up. "Three years ago, Katrina mentioned something about hitting a deer. She said she totalled the car and her insurance replaced it with the exact same model and colour." Bertie looked at Constable Wright. "Maybe you should make a call to her insurance company and check things out with them, Scotty."

"Yeah, and I'm sure forensics with have a blast lifting Smith's DNA off this car," Reid added. "I betcha that's why she sold this land to Moody. She needed the cash for some wheels."

Constable Wright scratched his square chin. "I'll get Sara to haul Katrina in for questioning once all the mess is cleaned up at the shelter with Moody and Holmes." Then he adjusted his blue Stetson-style hat which made him appear serious. "You kids should be proud of yourselves. It was a damn brave thing you did. However, you did break several laws, damaged police property, and almost started a fire in the station with your mini fireworks display, so there's no way I'm letting you off scot-free. I propose a solution."

Reid bit his bottom lip. "Um, what solution would that be, Constable?"

Constable Wright crossed his arms over his dark blue uniform. "Starting tomorrow, you and Meagan will report to the station. Instead of a fine, I've decided to put you both to work cleaning up all the mess, garbage, and broken glass outside and inside the building. After you're finished with those tasks you two will serve your community further by giving a fresh coat of paint to the police station's reception area, hallways, and lounge. Got that?"

"Got it," Reid replied, giving the constable a thumbs up sign.

Although Meagan was grateful for Constable Wright's conditions and change of heart, she didn't answer him. All her focus was on Nat. Meagan's scalp prickled and her mouth went dry. Nat's fists were balled as if she were struggling with her past, trying to remember what had happened. Her face reddened and her lips thinned. Then, as if something snapped inside her, Nat opened her hands, relaxed her shoulders, and exhaled. Her colour returned. She looked at Meagan and grinned.

"See, Meagan, what goes around, does come around. Karma rocks."

Meagan twisted her mouth to the side. "Speaking of karma, you do know that you're gonna have to deal with the consequences of stealing your stepfather's Argo, right?"

Nat hung her head and sighed. "Yeah. I'll probably be grounded for most of the summer. Touche, karma."

Suddenly, Whiskey wheezed and sputtered. Pink liquid shot out her nose.

"Oh, my poor sweetness," Aunt Izzy said, kissing Whiskey's head.

"You can make her better, right, Aunt Izzy?" Meagan asked, leaning into the Argo.

Aunt Izzy stared blankly at her. It was the same look she had when Meagan found Tess.

"I'm afraid we can only make her comfortable at this point, my darling. There's nothing I can do for her. Whiskey's just too weak and too old."

Tears welled in Meagan's eyes. "But...can I hold her, then?"

Aunt Izzy passed Whiskey to her. "You know nothing is forever, don't you, Meagan?"

The question was absurd. Of course she did. Meagan nodded. Some of her tears fell on Whiskey's head. She purred. "Don't...be...sad," Whiskey wheezed.

Meagan cuddled her. "Can't help it. I lost you, and then I found you, and now I'm going to lose you for good."

"Nothing's...ever...lost, Meagan. Just...changed," Whiskey mewed softly.

Meagan forced a smile. She turned away from the Argo and headed into the middle of the clearing, then sat down on the damp ground. "Whiskey is...changing. She's sick and doesn't have much longer."

Rustling leaves announced a multitude of cats coming out of hiding. Many from the bushes, the rest from under the car. All the cats were heading toward Meagan. George, Jules, and Oscar were the first cats to arrive at her feet.

George rubbed against Whiskey's cheek. "Please say hello to Tess for me, Whiskey."

Whiskey gave George a weak nod, then pawed her son's nose. "Oscar, take...care...of ...Meagan. She's...only...human."

Oscar licked her. "I know, mother, I will."

Jules pawed Whiskey. "Thanks for setting me free, old...Whiskey."

Other cats gathered around her—all colours, all breeds, all sizes—thanking her, saying their goodbyes. The huge grey and white cat Meagan had seen cowering in the fighting pit was the last cat in line. His ears were red-raw, like they'd been scratched from the inside-out.

"Forgive me, old calico. I should have listened to you." He bowed his big head.

"Et tu, Brutus?" Jules meowed.

Whiskey's breathing slowed. Meagan stroked her, consciously, slowly, letting her enjoy what cats' love best—a good scratch under the chin. "I guess it's my turn, old girl," Meagan whispered, tears streaming down her face. She bent to kiss Whiskey's furry cheek. "Thank you for reminding me who I am. I'd forgotten about what was buried deep inside of me. Then you came along and dug it up. Thank you for allowing me to see through your eyes. I-I'll never forget you."

Nobel whined. He jumped out of the Argo and strutted over to where she sat with the cats. Oddly, none of the cats ran, they all remained calm; in vigil. He put his head down on Whiskey's weak body, closed his blue eyes, and wagged his tail.

"Cats may still confound me, but you're the best darned cat I've ever known, Whiskey." Then Nobel opened his eyes, tilted back his head, and released a morose, ear-piercing howl.

Whiskey fell still. Releasing, relaxing, letting go.

"Is she...?" Reid asked, coming to sit beside Meagan.

Meagan nodded. She couldn't speak. Her throat ached.

Reid wiped her tears away. "She's not in pain anymore, Meagan."

Meagan licked her dry lips. "I know, I know. It's just that I wish she didn't have to go."

I'm here, Meagan, I'm here, whispered in Meagan's ear.

Meagan sat up, still hugging Whiskey's lifeless body. She knew she didn't imagine it. She heard it clear as a bell. To deny it was to deny her gift of animal gab. Meagan took a deep breath and let it go. Today she would celebrate Whiskey's life. An old, cantankerous calico who talked too much and thought humans were stupid and silly. The Fairy Falls Animal Shelter's observer, and friend to dog and cat. Whiskey's teachings seemed limitless, and her wisdom vast. Meagan smiled, knowing Whiskey's life had had a purpose, and she would honour this truth in the best way she knew how. By being true to herself and seeing with her heart.

Meagan leaned against Reid's shoulder, kissed his freckled cheek, and whispered, "Now that there's a job opening at the shelter, do you think I've got a shot?"

The End

Acknowledgements

As always, life is a team effort and a cooperative venture. Nothing is done without the help and support of others. The following people are in some way connected to the fabric of Lost and Found, to which I am eternally grateful:

A huge thank you to Lacey L. Bakker, who saw potential in my vision and rebranding possibilities for Mysterious Tales from Fairy Falls, and took a chance on breathing new life into my teen psychic mystery series through Pandamonium Publishing House. I truly appreciate your support, investment, and creative expertise during our journey together.

I'd be remiss if I didn't thank Justine Alley Dowsett and Robert Dowsett for their exceptional editing skills on the first edition of Lost and Found. This book shines because of your talents and gifts. Thank you to my mother and fellow animal lover, Peggy, who believed in this book from the get-go.

A special thanks to my first beta reader, Linda Toner Fisher, who provided some great feedback to make this book better, and Brenda Paterson, who never stopped supporting me.

And always, big hugs to my hubby Mike, my faithful companion and best friend.

A special shout out goes to my former cohorts and fellow animal care attendants: Susan Winther, Robin Pankhurst, Christie Knight, and Catherine Adams. You ladies could scoop poop with the best of them! I appreciate all you taught me, and I'm so grateful for the bonds we created with every dog and cat that found their way to us.

Last but not least, I want to thank all the women and men who, in some capacity, take care of the welfare of animals whether professionally or on a volunteer basis. You make this world a better place through your kindness, generosity, dedication, and love for all creatures great and small.

About the Author

Sharon Ledwith is the author of the middle-grade/young adult time travel adventure series, THE LAST TIMEKEEPERS, and the award-winning teen psychic mystery series, MYSTERIOUS TALES FROM FAIRY FALLS. When not writing, reading, researching, or revising, she enjoys anything arcane, ancient mysteries, and single malt scotch. Sharon lives a serene, yet busy life in a southern tourist region of Ontario, Canada, with her spoiled hubby, and two shiny red e-bikes.

Blackflies and Blueberries

Mysterious Tales from Fairy Falls

Book #2

Prologue

An icy breeze from the kitchen window sliced through Catherine Stewart. Her stomach tensed and she frowned. Something is about to happen. Something bad.

She drew her mouth into a straight line and bit her bottom lip, leaning against the kitchen counter. Her coral T-shirt rubbed across the counter's lip and her worn jeans lightly brushed the chestnut cabinet. She drew a deep breath and closed her tired, powder-blue eyes, allowing the ominous energy to consume her. Images filled her head. Images of bone-weary migrant workers harvesting vegetables in a sea of green, of blistered hands and grimy, sweat-stained clothes. Startled by these visions, she opened her eyes and looked into the sink. Her long, thin fingers were immersed in a strainer full of shredded lettuce. A laugh escaped her, allowing the uneasy moment to dissipate. Ever since Catherine was a young girl, her hands had possessed a special sight all of their own.

A shadow crawled across her oval face, like a spider stalking its prey. As a child, Catherine had often been dubbed a freak by her peers. Just because she was different; just because she possessed unusual powers. She had found out early in life that objects talked to her. Not talked in the same way that two people could carry on a conversation, but talked as in Catherine sometimes received subtle information from holding an object about its history and who had owned it. Personal objects like jewelry could tell her loads about the owner: what he or she did for a living, who they loved or hated, where they lived, and more. Catherine could get a person's whole life history if the object communicated this information to her. Sometimes what she found out was too emotionally overwhelming, too burdensome, so Catherine decided to keep her psychic ability a secret. That is, until she discovered it was possible to make a living using her powers.

Psychometry. That was what the fortune teller at the Toronto Exhibition told then thirteen-year-old Catherine her special power was called. That was over twenty years ago. Nowadays, Catherine preferred to call it her meal ticket. Over the years, she went from skipping classes to dropping out of school completely, choosing to sell her *object-talking* craft on the slick city streets. When her mother found out what she was up to, she went ballistic. So dear sweet mom packed Catherine's bags and sent her up north by bus to live with her aunt and uncle for a while. Catherine swallowed hard, tasting a lump of sour bile. The bus depot was the last time she had seen her mother alive.

Another sharp breeze broke Catherine's concentration. Her skin prickled. She reached over and slammed the window shut, knocking the jagged, purple rock she kept on the window sill into the sink. She scooped up the rock before it could land in the lettuce. A smile spread across her freckled, pale face. The small piece of amethyst had been given to her by her mother's older and only sister, Gertie. Catherine's thumb gently grazed over her childhood memento. *I wonder if Aunt Gertie still lives up in Fairy Falls?* Then she stiffened, thinking how she had no choice but to endure the last few good years of her youth in rustic Fairy Falls after receiving notice that her mom had been killed in a subway accident.

The amethyst cooled Catherine's palm. Her nose flared, picking up the scent of pine needles and fresh country air. She relaxed and half-smiled. *I guess it wasn't all that bad living in Fairy Falls.* There had been morning and evening canoe rides on Blueberry Lake, campfires, toasting marshmallows, and telling ghost stories. There had been swimming lessons in the warm afternoons and cool skinny dips in the hot, sticky evenings. But the best by far was blueberry picking on Aunt Gertie and Uncle Pete's extensive bushes in late July and early August. Blueberries were their main source of income in the summer, and enough had to be picked to fill the orders of local resorts and restaurants. After that, any berries left over were sold at the local Farmer's Market. This was where Catherine had honed her skills as a sharp saleswoman. Skills that had served her well through many years of participating in psychic fairs.

As these memories flooded Catherine's mind, she brushed her straw-blonde hair back behind an ear and brought the crystal up to her face. She rubbed it against her cheek and her smile increased. *No, it hadn't been all that bad in Fairy Falls.*

One particular day at the market fate had intervened in the form of a very handsome, and very sexy, tawny-haired boy named Tony Benton. Her aunt had taken an instant dislike to him. Her uncle, however, had been subtler, pulling out his rifle and cleaning it whenever Tony showed his face on their property. *Tony Trouble.* That's what Aunt Gertie had dubbed him, but Catherine didn't listen to her aunt, and she avoided her uncle like a swarm of blood-sucking blackflies. Soon things got serious between the pair of lovers, and Catherine confided in Tony about her special ability to talk to objects, about her psychic career on the streets of Toronto, and about the incredible amount of money she had made. Soon after that, she became Tony's meal ticket. She also became pregnant.

At seventeen and with only a minimal education, Catherine felt she couldn't tell her aunt and uncle about her pregnancy. They would have had Tony lynched in seconds. So one night, under the cover of the stars, Catherine and Tony hitched a ride to the nearest bus depot, leaving for Toronto. Catherine sighed heavily. She had never told her Aunt Gertie and Uncle Pete about Hart. The only information she had shared was a letter written in haste to let her aunt and uncle know she was safe, and that Tony had been offered a good paying job by a cottager who owned a business in the city. That was it. No mention of her pregnancy. No return address.

Soon, Catherine's dream for a better life turned into a nightmare when Tony broke her legs by pushing her down their apartment building's stairs, because according to him, she hadn't made enough money from her side-street psychic readings. He needed that money to supply him with enough beer and smokes for the week. Catherine winced, reliving the haunting pain of torn muscle and splintered bones, as if it had happened yesterday.

A bead of sweat ran down the side of Catherine's face, thinking back on the effort it took to try to crawl up those same stairs she'd been pushed down when she heard her three-month-old son, Hart, crying for her. A neighbor finally had the sense to call 9-1-1, and all Catherine could remember after that was waking up in the Toronto General Hospital, her legs plastered and in traction. Catherine's chin trembled as she wiped her slick cheek.

Six months of physiotherapy followed, while Hart was placed in a foster home. Catherine was determined to heal her legs and get her son back, at any cost. She was ready for a change in her life and she knew only she could make that happen. And change would have started by pressing charges against that abusive sleazebag she had once loved, but by the time a warrant had been issued for Tony's arrest, he was long gone. It was like he had disappeared off the face of the earth, or at least Catherine's tiny part of it.

Social workers helped her through the tough times, finding her a decent place to live, and a respectable job at a nearby food market. It wasn't much, but it was a new start. Once Catherine got Hart back, she started doing psychic readings at home in the evenings to supplement her income and pay for the extra food and clothing she needed for her growing boy. Her reputation as a psychic grew again, only this time she chose more wisely, deciding to help people the best way she knew through her gift of psychometry. News of her amazing abilities spread and soon she was invited to join the psychic fair circuit. Even the police had asked her to help out in a few baffling cases, getting Catherine to commune with articles of clothing from a missing child, or pieces of evidence left at a crime scene. Most of the time, Catherine would shine, but then there were those cases that would simply stump her and leave her in the dark, grasping for answers. Sometimes the object she held remained silent and there was nothing she could do.

A loud crash from Hart's bedroom startled her. Twisting, Catherine smacked the amethyst against the yellowing counter and lost her grip. The rock hit the floor and split in two pieces. Swearing, Catherine took a deep breath and headed toward the hallway.

Damn it. Hart must have left his window open again and another stray cat got in. The last cat that had managed to sneak into his room and sprayed everything he owned. Catherine shook her head. She'd told him to lock his window the other day. There had been a rash of burglaries in this area and last week the police had gone door-to-door warning the residents to tighten their security. Her skin prickled. *I have half a mind to wring Hart's freaking neck when he gets home from school!*

Catherine chewed her bottom lip. She wasn't looking forward to another homework session with Hart. His reading and writing skills were appalling, yet he managed to squeak by each grade. Maybe she was partly to blame. Catherine couldn't count the number of times they'd moved. Better chances and better opportunities in her line of psychic work had opened so many doors for her. And with the moves, came new schools. And with the new schools, came the frustration of misplaced records, making new friends, and starting over for Hart. Now an intermediate attending his third high school, she would see to it that this would be his last.

Standing at the entrance of Hart's bedroom, Catherine cautiously peered in. A messy bed, clothes strewn across the floor, scattered video games on the dresser, and a broken lamp under the window greeted her. Catherine wrinkled her nose and grunted. *When is he going to learn that I'm not his maid?* She brought her tongue to the roof of her mouth and clicked, "Here kitty, kitty, kitty. Come out, you flea-bitten hairball."

Catherine caught a moving shadow on her left. Before she could turn around, a pair of hands encircled her thin neck and squeezed hard. Catherine's eyes widened and her mouth went dry.

Instinctively, she reached up to grasp her attacker's hands. Even through the latex gloves, she could feel the ugliness of bulging veins, like an anaconda's coils rippling around its prey. She slid her hands up until her right thumb connected with a man's chunky, thick bracelet. Gasping, Catherine begged the bracelet to talk to her, to tell her what this man wanted.

Her stomach tightened. He wasn't here to rob her. He was here to kill her.

We want to hear from you! If you enjoyed this book, please consider leaving a review online or at pandapublishing8@gmail.com.

Discussion Questions:

1. How do you think Meagan feels about her ability to hear animals? Would you see this as a gift or a curse if you were in her shoes? Why?

2. Meagan is forced to move to Fairy Falls, a town she finds boring at first. How does her perception of the town change throughout the story? Have you ever been in a situation where you had to adjust to a new place or circumstance?

3. The story is partially told from Whiskey's point of view. How does seeing the world through an animal's perspective change the way we think about pets and their relationships with humans?

4. The animals in Fairy Falls use telepathy to communicate with Meagan. If animals could truly talk to humans, how do you think society would change? Would it be a good or bad thing?

5.Meagan starts off in trouble with the law but grows throughout the book. What lessons does she learn from her time at the animal shelter? How does this change her outlook on life?

6. How do Meagan, Reid, and Natalie work together to solve the mystery of the shelter's troubles? What strengths does each character bring to the group?

7. The antagonist in the story is trying to destroy the animal shelter. What do you think motivates them? Do you think they believe they are doing the right thing, or are they purely selfish?

8. The book explores the idea of humans having a responsibility to protect animals. What do you think are some real-world issues animals face, and what can people do to help?

9.Meagan has to learn to trust both the animals and the people around her. Why is trust such a big theme in the book? Can you think of a time in your life when trusting someone made a big difference?

10. What does home mean to Meagan at the start of the book versus the end? How does the animal shelter serve as a home for both animals and people in the story?